LOST LANE

CHARLIE GARRATT

BUNLACKY PRESS

ISBN: 978-1-9191817-0-7

This novel is dedicated to everyone who's reading
this book or read any of my others.
Writers are very little without readers.

ACKNOWLEDGEMENTS

For a number of years, I've enjoyed the company and support of the members of Writers on the Edge. I thank them for this and for their eagle-eyed reading of my chapters as they were created - and, of course, for the cakes.

A special thanks goes to Steve Dewhirst for his writings and his advice on some historical aspects.

As always, I couldn't have written anything without Ann, my constant companion, my muse, and the source of so much guidance and happiness.

ONE

Broseley, Shropshire, September 1751

You sit at your table, trinkets arranged in neat rows before you. Each lovingly taken from a velvet lined box where you store them. Each telling its own tale. You mourn a little for all the ones you've disposed of, but the recollection of how others were gained takes the edge off that disappointment. Some, those farthest away, simply the spoils of thievery and hold no special affection. They will be sold next. Through a man you know, and on to a wealthy lady or gentleman. Perhaps even to be stolen again.

Lifting a ring from the second row, you cradle it in both hands and hold it close to your nose. Can you smell the man this came from? Is it possible for such a jewel to absorb the essence of the person who died wearing it? You fancy it can, for you see the scene clearly. The crescent moon reflecting on a flat-calm sea. Music and song floating along the harbour from the tavern you'd both left behind. Not together, of course. He'd argued with a drinking companion and staggered out. You'd followed close enough to keep him in view. Not so close he could hear your footsteps. All night you'd had him in your sights. Well-heeled, which mattered. Not a strong brute of a man, which was also important.

The ring had caught your eye when he'd raised a mug of ale to his lips. A merchant, wearing his fortune on his fingers. Probably in this port carrying out trade to swell his coffers even more. You, there for business of your own. He'd not miss the gold you'd take. Though he *would* miss the breath you'd choke from him.

It had taken only a moment, like most of the others. Sometimes they'd put up a fight, but surprise and the deftness you'd developed usually made their resistance short and ineffective. You feel this was a shame, as a struggle heightened both the fear that you might not succeed, and the excruciating pleasure when you did. On the other hand, struggle or no, joy sprang from their last gasp. The delight in laying on the ground what had been a living, breathing, being. Glassy-eyed and still.

You lift a new bauble and smile, reminiscing on another life snuffed out in a different town.

At my feet lay my last remaining coins. No silver, only coppers bearing our second King George's head. Enough for food for the next week, or my next rent payment. Not for both. Meg Valentine might soon be on the charity of the parish.

I'd miss my Bridgnorth home if I'd to leave it. Not much of a place, two rooms, but that's one more than the rat hole of a stable loft I lived in before, and at least none of the windows are broken. In this cottage there's my own hearth and even a palliasse not riddled with fleas. I've promised myself a table and a better chair when funds allow. It only became mine when Edwin Hare left a bit over a year ago.

The thief-taker had covered my rent for six months, and I'd managed to eke out the wages he'd given me as his assistant until work started to trickle my way. Small, mindless, jobs they'd been. Chasing debts, finding the odd husband who'd gone astray, usually in a tavern somewhere. One case of tracking down a tradesman who hadn't delivered the goods he'd promised. That kind of thing. Nothing to tax the brain. None of the exciting thief-taking work I'd imagined would arrive on my doorstep from the goodwill of Edwin's contacts. It had paid well when the jobs arrived, but not enough to keep the wolf, in the shape of my landlord, away from my door for very long.

A call of "Meg" from outside, and Peter Turnstone was standing in the doorway, the sunlight behind him and his head well below the frame. I'd seen Edwin duck under that frame on more than one occasion. Peter doesn't share Edwin's height and isn't so broad-shouldered. Even so, I found him attractive. Wiry, curly brown hair, and a permanent grin. Not like Edwin at all.

I squinted against the glare to see if the grin is there. It was, as I knew it would be.

'Come inside and sit, Peter. Tell me why you look like you've found a golden guinea.'

Without waiting to be asked a second time, my friend bounded in, then flopped, cross-legged, across the room from me. Once there, he didn't speak, just looked around as if he's never been inside before. His eyes roamed from place to place, lingering for a moment on each object before moving to the next. Anyone watching would have thought he'd entered a treasure cave rather than my sparse cottage. I'd noticed this habit of being in his own place soon after we first met outside a murdered man's house in Bridgnorth. I first put it down to Peter being simple. It didn't take me long to discover he wasn't. Not a bit of it. The lad has ideas, and they might make him rich one day. I spoke quietly to pull his attention from the world around him.

'Peter. Are you there?'

He blinked, then fixed his chestnut brown eyes on me as if I'd just appeared. That smile widened and, for a moment, I thought how much I liked him. Peter pointed to the coppers on the floor. 'Getting thin are they, Meg?'

'My landlord came round this morning. He had to, sooner or later. It isn't his fault, he needs to put bread on his plate just as I do, and my unpaid rent denies him that luxury. He turned up, kept saying he was sorry, but he was firm, and I had to hand over half the cash left in my purse.'

'Do you think you'd be better going back to being a gardener? Wholesome, honest, work. Respected, wages every week, and the joy of watching the seasons go past day by day.'

I snorted.

'Never. Break my back to feed a master? A man who has all the money he'll ever need and still be willing to steal from his friends to put away a little more. Not on your life, Peter Turnstone.'

'So you're determined to go on being a thief-taker then?'

'God willing ... though ...'

'What?'

'Last time I went home my mother made it plain she depends on the bit of cash I've been able to send her. Since the Beaumont's house closed, there's not been as much work for Dad and I think they're struggling. If I'm not able to throw a few pennies into the pot I don't know what they'll do.'

'Then it's just as well you've got me around.'

'And why would that be?'

'Because I keep my ear to the ground whilst you sit here just worrying.'

'Have you heard of something, then?'

'I have. Last night, I was talking to Thaddeus Jackson, who runs the White Horse tavern, and he passed on gossip of some thefts up the road in Broseley. Several folk have been burgled. Thaddeus said it's a shame Edwin Hare isn't around because one of the ironmasters in the town has offered a reward to capture whoever is behind the housebreaking. I wheedled the man's name out of Thaddeus so sent a boy over first thing this morning to tell him you're available. I said you're just as good as Hare.'

'Peter!'

'It's only the truth, isn't it? You are available, and,' he winked, 'as Hare's a week's ride away from Bridgnorth you'll be at least as useful as him.'

Almost as soon as Peter finished speaking, his messenger knocked on my door, thrust a note into my fist and demanded a ha'penny for his trouble. I picked up a coin from my tiny hoard and told him he'd make do with a farthing. The boy grumbled but I guessed he'd still go off with a smile on his face once I closed the door.

Tearing open the seal, I traced each line of the letter with my fingertip, and went through the words twice, just to be sure.

My friend leant forward. 'Well?'

'You've done me a big favour, Peter. The ironmaster, Mr Matthias Bagnall, wants me to call on him in the afternoon.'

Two

They say it's four miles from Bridgnorth to Broseley. To me, the walk seemed longer with the hills and the rutted winding road. Peter's strides are worth two of mine, so I was glad to rest for a bite of bread after an hour. We'd seen no other travellers on foot, though plenty of carts had passed in each direction carrying goods to and from the river. Had I been alone I might have begged one of them for a ride but I was enjoying walking with Peter. All of the time he talked of what he called 'inventions' and new ideas he'd heard of in mining and iron-making, and where he thought there could be improvements. Most of it meant nothing to me, though I could tell it meant everything to Peter.

Sitting in the weak sunshine, me getting my breath, him sitting with his smile and his wonderment at the birds and the falling leaves, we fell silent for a while until I broke the spell.

'Do you ever think of marriage, Peter?'

He didn't react. In fact he didn't even reply until I nudged him with my elbow and glared at him.

'Marriage? You mean for me or in general?'

I shrugged. 'Both I suppose.'

'In that case I'd have to say I don't really favour it. Not at the minute.'

'How so?'

'Well if we're thinking of the general, I can only go on my own father and mother.'

'Are they not happy?'

'Content, more than happy, I think. They both seem so bored. Almost like they were excited to be together once, when they were young, but now they're treading water. No, not even as active as that, more like floating down the Severn just waiting for something to happen.'

'And will something happen?'

Peter pursed his lips and stayed quiet again, before shaking himself back to life. 'I doubt it. It must be the same for a lot of people. Aren't your parents the same?'

Now it was my turn to pause and think. Whilst I did, Peter's attention went away to a thrush which had landed close by and was tugging at a worm. I thought I might lose him again if I took too long. 'It's hard to tell. They'd hardly ever see each other until recently. Dad was working with me at Cliffe House, and my mother was at home in Hampton Loade. The master would let him go home for a weekend once a month and he'd come back in much better humour.'

Peter smirked.

'What you grinning at now?'

The smirk turned into a full-blown laugh. 'I can think of one good reason he'd come back with a smile on his face.'

Blankness for a second, then I felt my face redden and I swiped him with the back of my hand. 'Peter Turnstone. You are a very crude man. I thought better of you.'

'Oh, nonsense, Meg. The church tells us that marriage is for making babies and I imagine this is why the good Lord made it pleasurable.'

This seemed a sad view of marriage. I knew a man and wife couldn't hold on to the joy they had in each other when they were young though, surely, they could still have something lovely as time passed. Like the plants in the garden, Spring would bring them fresh and green, then they'd grow closer together, some putting out wonderful flowers, and some saving their best colours until the autumn. Was this too much to hope for? Or would it all be work, long silences, grunting in the night like I'd heard at home, and the inevitable children to follow?

I looked at Peter, still chuckling to himself, and wondered which path I might walk along with him. He was a quiet, kind, lad. Is that enough? He had ideas and dreams which might make him rich, though I feared they may just stay as dreams. If they did, we'd end up poor, and I didn't want to be poor for a minute longer than necessary.

In some ways I think Peter's like my father. I've seen Dad leaning on his spade, staring up at the sky, with a quiet smile on his face. When I was very young, I thought he might be thinking about my mother. Later, when I worked alongside him in the garden, I could see it was being surrounded by trees, vegetables and flowers that took him to a special place. A place where he could relax and where there'd be no expectations on him. A place where poverty and destitution would be someone else's worry.

Peter had only told me what he thought of his parents' marriage, not what he wanted from it for himself. I was about to ask, when a cart came up the lane and Peter was on his feet. He waved it to stop and asked for a lift. The carter looked us up and down. He appeared dubious until Peter mentioned his father's name.

'Jack Turnstone? You his son, are you? Good man all round. You and your sweetheart had better hop on the back.'

At least someone had the right idea. And the look on Peter's face was priceless.

Our transport dropped us on the edge of the town, where the way split in several directions. The carter pointed to a church only a short walk away and told us Matthias Bagnall, the man we were looking for, lived opposite.

The house we'd been directed to stood out. It didn't appear to have been built long, and was just as grand as Cliffe House, where I'd once been a gardener, though in a different way. A solid, square building with a tiled roof and large fine windows in the modern style, it faced the road and told the world that money lived here. The shining brass plaque by the door, declaring it as "New House", confirmed both my first thought of its age, and that we were at the right place.

A maid answered my knock and scowled, as if we should be round the back. I explained that we'd been asked to call. She ignored me and spoke to Peter. 'Ah, I see. You must be the thief-taker, sir -'

Without a second thought I put her right. 'No, he's not. I am.'

The girl couldn't disguise her bemusement. 'Really? Well I never. Please wait a moment, ... er ... miss, and I'll tell the master you're here.'

Two minutes passed with us shuffling our feet on the step before the door was reopened by a giant in breeches and a red waistcoat. He thrust out a hand. 'Miss Valentine. Matthias Bagnall. How good of you to come.' He nodded in Peter's direction. 'And this is?'

'Peter Turnstone, sir, a friend, and occasional helper. He accompanied me here on my walk today.'

Mr Bagnall raised an eyebrow. 'Walk, you say? You have no carriage?'

I shouldn't have felt ashamed of being not so wealthy as him, but I did. 'I'm afraid not.'

'Then you must have the use of mine if I take you on.' He stood aside and gestured for us to enter. 'Eliza will take your coats and then bring you through.'

A moment later, the maid led us down the lobby into a large hall, with a grand staircase at its centre, then through to what she called the "drawing room". I looked forward to the day when I might have a house with more rooms than I needed and could give them special names. This one alone was easily three times the size of my cottage.

Mr Bagnall asked us to sit. I brushed the back of my skirt, hoping no remnants of straw from the cart we'd ridden in would end up on the handsome pink fabric of the furniture. Peter and I had been told by the maid to leave our boots by the door, so at least I didn't need to worry about depositing mud, or worse, on the sumptuous rug.

Our host leant back in his chair, his massive hands pressed, palms together, under his chin when he spoke. His voice had little of the refinement I might have expected from the owner of such an imposing home. 'How much do you know already, Miss Valentine?'

'Only what Peter has told me, that there've been thefts from people's homes and you want someone to find out who's doing it.'

'Well there's little to add to that.'

'And you've had something stolen yourself?'

'No, I haven't, though my friends have. As you might imagine,' Bagnall waved his hands as if to display the room, 'I am a man of some standing in this community and in the absence of a local magistrate - we have none in Broseley - they look to me to help solve such problems. Are you up to the job?'

I told him I'd worked under Edwin Hare, in Bridgnorth, helping him to solve a murder, and of the work I'd carried out on my own account since he'd left. Even to my ears it sounded feeble.

When I'd finished, Bagnall waited a moment before he spoke. 'I have heard of the exploits of your Mr Hare. Some say he's a rogue, others say he was the best thief-taker for a hundred miles around. What would be your view?'

'There's no doubt it's the last of these, sir. He treated me well and though his methods sometimes appeared unusual, he showed me you need this to get results.'

'Such praise indeed. Then it's a shame I can't get his involvement. Still, if he had faith in you then I expect I should too. However, it is not really as easy as that. My friends are relying on me to find a solution and I must be sure the person I engage is up to the job. Tell me about how you might go about it.'

I glanced at Peter, who nodded as if to say, "go on then, tell him". Not a helpful response. Thinking on my feet hasn't been a skill I've grown over the years. In gardening there's not often call for it. Mr Bagnall must have believed I was a complete dullard as I scratched my head and mumbled about talking to the victims and asking questions around the town. When I'd finished making a fool of myself, he leant back in his chair and smiled.

'Do not fret, Miss Valentine. I know you are new

to this calling. Your answers tell me you are a thoughtful person, not prone, I would guess, to rushing off and stirring up difficulties where they shouldn't exist. If you keep me informed as you progress, and come to me if problems arise, I am sure you will do an admirable job.'

He offered two sums of money, one, to be paid if I undertook the task, would cover my rent for a few more weeks. The other, which made my eyes water, could be claimed if I was successful in identifying the thief. I glanced at Peter, who winked back.

The maid returned with a tray containing cups, a fine-looking apple tart and a pear-shaped teapot, possibly the prettiest, and certainly the shiniest thing I'd ever seen. A painfully thin lady followed her in. From her fine clothes this must be the mistress of the house. I couldn't help wondering how such a tiny sparrow would end up with the larger-than-life Mr Bagnall.

Her husband clapped his hands like a child and his face split with a broad smile. 'Dorothea, my dove, come and meet our new friends, Miss Valentine and her assistant Mr Turnstone.'

Peter scowled at Mr Bagnall's words, though I giggled inside at his assessment of our status. I'd need to be especially nice to Peter later if I wanted to make sure he'd continue to help me when needed.

Mrs Bagnall came over to Peter first, bowing her head in greeting and offering a hand to shake. Her only words, almost whispered, were her name. She brightened when she turned to speak to me. 'Miss

Valentine, it is lovely to meet you, my husband said you were coming. I do hope you will be able to help with his little problem.'

I was struck by the limpness of her hand when she lay it on my wrist. I also envied her the gold bracelet she wore, and I told her so.

'How nice of you to say, my dear. It was a gift.' She looked, smiling, towards her husband, 'From an admirer.'

Mr Bagnall came and took his wife by the hand, lifting the bracelet for closer inspection. 'It is an exceptionally fine jewel, just like Dorothea, and no more than she deserves. Now, let us all sit and talk of how you will proceed.'

We spent another hour with Mr Bagnall and his wife, in which I teased out of him as much detail as I could of the thefts taking place in the town. Several were from friends of his and, in each case, only a few things were taken. Few, but valuable.

When the crimes had started some years earlier, owners had been away from their homes for a few days. More recently, one or two had occurred when victims were in their beds. Perhaps, in the past, the thief had received information that his targets had been away. It looked like he was now becoming bolder, not concerned if they were home or not.

When we'd finished our discussions, the maid, who'd been introduced to us as Eliza, showed Peter and I to the second floor. Not with the family. Not with the servants either. She'd led us up the main staircase though, to be truthful, she'd kept glancing over her shoulder, probably certain we wouldn't go this way in the normal run of things. And she wasn't wrong.

The stairs came out on a corridor the full width of the house, with a window at each end, where dust motes shimmered in the sunlight streaming through. She asked me to wait for a moment, then led Peter towards the back of the house and another short flight of stairs, to show him to his sleeping quarters.

When Eliza returned, she opened the second door along, standing back so I could pass her. 'The master said this 'un would be yours ... er ... miss.'

I stopped, with my hand on the doorknob and my mouth open. This room also had two windows, large and sparkling, and the light streaming in made the carpet shine, blue as an autumn morning. The bed, with curtains around, would have filled my entire floor at home, even if I could have fitted it below my ceiling. On the walls, against a background of woodland greenery, flew birds of every colour, unlike any I'd seen in Bridgnorth gardens. If Mr Bagnall had given me this one as his guest, what was his own like?

Once I had made a pretence of inspecting the room for its suitability, I told Eliza to ask Peter to join me by the front door, so that we could begin our work.

'Yes, miss. If there's anythin' you need just ask.'

With this, she turned and hurried away, looking back only once, perhaps afraid I *would* actually ask for something.

Our host had suggested we first visit a Mr Edward Powell, his mine manager, who only lived a short distance away. He had arrived home from a night's stay in Ludlow earlier in the week to discover a window forced and a number of items missing. From the way Mr Bagnall spoke of him, I guessed Mr Powell might be a little sticky so I would be glad to have Peter's company.

THREE

The Powell house was nowhere near as fine as Mr Bagnall's, though fifty times better than my own. It lay a little off the main road, shielded by a tall, neatly trimmed hedge. The building stood two floors high so, given the position of the town on a hill, upstairs windows would have fine views of the countryside below, across the River Severn gorge. A man a little older than me opened the door. A bit taller than Peter, and much better looking, he folded his arms and raised an eyebrow. This was no servant.

'May I help you?'

I explained who we were, and that Mr Bagnall had sent us. The suspicion in his eyes melted into a smile which made my toes tingle.

'Then it will be my father you wish to speak to. Please come inside.'

He led us to the parlour at the front and introduced us to Mr Powell, seated at a desk. There was no welcome on this face when he looked up from his papers. We had clearly disturbed his train of thought.

I took a deep breath. 'Thank you for seeing us, sir. Mr Bagnall sends his regards. He tells me that you've recently been the victim of a theft. This must have been most upsetting.'

'Upsetting, no. Upsetting is when one of my men is killed in the mine. Upsetting is when a seam runs out unexpectedly and Mr Bagnall's investment is lost. The theft was merely inconvenient, though, on the other hand, I *was* a little sad to lose a watch left to me.' He glanced at his son, 'I had hoped to pass it on to Daniel here when the good Lord chooses to take me. Not that he'd be at all grateful.'

This Daniel shook his head. 'Now, now, no need to be so contrary. This nice young lady has been sent to help.' He turned to address me. 'Mr Bagnall is my godfather and a great friend to us, as well as being our employer. Father does not like to be beholden.' Turning back, he shook his head again. 'Do you?'

Grateful as I was for his protective interest, it did nothing to raise me in the mine manager's estimation. I needed to rescue the situation. Quickly. I smiled at the son. 'I can understand Mr Powell's resistance, sir. It's perfectly reasonable for your father to avoid being in our debt, especially if he's never met us before and knows nothing of us. Mr Bagnall has asked me to assist if I can, but perhaps coming here today was a mistake. Peter and I should leave and return when Mr Powell and Mr Bagnall have had an opportunity to talk.'

This necessary grovelling done, I spoke directly

to the mine manager. 'Is that what you would prefer, sir?'

Mr Powell's face was hard. I almost shrivelled under the glare which came my way.

'It is indeed, young woman. Though I doubt you'll be returning. Matthias Bagnall may be my employer, but he'll not tell me what to do in my own home. I will bid you good day.'

When he walked away to look out of the window, I knew our talk was over. It was not quite the result I'd wanted my words to have.

Daniel Powell cocked his head toward the door, and I was glad to follow him out of the room. In the hallway he bent and spoke to us in a whisper. 'Please do not take against my father, Miss Valentine, he has a lot on his mind. He constantly reads his Scriptures, and takes them seriously. Since he was a child he has tried to live by them. From time to time he finds a passage which is at odds with the day to day events in his life, and it troubles him. I believe this has happened recently. He is also used to managing the roughest of men at the mine, so his manners are not always of the finest. Leave it a few days for Mr Bagnall and me to talk some sense into him, and we'll have you back. I guarantee it.'

The son seemed as charming as the older man seemed obstinate, and he appeared to like me. At least he'd tried to protect me from his father's annoyance, and I guessed he'd turned on that smile for my benefit and not Peter's. I considered the fine house and wondered if he had a sweetheart.

The thought brought a blush, and I almost choked on my next words. 'Th ... then I'll need to wait, won't I.'

When I reached to open the door. Daniel Powell stayed my hand. 'Let us hope that isn't too long. But before you go, miss, I can tell you that the items stolen were of some consequence, regardless of what my father said. As well as the watch mentioned, there were jewels of my grandmother's. She died when he was young, and her things are still very precious to him. A bag of gold coins and some other small items were taken, though these are not important. Please do all you can to recover the rest.'

He closed the door after he spoke and as we walked away, I fancied I heard raised voices from inside.

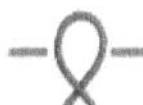

Daniel stubbed his toe on an unseen stone. A curse and then a snort. He shook his head. That ale tonight must have been stronger than usual. Or perhaps he'd taken more than he should. He laughed at the thought, and it came to him what a lucky fellow he was. A decent job, good prospects, and nights like these. The music in The Angel had been of the best and he had to admit his dancing partner, Becky was pretty, even thought they'd parted on sour terms.

Any other night, Daniel would have been happy to walk out with her, she was a fine girl who made him laugh. Tonight, though, he'd not been able to shake Meg Valentine from his mind. The girl had something about her. Unlike the ones his father wanted him to mix with. None of those worked to earn a crust, every last one supported by a father and each looking for a husband to take over the responsibility. Meg held her own on that front. And she had something beyond the local labouring girls as well. A thief-taker. Daniel repeated the word over and over out loud. 'Thief-taker, thief-taker.' He would seek her out in the morning.

Daniel approached the corner of the lane where his home stood, shrugged his shoulders, and dropped to sit on the milestone marking the distance to the Jackfield ferry. His thoughts had been troubled for the last few days by something at the mine. Though he knew he should discuss it with his father and with Mr Bagnall, he hadn't wanted to bother them, nor to raise any concern that he wasn't up to his job. He had asked advice from someone he thought could help, and the dear man had tried to put Daniel's mind at rest. Still the problem niggled. Before too long he would need to decide what to do. Let sleeping dogs lie, or stir up a wasp's nest? A noise to his left stopped him in his tracks. 'Who ... who's there?'

A cracking twig could be fox, badger, deer, or human. In the dark he'd prefer to know which. Daniel peered into the thicket. The meagre moonlight gave nothing away. He waited in silence, ears straining, though no answer came, nor another sound.

After a few moments he relaxed, deciding the

noise must just be the nocturnal activity of some animal, and he returned to thinking about the problem he'd been faced with. Five times he'd checked, and he was certain there must be an error. He was blowed if he could find it. Easy enough to make a mistake, he'd done it many times, though would usually spot it at the end of the day, or at worst, at the end of the week. This was different. Not his coalmine, though still his problem.

Daniel's chin dropped to his chest and his eyelids drooped, the beer and the late hour taking its toll. When St Leonard's struck ten, he almost toppled from his seat and it snapped him awake. He grunted and stood, glanced round once more, then walked the last couple of dozen steps to the gate. He pushed inside. On skirting the stables, Daniel was grateful at last for the glimmer of light from the house.

Once again, he paused, listened for the sound. There was nothing, only the wind sighing in the trees and the crackle of leaves falling to rot on the soil.

He reached an arm to unlock the front door. Felt warm breath on his neck. A tightness at his throat. His fingers snatched at a rope. Now a knee in his back and the darkness deepened. He fancied he heard the words "I'm sorry, Daniel" but couldn't be sure. They were muffled by a strange choking sound.

Four

You stand over Daniel Powell's body, yellow lamplight dripping from a hall window. Such a peaceful scene. He could be mistaken for being asleep if not for the fear-stretched neck muscles where he had struggled to escape the rope. That rope, three feet of it limp in your hand, came with you. Now you fling it into the bushes, its job done. There will be a fresh length for a fresh victim when there is one. You wait, silently, quietly savouring his lifelessness. It cannot be for long, you know this. Daniel's parents, inside, unaware their son has breathed his last, will soon wonder why he has not joined them. They will have heard his key in the lock. Perhaps their dog stirred too.

The emotions are strong. Daniel was said to be decent, honest, his father's son. Though you know this not to be true when it comes to women. You experience satisfaction, certainly, at a threat removed. More than this, hearing his dying gasps felt so, so, wonderful.

An inner door opens, a man's voice. A hint of concern? Fear? 'Daniel? Is that you?'

He receives no answer. The father will never hear a word from his son again. His shape moves towards the glass.

You half wish you had not thrown your rope away. It would be good to taste that sweetness once more when the father comes outside. Instead, you slide into the darkness where you are able to watch the grief explode from his heart.

When it comes, when his cry goes up to heaven, it is almost as fulfilling as the act itself. Almost. That pleasure will need to wait for another day. You pray it will be soon.

$$-Q-$$

I'm not a light sleeper, so for something to wake me during the night it has to be loud, and the shouts from outside *were* loud.

'Open up! Open up, Master. There's been a killing. For the good Lord's sake, open up.'

I threw off my covers and peered from the half-open window. In the yard below, two men, both with lanterns, continued to bang on the door until Mr Bagnall stepped out to speak to them. I couldn't hear all that was said, only the words "Daniel" and "strangled". It took me a few seconds to put those two words together, then my whole world shook. How could it be? Only a few hours ago I'd considered how it might be spending a lifetime with him. Now he was gone. It had been a stupid fancy. I hardly knew the man, though something inside was making me mourn what I'd imagined might have been. I shook myself free of these thoughts and minutes later I was downstairs, dressed, and at my host's side. Not knowing I'd been eavesdropping, he asked one of the men to repeat the news for my benefit.

The man looked me up and down and shook his head before he spoke. 'Mr Powell heard the key in the lock but no-one went in. The poor man found his son on the ground outside. Still warm, though not breathing.' He shook his head again, more slowly this time. 'The lad had been out dancing at a tavern, The Angel, just enjoying himself, and now he's gone from us all. We were sent for and told to search the garden. There wasn't a sign of anyone. Still a crowd there looking though. Mr Powell pulled us two off the search and told us to come round here to seek help from Mr Bagnall.'

I asked Mr Bagnall if I could speak to the men. He nodded and told them to answer me truthfully. I addressed the one who'd already spoken. 'My name is Meg Valentine. What's yours?'

'Frank Smitheman, miss.' He turned a thumb towards his companion, a man barely taller than me. 'This here's Ernest Kite.'

'Thank you, Frank. Do you know how long ago Mr Powell found his son?'

Smitheman scratched his whiskers. 'No more than an hour, I'd say. Church bell had struck ten before we were called for. We looked all around the outside of the house, the outbuildings, and the lanes about. Didn't go too far 'cos there'd be no point. Anyone who'd had chance to get beyond the hedge could have gone in any direction.'

I glanced upward and pointed at my bedroom window. 'From up there I heard you say the young man had been strangled. How could you tell?'

'The lad has marks on his neck. He'd not been shot or stabbed, not as far as I could see anyway. So what else could it be? Hadn't just taken a fit and died, that's for sure.' He turned and grinned at Ernest Kite, snorting, and cocking his head in my direction as he did so.

I needed to bring him into line. 'Is the death of a man something to laugh about, Frank? Perhaps you'd something to do with it? Shall Mr Bagnall lock you up so we can settle this affair quickly?'

I shook inside as I spoke, but I wasn't going to let this man think himself better than me. Besides, I was confident Mr Bagnall would let no harm come my way.

Smitheman stiffened and turned back. 'Surely, there'll be no need for that, miss. I meant nothing by it. I too want to see the devil caught who did this. I'm most sorry if I've offended. Is there anything else I can tell you?'

'Not at the minute. Go back to Mr Powell and tell him I'll come to the house shortly. Give him my condolences and ask him not to move his son's body or disturb the area, so I can examine it properly when I get there.'

The two men left. Mr Bagnall, who had stood

silently beside me, pulled his gown more tightly across his chest and laid a hand on my shoulder. 'This is indeed a sorry affair, Miss Valentine. I have known Daniel almost all of his life. He is ... was a fine young man, with a keen brain and good at figures. He had a bright future in front of him. I am pleased you will investigate his death.'

I stepped away. 'I'm not sure that's something you'd want me to do, sir. Murder's a serious business, and possibly beyond my meagre skills. I'll take a look to see if we can fathom any idea of who might be behind young Mr Powell's death. Then, if not, you may wish to seek someone more experienced.'

'But you said you had aided Mr Hare in finding a killer.'

'And so I did. I aided him. Edwin had been at his business a long time. He knew where to look, and what to look for. I only did his bidding and helped him think it through.' I was beginning to regret using my association with Edwin to get me work. Catching petty thieves is one thing, chasing murderers something else entirely. 'I'm afraid you'll need to find someone more fitting for such an important job.'

My new employer frowned and folded his arms. 'Then perhaps I may as well engage them to look at the thefts too. There is very little point in me paying for two when one will do all.'

I saw my recently promising financial future slipping away. 'Please don't do that, sir. As I said, I'll take a look at the place where Daniel died, and it may be clear from there. If not, I'm more than happy, at no cost to yourself, to assist someone who has the necessary skills to catch a killer. In the meantime, I can chase whoever's been stealing from your friends and neighbours.' Mr Bagnall didn't reply, though I could see he was thinking. 'Would that be acceptable to you, sir?'

He shook his head and sighed. 'You are a persuasive young woman, Miss Valentine. I can see why Mr Hare let you work with him. Now, I will go and dress properly, and you go to see Mr Powell. I assume you will take your Mr Turnstone with you?'

I said that I would. Peter, in his room at the back of the house, had clearly not been woken by events, so I sent for him to be roused. I asked Mr Bagnall if he wanted me to give any message to his mine manager.

'Just tell him I will come to see him as soon as I am able, and that he has my promise his son's murderer will be caught and hanged.'

When Peter and I walked through the Powell's gate a cart almost knocked us over. Two men pulled it from the front and two more pushed from behind. On top of the cart, its outline clear under sacking, lay a body. I assumed it must be Daniel's and shouted to the men to stop. They ignored me and were off into the night before I could do more.

I muttered an oath, and Peter heard me. 'Meg, that's a bit strong, even for you. What is it?'

'I told them to leave the body where it was found. And look at this lot.' Lanterns hung on every bough and bracket around the Powell's garden, making it bright as day. Men and women searching for the killer cast long shadows in every direction. 'There'll not be a trace left of what happened. Can't they see that?'

'Surely the father would want his son to be properly attended to?'

'Of course he would, but he could have waited an hour. Suppose the killer had left a boot print or dropped something on the ground which would identify him. That would be trampled away by now. I'd also like to have seen how Daniel lay. From that we might get an idea where his attacker had been hiding.' I balled my fists in frustration. 'Even seeing the body myself might have confirmed what the men at the house told me about him being strangled. Nothing to be done about it now, I suppose, that cart is well away.'

Halfway between the gate and the house, two figures stood, Edward Powell and a short, plump, woman who I took to be his wife. He looked in command. She looked bewildered. We approached them, though Mr Powell didn't appear to notice until we were a couple of paces away. The woman nudged him. Close to, I could see that although his face was hardened for giving orders, his eyes held more than a hint of horror.

The edge to the man's voice told me he wasn't glad to see me. 'What do *you* want? Have you not heard what happened here? I've no time to talk to you about stolen goods now.'

'I'm ... I'm not here for that, sir. Mr Bagnall will be here presently and has asked if I will look to see if there are any clues to how your son died.'

He spat on the ground at my feet. 'Look around you, girl. Do you not see what we are doing here? Every man available is searching for the killer. What can a woman barely away from her mother's skirt hem possibly do?'

He wasn't wrong, I'd no idea what more I might

do. Nothing other than to stop this madness anyway. I wanted to rail at him that me being a woman had nothing to do with it, but I needed to remain civil if I was to make progress with this man. 'Sir, it seems to me that the person who took your son's life will no longer be anywhere nearby. Two dozen pairs of feet tramping the ground will do little to enlighten us on who else might have been here. You might consider calling off your men or send them out more widely round the town in their searches and allow me to do what Mr Bagnall has requested.'

Mr Powell opened his mouth as if to hurl another insult at me but was stayed by the woman's hand on his arm. She spoke surprisingly calmly, despite her freely flowing tears. 'The young lady makes sense, my dear. Daniel is gone from us,' Her chest heaved, and she clenched a pudgy fist to her mouth for a moment, 'and we must do all we can to find who did this. Barking orders and running about has not achieved anything yet. Perhaps a gentler approach might.'

Her husband opened his mouth again, then snapped it shut and shook his head before walking to the middle of the garden. His voice rang out clear and drowned all the other noise. A man used to being obeyed. 'Hold on. Stop now. Everyone. There's nothing more to be done here. Those of you with horses ride as far as someone could run in an hour and work your way back. The rest, either go home to your beds or spread out amongst the streets and lanes until you meet the riders returning. All of you watch for strangers or anyone suspicious. Bring me news straight away if you find anything.'

Mrs Powell grasped my arm. She repeated the same excuses for her husband's uncivil behaviour that their son had used the previous day. 'Edward seems a little fierce at times. He has to be that way if he wants to keep control of the miners. They can be a rough lot to handle. Underneath, he is a considerate man and is only doing what he thinks best. He will be quieter now and let you do your job, I am sure.'

The mine manager came back, and he stared at me for a few seconds, his face creased with concern. 'You had better get on. Let the yard clear then do what you must. I will have words with Mr Bagnall when he arrives.' He called a lad over and spoke to him in a kindly fashion, his mood completely changed. 'Natty, you help Miss Valentine and her friend here. Show her where my ... my son ... died, and around the yard and anywhere else she wishes to see.'

Mr Powell bent and whispered in this Natty's ear, then put his arm around his wife's shoulders and steered her down the path back to the house. A couple sharing their grief.

I took in the scene again from where we stood, now that it was clear. The garden seemed magical in the lamplight, although, strangely, this made the blackness of the trees beyond more threatening. The hedge beside the lane let in two paths, one wide enough for a cart or carriage. The other, facing the front of the house, split in two, with a branch leading around the back, and a branch which Natty said led to the main door at the side. Within the spaces created by this arrangement grew all manner of shrubs and trees. Excellent cover for a killer.

Given all the activity, I thought it unlikely Peter or I would see anything new, but I asked Natty to grab a lamp and take us to where Mr Powell had found his son. It was by the main door, a spot which would not be easily seen from the lane and not at all from the front windows of the house. Could Daniel's killer have known where he would be invisible?

Starting from the corners of the house, Peter and I criss-crossed methodically for about twenty paces in all directions, until we had the entire area covered between us. We found nothing other than the searchers' boot prints where the ground lay damp. I could see the garden was looked after, with many plants and bushes, some of which I hadn't seen before, and hoped I could get back during daylight hours to see them better.

When we returned to the main door, Peter and I left Natty for a few moments, to admire a magnificent small tree, with hand-shaped leaves shining a most glorious red under the lamps. Something hanging from a branch caught my eye. A piece of rope, half an inch thick and perhaps a yard in length, easily long enough to strangle someone. This rope was out of place in the well-tended garden, where such an item wouldn't just be discarded. I've seen rope used to bind a broken branch, supporting a graft to heal, and I've used it often to tie apple boughs level with the ground to improve the yield. Neither of these were its purpose here and I could think of no job it would be performing. I waited until I saw Natty turn away, then grabbed the rope and slipped it in my bag.

A couple of minutes later, Natty pointed down the second path. 'That one goes round the house and comes out lower down the lane.'

"Show me."

He led the way and we checked both sides as we went. I saw nothing further to interest us, though it was thickly dark beyond the lamp's glow so wouldn't have expected much else. I sent Natty to fetch his Mr Powell when we arrived at the front again.

While we were waiting, Mr Bagnall came through the gate. He raised a hand when he saw me and came over. 'How is it going, Miss Valentine? Have you found anything?' I shook my head and ignored Peter looking baffled. I wanted to keep quiet about the rope until I was sure who I could trust. 'And you have looked everywhere?'

'Not everywhere, sir. Even though I'd asked them not to disturb the area, Daniel's body was taken away, and I haven't had chance to look inside yet. Your friend doesn't seem to like me much, so it'd be good if you can ask him to let me see his son's room.'

Mr Bagnall nodded, 'I will do my best, but Edward is grieving, so may not do as you wish.' The house door opened, and he left to console Daniel's father. The two spoke quietly for a few moments before coming back. Mr Bagnall stayed a pace away, and Mr Powell addressed me. The frown had returned to his face. 'Mr Bagnall tells me you would like to look in my son's room. Is this correct?'

'Yes, sir.'

'Then I must tell you the answer is "no". As far as I can see, you have little experience in these matters, and I will not have a slip of a girl digging through Daniel's private affairs. My wife convinced me to let you look outside and, as far as I'm concerned, that's enough. I won't have you in the house.'

I glanced at Mr Bagnall. He shrugged and tilted his head towards the gate. I took the hint and left, with Peter trailing behind.

In this dark garden, you lick your lips with the deliciousness of it, feeling you can almost take the grief in your hands and stroke it. To make it better, it is not just the lad's father, nor the mother, distraught, but every man and woman here is spilling it out. Horror and fear lap against the walls of this house.

After the deed was done, you went home to your bed. You couldn't sleep, so came back to watch. Edward Powell greeted you with tears, as he did everyone, suspecting nothing. Only grateful for the concern you displayed.

He directs you to go with some of the searchers, and you strain to contain a laugh, knowing their searching will be fruitless. You hope the men might come upon some hapless soul who cannot explain his presence and the blame will rain down on him. They collect around the coach gate then, in dribs and drabs, spread out along the lane. It is easy for you to slip away into the garden again to take up your vigil. If you'd been challenged you would have said you thought it a good idea to wait, in case the killer returned. The fools would have praised you for your cunning. There will be nothing to amuse you with the mob who have left. There will be plenty where you are.

A girl arrives, along with a lanky male. You have no idea who she is, or why she is here. She's dressed not even with the quality of Powell's clothes. Not in the style of a poor labouring girl either. The way she holds herself shows she's no idler and expects respect. If you met her in the street, you might take this woman to be a clerk, or a wealthy man's assistant, though it's clear she's more than that. You watch her speak to Powell, then to his fat wife, before she starts to examine the garden like she knows what she's doing. Not running every which way like Powell's idiots had. She moves slowly, with deliberation and precision.

You curse when she finds the length of rope, wishing once again you'd kept it with you. It's unfortunate, though something inside glows with the excitement of a link being formed between the two of you. A find which will puzzle her. Or does she already understand why it was there?

You consider it odd she doesn't show it to Matthias Bagnall when he questions her, and you sense the disappointment she must feel when he and Powell send her away. For a moment you think of her by your side. A soulmate perhaps.

Six

I couldn't sleep after we got home and suspected none in the household slept much either. A storm had broken soon after I went to bed and my mind raced with thoughts of stolen jewels and stolen lives. It was the middle of the night before I dropped off into a deep slumber.

By the time I stumbled late from my bed, the air felt much fresher. Mr Bagnall wasn't downstairs. I was told the family had eaten and gone to church. I dashed from New House and across the lane, shrinking under the barbed stare of the minister when the church door creaked open. Labourers and other poor folk huddled at the back, and I took a place amongst them. St Leonard's was full, with thanks being given for the harvest-time. It seemed to me that half the town must have been there. The minister, with many sickly-smiling glances at Mr Bagnall and Mr Powell, said prayers for the dead man.

After the service finished, I hung around outside,

hoping that Mr Bagnall would see that I hadn't neglected our Maker on a Sunday morning. It wouldn't have escaped his attention that I was still in my bed when he left. My wait wasn't in vain and he approached me after he'd spoken to many of the congregation, wealthy and poor, on his way from the church. My employer told me he'd heard of no more discoveries and asked me to reconsider taking on the case. I refused again. We walked back to New House in silence until, once inside, he asked me to join him in the drawing room.

By the fireplace, Mr Bagnall folded his arms and shook his head. 'Tut. You are still saying you will not help find that young man's killer, Miss Valentine?'

I didn't appreciate his disapproval, though couldn't afford to show it. 'It's not that I won't help, sir. As I've said. I can't. I don't feel I have the tools to do it. If you engage someone else, I'll be more than happy to assist.'

A year ago, I'd earned my living tending my master's garden. I'd learned how to do most jobs, but the heavy ones I'd had the wit to leave with my father or one of the other men. They'd the strength and the skill with spades, forks, and picks to do them in half the time, and with half the effort I would take. Why shouldn't it be the same with solving crimes? My teacher, Edwin, would have found his way through any maze with little effort, I was sure. He'd taught me never to take people or events at face value, to always ask questions, and to keep trying to fit pieces together until they made sense. What he didn't manage to pass on in the short time we were together, were all the little tricks making it possible. Gathering facts is one thing, putting them in the right order is quite another. Despite Mr Bagnall's confidence in me, I knew, deep down, I was an impostor.

He raised an eyebrow. 'It seems to me that if we don't have the tools to do a particular job, we buy them, make them, or find a different way of doing it without them. Are you saying you could not manage one of those, even with my help and the assistance of your Mr Turnstone?

I hung my head, grasping for excuses. 'I don't know the area, sir. This would be a real disadvantage.'

'A matter of little importance I'd say. We have no one of your experience in the town so if I were to engage another, they would face the same problem. It is easily remedied. I will give you someone who knows Broseley like he knows his own mother.'

'But I can't give it the time it needs, Mr Bagnall. It may take weeks and would be too far to travel from Bridgnorth every day. And ... and if I'd to be here late, I wouldn't want to travel that road back in the dark. I'd only planned to be here a few days to sort out the burglaries.'

'Nonsense. You can stay here as long as you need; I have already said as much. Look around you, Miss Valentine, is this not a fine house? You would continue to stay as my guest — not as a servant— and I'm sure you'll agree, your accommodation is quite comfortable.'

I told him it was more than adequate, and he began pacing the floor, back and forth, wringing his hands. I hadn't seen him so agitated since we'd arrived. Clearly, Daniel's death meant a lot to him. After he'd covered the whole room twice he stopped, looked from the window, then turned back to me and clapped.

'That's it. I provide you with someone with local knowledge, you stay in my home as long as you want, and you can bring in Mr Turnstone whenever you need him. You will have as much help as you require, and we will have the murderer swinging from the gallows before we know it.'

'But -'

'No, no, Miss Valentine, that's it settled. Do this for me and you will be well paid, make no mistake. I have every confidence in your ability to do what is required. Now, I believe you said your friend needed to go back to Bridgnorth. Walk with him to the edge of town then you can return and start your task.'

'Sir. Stop. This is not how it will be. If you wish me to look into the thefts, which is what you engaged me for in the first place, I'll do so. I won't take on the bigger job. I'm more than happy to accept your offers of accommodation and the help with local knowledge. Paying me fairly for my work goes without saying, I believe you to be an honourable and trustworthy man. I'll think about who might be able to assist you, and Peter can ask around when he returns home. Between us we'll find someone who's up to the job, and who'll not cheat you.'

Mr Bagnall paused, then sighed. 'If that is your decision then I must respect it, though I am not happy. Each hour which goes by makes that poor boy's killer harder to find. He was decent, and had his whole life in front of him, and I believe I owe it to his father to discover the person who took it from him.'

He started to say farewell to Peter, then beckoned him closer, and nodded in my direction, saying something which I didn't catch.

Peter didn't speak when we left New House. In fact, I don't think he would have spoken to me at all if I hadn't tugged at his sleeve when we passed the corner where I should leave him.

He turned and glared at me. 'What?'

'Are you going off without saying goodbye, Peter?'

He shrugged. 'Why shouldn't I?'

'Because I thought we were friends.' Friends? Is that what I think? More, surely?

'So did I, but friends don't make decisions without talking about it first.'

I let go of his sleeve, folded my arms, and stared. 'What decision is this?'

'You know very well, Meg.'

'Do you mean me refusing to do what old Bagnall told me to?'

He shuffled his feet and lowered his stare to the ground. 'When you put it like that ...'

'How else would I put it? The man's rich and used to getting his own way. I'm done with taking orders from people like that. And I don't need your permission to say no to him.'

'Don't forget there's money in it, Meg. Money and a leg up. If you were to catch that Powell lad's killer, just think how much work would come our way.'

'Our way? So there we have it. You've only your own interest at heart, just like all men.'

Peter's frown told me I'd gone too far. He may have been interested in the extra money we'd get, but he wasn't like all men. I'd always found him thoughtful and kind, ready to take one more step to help me when I needed it. In the early days working on my own, I'd needed it quite a lot.

As he turned away, I tugged his sleeve again. 'I'm sorry, Peter, that was unkind. I know a little extra money makes a difference to you and your family, as it does to me. All the same, I don't want to be forced into doing any wealthy man's bidding.'

'I can see why you wouldn't want to be pushed around, Meg. What I don't understand is why you're so against having a go. You'd be more than able to find whoever attacked Daniel Powell. You already found that rope which everyone else had missed.'

'You heard what I said to Mr Bagnall, I've not the experience to be taking on such a job. I found that rope, and I'm guessing it was used to strangle Daniel

Powell. But it *is* only a guess and I'm far from certain it really means anything. If I had Edwin nearby, I'd feel more confident, knowing he'd step in if I was struggling.'

'But you'll never get experience unless you try. We all sometimes face work we haven't done before. It's how we learn, isn't it? See the problem, step back, scratch the head, then give it the best we can. If the first idea doesn't work, try another.'

For the first time that day, I laughed. 'You make it sound so easy, Peter.'

'I didn't say it was. In fact I'm sure it's not. That's just the way *I* try to think. Anyway, will you do it?'

'I don't know. Ask around when you get back to Bridgnorth, see if there's anyone passing through who could take it on. Even if I shadowed them, or could ask for their help, it would be something. In the meantime, I'll talk to the locals about the thefts and stay listening for any clues on the other matter.'

I felt the time was right to ask the question I'd held on to since departing New House. 'What did Mr Bagnall say to you before we left, Peter?'

'Nothing. Just saying goodbye.'

'What, whispering? I don't think so. Come on, what was it?'

'He wanted me to convince you to find Daniel Powell's murderer.'

'Well you've done as he asked.'

'Don't be mad at me. I was going to anyway. And if a rich man like him has faith in you, you should have faith in yourself.'

For some reason, which came from nowhere, I took Peter's hand. 'I do appreciate your help, Peter, you know I do. If I can repay it, I will.'

He pulled his hand away quickly, then smiled, so I wasn't sure if it was my show of affection or my words caused his grin to return. He began to whistle tunelessly as he walked away down the lane. My own smile faded when he strode out of sight, and all the way back I wondered who was right. Mr Bagnall's offer of a decent payment was tempting. It would make me able to pay my bills for a good while. His recommendation for a job well done would also count for a lot and help secure more work in future. Of that, I was sure. What I was less sure about was being able to do the job well enough to gain his approval.

SEVEN

Beth Hurdley had enjoyed a good morning with her mother. They didn't always get on well, but today, in the kitchen, she'd shared her news, and the older woman had shrieked and clapped her hands with excitement, showering Beth with flour. The two had laughed so much. Ellen, Beth's youngest sister, had joined in and the four-year-old jumped up and down, giggling, until their mother told her to stop. The child, like all her brothers and sisters, did not need to be told twice.

Mother and elder daughter baked two loaves, prepared vegetable broth and, later, picked apples from the garden. Beth's father was away working in his fields, and wouldn't go hungry when he returned after dark. Her mother hugged her again before Beth left, kissed her on the forehead, and told her she must look after herself.

But you see none of this, other than the smile playing fresh on the pretty young woman's lips. You don't know the reason for her good mood, though you will later. You know nothing of her mother's excitement, nor of her little sister's joyful play, nor of a meal prepared. Your strong feelings inside, which returned so soon, tell you her parents' lives will never be the same come tomorrow.

You watch Beth close the gate from the cover of the bushes, where you'd jumped when you spotted her leave the house. It was only chance that you'd seen her. Dawdling the lanes when you should be working. Musing on your next theft. On the circumstances of your next release. You see her glowing skin, her long black hair, and you know, at other times, you'd want her in a different way. Now though, you have only one purpose, to satisfy this other longing. The desire to grab her, drag her into the field, and strangle the life from her is almost overwhelming, but she is strong. She would struggle in your hands and probably scream. In daylight, so close to this house, such an attack would be rash. Reason tugs at you. Wait, follow her to the cottage. Take her indoors and by surprise. Better, also, to savour the expectation, let the vision of the act grow inside your head. Smell it. Taste it.

Fifty yards behind, you now join Beth in her smile. Step by cautious step, you follow. Keeping close against the hedgerow, ready to duck into its cover if she turns. There's a danger, even in this. A snapping twig, or a startled pheasant, could alert her. She would stop. Listen. Turn. Then you'd need to act quickly. Speak to her as if met by luck? Take the chance and satisfy your need after all?

Beth meets no-one as she walks the ten minutes home. You note, not for the first time, the thatch is in need of repair. If only it was cared for as well as Beth's herb beds. You recognise the tall angelica and the fading pink flowers of mallow, but that is as far as your knowledge goes. She lifts the latch and goes inside. You find a space to stand unseen. Watching.

Five minutes pass, smoke begins to issue from the chimney. She will be in the kitchen, you are sure. When you shift your position to see inside, this is confirmed, her shape moves back and forth from stove to table. The thought comes. You will slip through the door if she goes into another room or the back garden. You fondle the new length of rope in your pocket and feel a tingle in your fingertips. The job will be quickly done, with no call for help escaping the thick cottage walls. What a delightful game.

As if at your bidding, Beth disappears. You are about to dash across the lane when you catch a movement from the cottage next door. The bent-backed woman carries a broom and begins to sweep fallen leaves from the flagstones. You wait until you sense the neighbour won't be going back inside soon. You turn away, and skulk through the bushes until you are clear from view, to emerge just a man on the road. There will be no satisfaction for you now. At least not for a few hours.

Having left Peter, I went up to my room and lay

down, weary from my late night. I'm not one for resting in the morning, not often having the chance to do so, and my straw-filled palliasse at home doesn't compare with this bed of the Bagnall's. For a few moments, sleep hovered over me. Peter's face, smiling, handsome, dragged me deeper in. Then a cart, with sacks covering a corpse, rolled through my head, and I was awake again. Why, in this tiny working town, would anyone want to kill a young man outside his front door? Not a fight or street argument, at least none that was heard by his family inside. The scrap of rope, did it matter? From what I understood of murder, taking that length of rope and stripping the life out of Daniel must have been planned. A cold-blooded act. Senseless, beyond any real reason or logic. I'd told the ironmaster I didn't feel able to enquire into Daniel's death, but this didn't stop the questions coming.

What would Edwin do? He'd not rush in, that's for certain. His interest was in getting a result where he'd be paid. He'd wait, consider what every scrap of evidence might mean, and only then take action. He'd talk to his contacts, lots of them throughout the county, His experience would tell him what was important and what wasn't. I smiled as I thought of the first time he'd helped me, and the pride I'd felt when he'd thanked me for helping him to catch a killer.

It must have been only seconds after this that the tiredness won, with me not surfacing until Eliza knocked my door to say lunch was being served.

The dining room table was laid with all manner of cold meats, and a bowl of plump, red apples. A large jug of beer stood at the centre. Mr Bagnall waved a hand across the feast. 'Help yourself, Miss Valentine.' He lifted the jug. 'Will you take a drink?'

I nodded and he poured a mugful for me and for himself. His wife declined. Both wore a pasty expression, as if they'd just risen. Mrs Bagnall must have anticipated my thought. 'I trust you slept, Miss Valentine? My husband and I also took the opportunity to rest, though I find daytime sleeping is very taxing. It seems impossible to properly wake up afterwards, do you not think? Still, I expect we needed it after a night such as we had.'

Mr Bagnall was largely silent whilst we ate. His wife chit-chatted all the time, asking me of my home in Bridgnorth, my parents, and digging for every detail of the murder I'd worked on with Edwin. To spare her nerves I kept the more unpleasant facts to myself. I have to admit I enjoyed telling her how I'd started out as a mere under-gardener but soon after I'd met the thief-taker I was interviewing suspects and even wielded a pistol to protect us. I may have built up my part a little more than was true, though she didn't appear to notice anything amiss. Her eyes sparkled as I told the tale.

After we'd finished eating, Mr Bagnall asked me how I would approach finding whoever was house breaking.

I'd given a lot of thought to this since our discussion in the morning. I'd to show some fitness for the job, so I hoped my answer sounded confident. 'The first step, I think, will be to take a look at the town so I can see if there's anything connects the properties broken in to. Are they all hidden from view, or close together, that kind of thing. Then I'll talk to the victims, again to find out what their burglaries have in common. After that, we'll have to see where it takes us.'

Mr Bagnall nodded as I spoke and rubbed his chin before he replied. 'You appear to have it well mapped out Miss Valentine. There have been thefts on and off for years, though the severity has increased recently. Bolder, if you will. Higher value items taken, and so on. From the top of my head I know of nothing which would make these houses targets more than any others. True, they tend to be bigger than most, reflecting the wealth of their owners. They would not be worth burgling if they weren't. As for the victims, as I say, they would all be affluent, largely men of business, and I would be acquainted with most of them. One strange thing is that the thefts ceased for a month this summer, then began again about three weeks ago. This is why I decided to engage a thief-taker.'

'Do you have any idea, sir, why they stopped then started again?'

'None, I am afraid. We had all hoped the thief had moved on to another place, but it seems not. This cannot go on, so I hope you can find the scoundrel.'

After lunch, I told Mr Bagnall I would take a walk. I needed to clear my head. I also wanted to begin to get the lay of the land. New House stood at the south-eastern end of the town, close to St Leonard's Church and a few cottages, hardly more than a hundred steps from where I'd left Peter that morning. Other than the short walk to where Edward Powell lived, I'd seen nothing of the place. I wandered away from the Bridgnorth turnpike, and the lane clearly sloped uphill all the way, for I was puffing by the time I reached the centre. Several shops and taverns surrounded a pond, and I waited to catch my breath at the waterside. When I'd rested for a few minutes, I carried on with my walk. The land continued to rise. From the top of the hill I could take in the roofs of all the buildings back as far as New House and St Leonard's.

All of the road in this part of the town was deeply rutted and black. I understood why when a cart, piled high with coal and pulled by six horses, thundered past. I'd seen similar by the Severn in Bridgnorth, so now knew they must come from the Broseley mines. Two old women, sitting in front of a cottage, stopped their conversation and eyed me as I went past. A gaggle of children, with ragged clothes and dirty knees, shrieked and splashed in a puddle in the cart track.

To the west and the north, the land fell away sharply into the valley and here were ramshackle cottages on top of ramshackle cottages, with muddy paths running between them. The pall of chimney smoke floating above was thicker than I'd seen anywhere and I guessed this was where the miners lived. These homes were hovels compared to that of Mr Bagnall, who owned the mine, and to that of his mine manager, Mr Powell. I'd lived in a loft above my master's stables, while he lived in a fine, big house, so this shouldn't have been a surprise to me. But it was. I'd only looked after my master's garden, providing him with a service, while these people dug the coal that gave their master his fortune. It all seemed so unfair.

Further on, the town started to thin out, with better tended cottages lining a lane which the milestone announced ran to Much Wenlock. As I turned back, a cold wind whipped up, reminding me autumn was well on its way. Minutes later, I needed to shelter under a tree from a sudden shower, with golden leaves falling around me. When it had passed, I hurried through the town in case the rain returned. I was pulled up by a shout from one side. The young lad, Natty Preece, who I'd met at the Powell's house, peeled away from a group of men. He, like all of them, was covered with coal dust from the crown of his head down to his boots.

'Miss .... miss, I have some news for you.'

I asked him what it was.

'The word in the mine is that the thieving had stopped, then started up again.'

'I know this, Natty. What has it to do with Daniel Powell's killing?'

He folded his arms and fixed me with a look suggesting I was stupid, 'Nothing, miss, only I heard you say you were *also* looking to find a thief. If you are, then you should talk to the folk camped out by Rough Lane. They were there until middle of June then moved off for a while. They're back now though.'

'Rough Lane?'

'Go past Mr Bagnall's and St Leonard's, to the corner. Do a quick left then the right-hand fork. That's Rough Lane. About a quarter mile down there you'll see some trees and they're camped this side of them.' He grinned. 'D'you want me to come with you?'

'No thank you, Natty. I'll find my own way.' His grin fell away and I was immediately sorry for rejecting his offer. 'It's very kind of you. You get yourself home and cleaned up for now. Perhaps you can help next time.'

Eight

The tinkers were where Natty had said they would
be. Four carts, made the corners of a square, all on
the side of the field sheltered by a coppice. Canvas
canopies were strung between two of the carts,
providing extra protection for the tents beneath. The
camp was a jumble of dogs, even scruffier children
than the ones I'd seen in the town, and ground
strewn with pots, pans, and the tools for mending
them. In the midst of all this, two men tended a
brazier. Father and son by the look of them.

The children, six in all, ran towards me, criss-
crossing each other and the dogs that barked
alongside them. One of the men shouted them back.
They stopped, looked round as if they might disobey,
then turned and sheepishly walked to where they'd
been playing.

The older man put his tongs, ends glowing red,
back into the fire, and walked to face me. A strong-
looking man, he reminded me of my father, with his
tanned skin and muscled forearms, developed

through years of hard toil in the open air. They'd have been about the same age as well.

The man's eyes, hooded and suspicious, told me he wasn't too keen on strangers. 'Whaddya want?'

I introduced myself. He didn't. 'I just wanted a word.'

'About what?'

'I'm looking into some thefts. Valuables taken from houses in the town.'

He laughed, then spat. 'Ha, I might have known. We turn up, only looking for a bit of work, something goes missing, so we're to blame. Happens all the time.'

'I'm sorry, Mister ...?'

'People call me Solomon. Plain Solomon. No need for that Mister nonsense with me.'

The scowl didn't disappear.

'Then I'm sorry, Solomon. I didn't mean to insult you. And you're right. Some things have gone missing, and the finger has been pointed at you and your friends. But I'm not doing any pointing. I'm only asking questions. You look me square in the eyes and tell me you had nothing to do with it. Then I'll believe you.'

Before he answered I already knew they'd not stolen anything, or at least nothing of any real value. Their camp said it all. These were poor people, earning what they could from the trade they practised. There'd be evidence of them living a better life if they'd the benefit of gold and jewels stolen from Broseley gentle folk.

Solomon folded his arms and stared directly at me. 'I hate to have to do it, though the good Lord knows the blame will stick if I don't. So I say to you, Meg Valentine, neither I nor any of my family have taken anything you need worry about. Now if you was asking about a few eggs or a gill of milk, I'd p'raps put my hands up and curse you for begrudging it. Never nothing valuable. That's not our way.'

He knew as well as I that the courts would be as likely to hang him for stealing eggs and milk as they would for taking a fine jewel or killing a man. I also knew *he* could see the difference, even if the judges can't.

'Then I apologise again, Solomon. Can I ask you two questions though?'

'What sort of questions?'

'Ones that'll help me find who's really behind this thieving. Won't do you any harm either, stop the finger pointing your way.'

He thought for a minute, then turned back towards where he'd been working. 'You'll need to come sit by the fire while I finish this job.'

I followed him across the field and watched him heat a lump of metal fire until it glowed. He lifted it out and beat it, sparks flying, to be round and thin, before punching a hole in its centre and plunging it a bucket of water at his side. Five minutes later he'd used the disc to fix a hole in a large, black, kettle. His care and skill were obvious. When he'd finished, he passed it to his son, who filled it from the bucket.

Solomon held the kettle high. He ran his tongue

slowly across his top lip as he examined his work. 'That's a good 'un. Now, what was them questions you wanted to ask?'

'You were here 'til the start of the summer, then left and came back a couple of weeks ago.'

'That's right. We do the fairs in July and August. Wandered from here down to Hereford, over to Worcester, then Stratford-on-Avon and worked our way back. Can be good money in it sometimes. Not this year though, no money about with the price of bread as it is. Men going to fix their own pots and pans rather than paying us to do it for them.'

'When you were here, was anyone with you not a member of the family?'

He shook his head. 'No. Just me, the wife and little 'uns, plus her brother and his lot.'

'Fine, Solomon, just one last thing. You heard about the lad who was murdered yesterday?'

'I did. But you're not trying to say we had anything to do with it?'

'Not for a minute. I just wondered if you'd heard word around about who might have?'

The tinker stood and pulled another piece from the fire and began hammering at it. He turned and held the smoking tongs close to my face. 'Heard nothing and want to hear nothing. Rich boy gets himself killed, that's sad, but none of my business. Now, I think you'd best be going.'

I didn't wait to be asked twice, so thanked him for his truthfulness and left him in the field. Behind me, the sound of hammer on anvil didn't drown out the taunts of the chasing children.

With no progress made, there seemed to be little point going straight back to New House, so I turned down a lane on my right, as soon as I was out of sight of Solomon and his brood. It was barely the width of a cart and hemmed in on both sides by shrubbery and trees, making it dark and still. Had it been in the evening I'd have been cautious about venturing far, but I could see it became lighter a little further along, so I continued. The bushes on the southern edge of the track carried on into the distance, whilst a large, flat, field spread out on the other. Almost as far away as I could see, a man appeared to be feeding pigs from a bucket. He showed no sign of seeing me, probably because my dark clothes blended with the hedgerow. I watched him for a while. Old or young I couldn't tell, nor anything of his complexion or features. He looked at peace, moving amongst the animals, stroking one, throwing a morsel to another. When I lived with my parents, I was never keen on pigs, always wary of their pointed teeth. This labourer was at one with them.

Straight ahead, perhaps quarter of a mile away, stood a cottage, thick smoke rising idly from its chimney.

Tom Hurdley lifted a post to move the picket ten feet across the field and before he could lift the next one, the pigs were already snuffling in the ground, ripping up the white and purple turnips, crunching them like they'd never been fed. By the time he got to the fourth post, the snouts were chewing more slowly. Before long, the pigs would be lying down, basking in the late afternoon sunshine. Tom wished he could do the same but knew he couldn't afford another break today. His wandering through the lanes in the morning was time he wouldn't be get any money for. Even so, there'd been other benefits. He moved another post and the pigs dived in to the next rows of turnips. The animals weren't his, he only tended them for his friend and neighbour, Jake. On days like this Tom felt so close to them, as if they did belong to him.

He dreamt of renting his own piece of land someday soon. It was almost all he and Beth talked about. Not quite all. When he'd returned home earlier to eat, she'd seemed like she wanted to talk about something else, and though he'd asked her what it was, his wife told him it was nothing, and it would wait until dinnertime. She'd been to her mother's in the morning and he'd thought there might be a problem with her parents, but Beth was in a good mood, so he decided it mustn't be too serious.

He'd heard of no land coming up for rent for a while, and even if there had been, he'd not have enough cash to put up front. Not yet. So he'd just keep on tending the plough, digging ditches, cutting hedges, feeding pigs, and whatever it took. Getting money from wherever he could, until he'd saved enough to approach a landowner with an offer. He knew he hadn't long. He and Beth had been married over a year, and children would be bound to come along soon. Then there'd be even fewer coppers to put away.

In his quiet, rhythmic world he tossed another few turnips on the ground and looked over the fields to Jake's cottage in the distance. The man was his closest friend. Even so, Tom couldn't help feeling envious of all he had. Jake's father owned his land and made a good living from it. Jake would inherit it all one day and, in the meantime, got a good wage for the hours he put in, while Tom got a pittance for tending Jake's pigs. Hard work and honesty were for fools.

He caught a movement in the distance. Was someone watching him? Tom squinted, covering his eyes to shield them from the sun. He stared for a few seconds more and decided it must have been the wind in the hedgerow. With a glance over at his own cottage, he bent his back to pull out the final fence stake.

As I drew closer to the cottage, I could see that it was, in fact, two, the closest one in considerably poorer condition than the farthest, apart from the well-tended herb garden at the front. The smoke which I'd thought thick was from the pair of chimneys, one for each cottage, rising from the middle of the thatched roof.

When I reached the first, a woman only a little older than me, was hanging washing on a line strung between two apple trees. She raised a hand and smiled. 'Fine afternoon. Out for a walk?'

I said that I was.

She tucked a stray lock of hair into her scarf. 'Not many come down here. "Lost Lane" they call it on account of you can't really see it from anywhere unless you're on top of us. Doesn't go anywhere either, just into the woods then drops to the river.'

'It's very pretty, and your cottage is ... nice.'

As I spoke, a lone magpie which had been looking down beady eyed from the thatch chattered and flew away, its blue-black and white wings stark against the sky.

The woman turned at the sound and looked back at her home. 'I suppose so. I'd rather be in the town, but Tom's dad built this years ago and we got it to ourselves when he went to his Maker last year. Distant cousin of his lives next door but we don't get on. I don't think I know you do I?'

'I'm not from round here. Just working in Broseley for a few days. Meg's the name.'

'Beth, Beth Hurdley.'

'Pleased to meet you, Beth.' I said it and I meant it. Though this woman had good looks which might make me envious, she seemed a pleasant soul, and as friendly as any I'd met so far in Broseley.

'And what kind of work would you be doing, Meg?'

A question I'm never sure how to answer in the day-to-day way of things. If I think there might be work in it, or if someone is trying to lord it over me,

I'll tell them straight out I'm a thief-taker. I've found with most other people it's better not to bother. They either scoff, act as if you've ideas above your station, or ask for stories of your escapades. I decided to be vague. 'Mr Bagnall, of New House, has taken me on for a week. See how I do.'

This appeared to satisfy her curiosity, and she pointed in the direction I'd walked from. 'You'll have seen my Tom in the field up yonder. Thinks more of them pigs than he does of me, I reckon.' Though her words were harsh, she laughed, then bent to pick up her basket and walked towards her door. 'Anyway, this isn't getting my work done. Nice talking to you, Meg, and maybe I'll see you again.'

NINE

Beth pressed her nose and cheek to the window to see as far down the lane as she could. There was no sign of Tom, and the sun had almost set. She hoped he hadn't gone straight to the tavern again without his supper, she had so much to tell him. It wasn't something he did often, only twice since they'd married. Both times, when he'd arrived home late, they'd argued, and Beth hated to fall out. Later he'd apologised, though she'd not let him off lightly. It was important he knew what she'd take and what she wouldn't. He worked hard and enjoyed a mug of ale now and again, so she didn't usually object. Like last night, as long as he came home for his meal first and he didn't have too much. He could get a temper on him when he did.

Tom's temper worried her. Mostly he was the gentlest, quietest man. Just, sometimes, he wasn't, and she didn't know why. Beth understood how the drink might make him different, but some nights he went out and when he came home, she could smell nothing of the alehouse on him. If she asked where he'd been he'd rear up, then sit silently by the fire until going up to bed. Occasionally, Beth would catch him glaring at her, as though a deep anger simmered inside.

She went back to stirring the pot, all the time rubbing her stomach with the other hand. Beth's mother had told her she'd feel nothing this early, but Beth was sure she could. She was also sure a bump was beginning to show. Beth had always been so thin, and Tom would surely notice. For the last week she'd turned away when she changed for bed so he wouldn't see.

Beth swung the crane off the full heat of the fire, left the pot to simmer, and went to the door. Before stepping outside she peered both ways into the gloom. All the way home from her mother's she'd felt watched and had kept the house bolted when Tom went back to work after eating. She knew it must just be her imagination, Broseley was such a quiet place. But the bats flitting through the dusk, and the story her mother had told her of the previous night's murder, made Beth unsettled.

Satisfied there were no strangers lurking in the bushes, she stepped outside and peered down the lane. From the direction of the town, the white moon of a face hovered in the darkness. She was about to duck back inside and lock the door when a hand was raised and Tom's voice rang out.

"Ho, Beth. I'll be there in a minute. Sorry I'm late.'

Soon, Tom was cleaning up, and Beth put the finishing touches to his meal, making sure the stew was good and hot. This mix of pork knuckle and greens, was his favourite. She needed him to be happy before she broke her news.

When he'd wiped the last dregs of gravy from his plate with a lump of bread, Tom leant back in his seat and laid his hands on his stomach. 'That was delicious. So what's it you want to tell me?'

Beth laughed. 'Who says I want to tell you anything, Tom Hurdley?'

'You did, or at least as good as, when I was here for my dinner. You've also not stopped grinning and taking peeks at me since I got home. Come to think of it, since when did I get such a fine meal on a workday? Come on, spit it out.'

Beth went and stood beside her husband and lifted his hand from his stomach on to her own. 'Do you feel anything?'

His hand strayed upward. She pushed it down again. 'Now you behave Tom and answer me. Do you feel anything?'

He shook his head. 'No.'

'Nothing moving?'

Tom pulled his hand away. 'You're not -'

'Yes, I am. We're going to have a baby.'

Her husband pushed back his chair and stood, pressing his fingertips to his forehead. 'You can't be ... we can't be ... how can we afford a child?'

Beth didn't say anything, just pinched her nose and walked to look out of the window.

Less than a minute passed before Tom stood behind her, wrapping his arms round her waist. She stayed stiff, not letting him in. Her words were a whisper. 'I thought you'd be pleased. A family. We talked about it.'

He softly kissed her neck. 'We did, and I'm sorry, Beth. It's just such a shock. All afternoon I've been thinking of how I can get money to rent some land, and now this.'

Beth wrenched herself out of his hug, swung round, and pushed him away. 'Land! Above me and our child! How dare you?'

Neither spoke for half an hour. She cleaned their bowls away, peeled vegetables for next day, and scrubbed the floor. Tom stared into the fire. When Beth took the other seat he looked across and grinned. She simply glared at him, wiping the smile off his face.

Tom stood and walked to the door. 'If that's how it's to be I'll see you later.' He lifted the latch and went out.

Now it was Beth's turn to stare into the fire. With Tom taking to the drink again, she wondered how this night was going to end.

Tom avoided The Angel. He hadn't enjoyed it the night before, watching Daniel Powell dancing with any woman he wanted. Why should that man be interested in his Beth when Powell could have any woman in the town? Tom had only stayed for a while, keeping out of sight, getting more and more angry.

Tonight he was angry again when he walked into The Plough. Not with Powell this time. That lad had got what he deserved. Now he was mad at Beth for pushing him so hard. It was just as well he'd bumped into Jake. Tom swallowed a long mouthful of ale, banging his tankard down on the table when he finished. 'Said I think more of getting a farm than I do of her, Beth did. Don't she know I'm only doing it *for* her?'

Jake clamped a strong hand on his friend's shoulder. 'Course she does. Just mad at you 'cos you said the wrong thing. Women is different, you should know that by now. Beth'd expect you to be as excited about having a little 'un as she is, and you weren't.'

'She shouted at me, then wouldn't talk at all, even when I tried to make up.'

Jake took a slow sip of his drink, nodding to a man at a nearby table as he did so, then turned his attention back to his friend. 'Look Tom, that wife of yours is a fine woman.' he laughed 'too good for you at any rate.'

'Don't you think I know that, Jake. Her dad rents ten acres, and here's me with nothing. Every waking minute I'm thinking how I can take that step up.' He leaned in close to Jake and whispered in his ear. 'There's always a chance to make a shilling if you've no scruples.' Tom tapped the side of his head with his first finger. 'I've a scheme or two.'

'Like what?'

'Oh, schemes, that's all.'

'Hah. Tom Hurdley, you're a rum one. Never known a man with such an eye on the money.'

'That's ripe from you with all *your* dad's land.' Tom took a swig and belched. "Who d'you think's behind these burglaries?'

'You? Tom, say it's not you.'

'Well the wish is there. Serving up a good shilling it's said.'

Jake laughed again, this time spraying Tom with drink as he coughed and spluttered. It took several minutes of him beating his chest and wheezing before he could speak again. 'God's teeth, thought I was gone there.' He lifted his empty tankard. 'You getting another in or not? With your pockets full from being this master thief you can afford it.'

Four drinks later, the two men had roamed a wide range of topics including the King, the cost of bread, labourers' wages, and ailments in pigs. No solution had been reached on any of them, and each had seamlessly moved on to the next and back again.

With every emptied tankard, the words flowed more freely and Tom had become more relaxed. 'Jake? Can I ask you something?'

'That sounds serious.'

'It is, or at least it might be. D'you think Beth's seeing someone else?'

'What?'

'Another man. She's been very quiet about the house these last two weeks, and I've caught her once or twice smiling to herself.'

A picture of Beth laughing at him earlier in the day came into Jake's head and he paused, for a second longer than he should, before berating his friend's fears. 'Don't be a fool, Tom. There's plenty of men out there would like to take a chance on Beth, but she'd have none of it. I'd say she's been totally mad about you since you met.'

'Took your time to think about that though, didn't you? If there's all these men fancy her, and she's not taking up with 'em, what's she grinning about morning, noon and night?'

'It would be my guess she's been thinking about this baby. Now you drink up, go home, and tell Beth you're sorry.'

Tom stood and flung his arms round Jake, before weaving his way to the door. Outside The Plough, the cool night air slapped his eyes wide. As the church bell struck nine, he knew he should be at home with his wife and their child-to-be.

TEN

Tom wandered through the town, no longer staggering from the ale. Not so steady as he might have been without it. His mind swam with thoughts of his wife, and of the baby she'd told him about earlier before he'd stormed out to the tavern. Thoughts of how he's going to say he's sorry.

As this last one gripped him, he increased his stride, hurrying as best he could in the darkness, the new moon barely forcing any light through the clouds which had gathered. The walk to Lost Lane took only a few minutes and Tom caught a glimpse of his cottage when lightning flickered.

He stopped in the lane. Watched his pretty wife through the window, the candlelight on her skin turning her into an angel. For a moment. Then the memory of the child and everything it meant for his plans came back to him and the anger bubbled up again. His breathing deepened and Tom closed his eyes. When he opened them after a few seconds, the angel was back.

Tom went indoors, tried to take Beth in his arms, but she pushed him away. He slurred words of apology. She gave him the coldest of stares.

There was confusion in his eyes. 'What is it, Beth, I can't touch you now, is that it?'

Beth's reply was a shriek, like he'd never heard her before. 'There's been too much touching already. Too, too much. More than a man like you deserves.'

'A man like me? What does that mean? 'You've found better I suppose.'

'Could hardly be any worse, could he?'

The insults and recriminations went round and round until there was a rap at the door. Both froze, then turn their heads to the sound. Tom opened the door to speak to the woman standing in the muggy darkness, their neighbour, Mrs Reader.

She craned her neck to see inside, though Tom blocked her view. 'What's going on? Screaming and shouting at this time of night. Where's Beth?'

'Beth's in the kitchen, not that it's anything to do with you.'

'Can I see her?'

'No you can't. We're busy.'

'Doesn't sound like you're busy, more like you're about to knock the skin off each other.'

'Even so, still nothing to do with you, is it? Just clear off and leave us to it.'

Tom shooed the woman away in the direction of her own cottage. With no further words, she did as he demanded. He watched until the first heavy raindrops splashed on the leaves, then slammed the

door and returned inside to dig out the stoneware
gin bottle his father had dipped into most nights.
Tom hadn't touched it since the old man died.

Beth stood with her back to the fire, arms folded
and still glowering at Tom. She didn't speak when he
slumped down at the table, uncorked the bottle, and
poured a large measure.

Tom kept his voice low. 'So who is he?'

'Who?'

'This man you're seeing.'

A harsh laugh. 'Are you joking, Tom Hurdley,
what man would I be seeing?'

'Don't lie to me, Beth. You already said he
couldn't be any worse than me.'

'That's not what I meant, and you know it.'

His fist on the table rattled round the room. 'I
don't know it, that's the trouble. Your mind's been
away for weeks, and I see you smiling when you
think I'm not looking.' Tom threw the gin down his
throat and poured another, which followed the first.
'And now you're expecting. Is it his?'

'You're a fool, Tom. A stupid, drunken, fool.'

Beth turned away and stared through the
window into the blackness of the fields behind the
cottage. She muttered something more, but her
words were lost in a crack of thunder. Tom stood
stock still and glared, the anger rising once more.

The morning light stung Tom's eyes. His head
throbbed and his mouth felt like he'd eaten a sow's

backside. He gagged as the stench of vomit on the pillow hit his nostrils. His father's gin bottle came back to him, and he groaned. He'd never been able to stomach spirits, especially on top of the two quarts of ale he'd downed in the town. There'd be an apology to Beth required. Something behind the fog tugged at him. A picture of them arguing. Strong words. Raised voices. Wanting to shut her up.

He turned on the bed to lay a hand on her shoulder but found fresh air. Tom stretched out his arm, thinking she may have moved away to avoid the smell. Still he found nothing. Raising himself on one elbow, he cursed when he opened his eyes and the light seared though his brain. His wife wasn't there.

Holding back his urge to throw up again, Tom staggered out of bed, thankful that he'd not undressed the night before, not even his boots, and though he felt soiled, at least he didn't have to face the torment of bending to pull on his pants. He stood for a moment, one hand on his stomach and the other on his forehead, until the dizziness took him again and he slumped back down.

Tom called his wife. 'Beth?'

No reply. He shouted her name again, louder. Still nothing came back. Now he knew he must force himself to get off the bed. Beth rarely left the house early. He'd be certain she'd not let him sleep in because he'd a drink taken. Not unless she was still mad at him from their argument. Was Beth just ignoring his call, or was she piling on the guilt by doing his morning's work? The only way he'd be saved from a severe telling off would be if he caught up with her, made her believe how sorry he was, and then tend Jake's pigs like he was supposed to. Perhaps then he'd get away with her not speaking to him for the rest of the day. Much better than any alternative he could think of.

He cursed again when he stood the second time, and when he took his first step. The third step got him to the wall and some support. By the time he reached the door at the bottom of the stairs, Tom had recovered a degree of balance and was ready to face the woman he'd despised so much the night before.

Eleven

I gulped the last of my bread when Eliza came to tell me Mr Bagnall wanted to see me in the hall. The men I'd met at the Powell house, Kite and Smitheman, were standing at the front door.

My host's face was ashen when he spoke. 'Ernest, tell Miss Valentine what you've just told me.'

The smaller of the two shuffled his feet. 'There's been another one, miss.'

'Another what?'

'A killing. Young Beth Hurdley. Found by a neighbour not half an hour ago. My place is on the corner of Rough Lane and Lost Lane, and she came a-banging on my door. I went back with her then fetched Frank and came round here.'

'How do you know she was killed?'

Kite shook his head. 'What else could it be, miss, Beth would be no more than early twenties? Fit and healthy woman like that, not going to just drop dead, is she?'

I knew he was right. Certainly she'd no signs of

illness the previous afternoon when I spoke to her. A second killing in as many days? How could this be? Two young people with their lives snuffed out. Two people I'd briefly met and instantly liked.

Soon, I was at Beth Hurdley's cottage on Lost Lane. Mr Bagnall had asked if I'd take a look and though I'd told him yet again I didn't feel up to the job, he'd pressed, I'd finally agreed, and he'd sent Frank Smitheman and Ernest Kite with me. I'd left them on the road with an instruction not to let anyone else into the house. Despite the coolness of the morning after the night's storm there was no smoke rising from the chimney. Just inside the door, a woman about my mother's age sat on a three-legged stool, staring with blank eyes at the body lying on the floor. I asked her name. I thought for a moment she hadn't heard me until she turned slowly and looked up.

'Annie Reader,' she cocked her head towards the wall, 'I live next door.'

'And you found her?'

The smallest nod.

'How?'

'I was worried about her. Such a row last night. Quiet this morning though, then I saw him running out of the house. Came round to take a look and there she was. Could see Beth was dead the minute I saw her. Raced up to tell Ernest as fast as my legs would take me. Should have done more last night ... I knocked the door ... he chased me away.'

'You say he chased you? Who?'

'The husband. Tom Hurdley. Drunk he was I reckon. Been out anyway, I saw him coming home. Next thing there's all this shouting and raving, so I came to tell them to stop. Told me to clear off, he did. He'd never have got away with that if his dad was still alive. Him and me were cousins, you know. Real gentleman his father was, always polite to me and mine.'

'What time was this?'

'Late. Was dark and fire was dying down, so a while after nine o'clock I'd say.'

'But Mrs Hurdley was still alive then?'

'She was. Caught a glimpse of her in here, face red as a beetroot. Didn't speak though, he wouldn't let me.' The woman stood, then sat again. 'Why didn't I make him leave her alone? Or ask her to come and stay with me for the night? Poor girl would still be alive then.'

I told her she wasn't to know something bad would happen, and the argument might not be connected to Beth's death. She laughed bitterly and shook her head.

'How can it not be connected? If Tom Hurdley didn't kill his wife, why isn't he here? Tell me that. Wouldn't be the first time a husband lost his temper and done for his wife. Won't be the last either, I'd say. Odd though.'

'Odd in what way?'

'First time I ever heard them fight. I'd hear a cross word now and then if they was outside, but no more than any other man and wife. This was different. Really full-blown row, both of them loud as can be. Her more than him. Stopped soon after I was here though. Big bang after I went back inside, like a door being slammed, then nothing. Seemed to me one of them had gone off to bed. Is that when he did it, d'you think?'

I repeated that I didn't know if Tom Hurdley *had* murdered his wife,

'Then I say it again, why'd he run away this morning? Saw him. Like a scared rabbit, he was, out the door and into the fields. Off to his friend's I'd expect. Thick as thieves them two.'

'Friend?'

'Jacob Slack. Jake, they call him. Lives about a quarter of a mile out the back of here. There's a track a bit further down the lane. Tom didn't go that way, in too much of a hurry.' I stood and asked her to show me the track. She shook her head. 'No point going down there now, he'll be off to market in Bridgnorth, won't be home 'til I don't know when. Probably stay over and spend all he's made in the alehouse. Might be tomorrow he'll wander back, even the day after.'

I thanked her for her time and told her she should go home. When I went to the door with her, I asked the man called Smitheman to search around for the husband, and sent the other to bring help to take the dead woman's body away.

Inside, I bent and looked her over. The only mark I could see looked like a burn around her throat, all the way from front to behind her ears. Had she been strangled?

A bottle stood on the table, empty. One chipped glass. I sniffed it. Gin? I knew it wasn't just ale. I checked there was no smell of it on Beth. So Tom Hurdley had been drinking, either before or after their argument. At first glance nothing in the room was out of the ordinary, other than, of course, a dead body in the middle of it, and the fire not having been lit. This suggested she'd met her end the previous night, not after she rose in the morning, though I couldn't be sure.

There wasn't much in the room. Two tables, one for eating off, with two chairs, and one for preparing food. All of these looked roughly made, probably by the husband. A pail half-full of water and a basket of vegetables stood beside the second table. What lifted the kitchen out of the normal was the collection of knick-knacks hanging on the walls and scattered on every surface. Beth Hurdley clearly liked to keep her home and garden looking nice, even if the cottage wasn't in the best of repair.

I raked through the hearth. Among the grey cinders and ashes, something thin and black, the length of my finger, stood out. When I lifted it and held it by the window, I could see it to be a piece of rope, too charred to tell immediately if was the same as the one I found in Edward Powell's garden. I slipped it into my pocket until I could compare them properly.

It took only a few minutes to have a look round upstairs. Again, I could see nothing linked to the killing of the wife below and when someone banged at the front door I was glad to get away from the stench of stomach contents.

Smitheman, the man I'd sent searching, stood on the step. Four others, including Kite, were by a cart in the lane. I asked Smitheman if he'd found Tom Hurdley.

'Not a sign of him, miss. Been up and down,' he cocked his head towards the other side of the lane, 'and through the bushes yonder. If he'd been there, I'd have seen him. Master's sent these lads to take Mrs Hurdley's body to be looked after. I'll go with them if there's nothing else?'

In as short a time as was decent and respectful, they'd put Beth's body on the back of their cart and covered her with a blanket I'd fetched from the bedroom. I watched as they rolled away, wondering why two young people had been so cruelly killed in this quiet little town. Also wondering what my next step should be.

Twelve

Matthias Bagnall was waiting for me when I returned, and stood as I entered his drawing room. 'Did you discover anything, Miss Valentine? Smitheman told me there was no sign of the husband. I've put more men out to search, but they've not found him yet.'

'Not much to see. That poor woman lay cold on the floor, looks like she'd been there all night. The only odd thing was she had some marks on her throat and there was a small piece of rope in the hearth. It's my first guess that Beth Hurdley had been choked to death and whoever did it tried to burn the evidence.'

Mr Bagnall gasped. 'Strangled? Like Daniel?'

'I think so.' I still had no desire to tell him of the piece I'd found in the Powells' garden. 'There are other things which seem the same, which I'd rather not go into until I'm sure.'

'That would seem to be a wise decision. We don't want to set hares running unnecessarily, do we? Are you telling me you've decided to examine Daniel's death after all?'

'I hadn't when I went to Lost Lane. At least no more than I'd agreed to.'

'But you will now?'

I was still torn. Though I didn't have the confidence to do the job, I'd liked both Daniel Powell and Beth Hurdley in the brief time I'd known them. There was also something fascinating about the deaths. This wasn't just some stupid killing in a street fight or a robbery, there was more. Two young people, with no obvious connection and nothing to suggest either of them had enemies, both seemingly strangled in, or close to, their own homes. What linked the son of an affluent mine manager with a farm labourer's wife?

Another consideration was the rise my fortunes would take if I was to solve both a series of burglaries *and* two murders. I'd have a path beaten to my door by paying customers desperate to have their wrongs righted. 'I've had no word from Peter to say he's found anyone willing to take it on. And I've had no inspiration myself. So, I think I must stay a little longer to see what I can find out. These killings are so shocking, the murderer can't go unpunished and, as you've said, the longer the trail goes cold the less likely we'll catch him.'

He beamed like a small boy. 'Good, good. You must stay here; you told me the room is satisfactory. And the lad, Natty Preece, will help. He knows everyone in the town, and I hear he knows everything that's going on. Do you need anything else?'

'I'm not so sure I need that boy, Mr Bagnall. Peter has helped me in the past and I can call on him again if I want assistance.'

'Mr Turnstone can be brought whenever you wish, but he must have work of his own. I'll send for Natty, you and he can talk, then you can put him to errands whenever you want to. I'll send a carriage to Bridgnorth for your friend, any time day or night. You just let me know and it will be done.'

Natty Preece stood in front of us on a rug in New House, with me on one chair and Mr Bagnall on another. I'd only seen the lad before in the flickering lamplight in Mr Powell's garden. Here, in the brightness of the day, stood a scrawny, under-fed, and grubby specimen of a boy with greasy hair as black as the coal dust caked in his ears. He'd have to clean up if he was to accompany me anywhere.

Natty looked at me, I looked at Mr Bagnall.

'Ask the lad a question, Miss Valentine. See if he's up to scratch.'

This bothered me greatly. Though I was used to asking questions of customers, suspects, and witnesses, I had no experience of what to ask someone who might be working for me. I came out with the first thing that entered my head. 'Why do you want to assist me, Natty?'

'Not sure that I do, miss.'

At least the boy didn't mince his words. 'Then why have you offered?'

'Didn't exactly offer, miss.' He glanced at Bagnall, 'I was asked by the boss and I'm always willing to do *his* bidding.' Out of the corner of my eye I saw Mr Bagnall pull a face. 'Besides, it must be easier than picking coal all day.'

I'd been a labourer like him. My days spent in my master's garden, with long hours, heavy lifting, and little pay. So I could see his desire to get away from that. 'This is a different kind of work though, Natty. Brain work. Where you have to be able to remember small details, and to think things through. Are you able to do that?'

Natty grinned. 'I reckon I can. After all, if a girl can do it, I'm sure it can't be too difficult.'

'Well if that's your view, perhaps I don't need you after all. You can go.'

A look of panic came on Natty, and his eyes flitted between Mr Bagnall's face and mine. 'I'm sorry, miss, I didn't mean to offend.'

'It doesn't matter if you meant it or not, Natty. You'll not be working with me. Please leave.'

Mr Bagnall raised a palm and intervened. 'Let us just wait a moment.' He turned to Natty. 'You go and wait in the hall, and I'll come to speak to you shortly. Miss Valentine and I need to discuss something.'

When he'd gone, Mr Bagnall waited for a minute then walked over and pulled open the door. The boy was standing just the other side. Mr Bagnall pointed along the hall. 'Down there, Natty.' He waited until

Natty had done as he had been told, then sat beside me again.

'There is a favour I must ask of you, Miss Valentine. I owe the Preece family a debt of gratitude. I will admit this lad is in many ways difficult. I do not think he is particularly trustworthy. He creeps around Edward Powell attempting to get into his good books all the while, and I cannot stand a sycophant. I know for a fact he is lazy, and I suspect he and the truth are often strangers. Even so, I want to make his life in this world a little easier in order to help repay my debt. I must, therefore, prevail upon you to let him work alongside you, at least for a little while. If he becomes too much of a burden, say the word and he'll be back on the coal heap where he came from.'

I resisted for a while longer with only a little conviction. Despite my doubts, I felt I owed the boy a chance, just as Edwin had given me mine. I only hoped I wouldn't regret it later.

Tom rubbed his shoulder and upper arm where he'd leant against the stone wall of the barn for the last few hours.

After he'd fled from home, Tom had found Jake returning from the two-acre field and begged him for help. Jake was doubtful at first and said he wouldn't do it unless Tom told him why. Tom argued that they'd been friends for a lifetime, so Jake should just trust him. This seemed to have done the trick, at least on the surface.

From Jake's father's cottage he'd hurried across fields and through woodland, keeping out of sight as much as possible. For about a mile he followed Dean's brook and doubled back across the Bridgnorth road to skirt Willey Hall. Tom hoped to find somewhere there to hide. He thought he'd succeeded when he found an abandoned cottage. It looked solid enough and stood a good distance from the other estate buildings. The door opened without him needing to force it and Tom was pleased to find it dry inside, if a bit musty. Just when he started to relax, he heard voices, so slipped out and ran as fast as he could. He had no idea where he was running to, only what he was running from.

Eventually he'd found the ruined and roofless building on the edge of a coppice, and dropped down in a corner. His head still spun, and his stomach still churned. For a while he'd tried to bring back what had happened, but it was a blank. Only the argument, the gin bottle and, in the morning, Beth's body on the kitchen floor.

Despite the raging in his brain, he'd fallen asleep, only waking when water dripped on to his head. It was close to dark, he was cold, and now he was getting wet.

It had been around three hours after daybreak when he'd left his home, and Tom considered it must be at least half past six now if the fading light and the rumbling in his belly were anything to go by. Surely any searching for him would have stopped for the night, especially if the rain was coming down. There seemed nowhere in the barn where he'd be protected from the downpour. So Tom decided to chance seeking better shelter and, hopefully, finding some food. He knew Linley Church couldn't be far, so climbed the tallest tree he could see and scoured the skyline. It was there, no more than a couple of hundred paces away, with only the top of its square tower poking above the woodland.

It took him no time to reach the building, but, once there, Tom hung back, cautious not to be discovered, and more than a little fearful of going inside a church in the near dark. The shadowy face of the Green Man over the entrance, with dark, sunken eyes, made him even less keen to enter. Ten minutes later, Tom pushed open the church door, fully prepared to drop down and pray if a service was underway. The church was empty. The day before it would have been full, packed to the aisles. The pile of apples, pears, bread, and barley on the altar testified to the harvest they'd been celebrating. There was much less fruit left by the time Tom had gorged his fill and settled himself on the priest's chair by the pulpit. Though he still shivered, it was dry inside the church, and not quite as cold as his first shelter.

Within half an hour, the night had darkened completely, leaving only a single altar candle flickering against the walls. Tom's eyes drooped once more. Twice he snapped them open, wrestling himself from slumber. The third time a dark silhouette towered over him.

Tom jerked his knees up to his chest. 'God's teeth.' The pale faced figure stretched a bony hand towards Tom shoulder and the young swineherd stifled a scream.

'Calm yourself, young sir, I mean you no harm.' The hand now rested, strong but reassuring, on Tom's shoulder.

As his eyes cleared from his dozing, Tom could see the man wore the black suit and white neck-piece of a minister. He looked to the door to see if he could escape.

The cleric appeared to sense this and pressed slightly more heavily to hold him down. 'There is no need to run, my son. What is your name?'

'Tom ... Tom Hurdley, sir.'

'And mine is the Reverend Henry Davies. Where are you from?' Tom heard the softness of a Welsh accent.

'Broseley, sir. Lost Lane.'

'So, Master Hurdley from Broseley, what is troubling you so much that you are hiding here in my church?'

'Who says I was hiding? Am I not allowed to come into church to pray?'

Reverend Davies glanced towards the decimated offerings of food on the altar and shook his head. 'Indeed you are, and I would not be bothering you if I thought that's what you were doing. But you were not, were you? You were sleeping and almost jumped out of your skin when I woke you.' He smiled gently. 'So come, tell me what it is.'

Tom didn't reply for a moment, then shrugged. 'I may be in some trouble.'

'You have done something wrong?'

'I don't really know, sir. My ... my wife. I found her dead this morning.' For the first time since leaving his home, Tom shook with grief. 'I wouldn't harm her, not for anything. Not in the normal course of things anyway. But I had bad thoughts and I'd been drinking ...'

Davies shook his head again and sat on a pew opposite Tom. 'The ale will do terrible things to a man, it's true. Tell me, my son, why would you kill your wife? Was she a wasp? Unfaithful?'

'Neither of those. She has the pleasantest nature, most of the time, even when I'd try it on. I accused her of seeing another man, and we argued. I didn't believe it. Not deep down. She said she was expecting our baby, and after I'd thought about it, I was really happy.'

'Then why?'

'We had a fight, husband and wife like, I took to the bottle and don't remember anything else 'til I found her in the morning. No-one else in the cottage, so who else could have done it?'

'So you ran away and hid in God's house?'

Another shrug from Tom. 'What else could I do. Had to think. Had to remember.'

'Then you must go back home and give yourself up to your neighbours. There's nothing to be gained by running, your guilt will keep up with you and never let you rest. Not if you're an honest and decent man, which I can tell you are. You can stay here tonight. Then, in the morning, take yourself back to Broseley. Will you do this?'

Tom nodded.

'That is good, young man. Now, let us say a prayer to get you through the night. You will need God's help in this, I am sure.'

Thirteen

When Mr Bagnall and I agreed how I might proceed, we talked briefly about payment. It was brief because his offer was so generous there was nothing to discuss. I then went to my room to worry about how I might fulfil the task he'd given me.

Already I was missing Peter's help. When we'd worked together, we'd usually sit and chat about how a crime might have been committed, who had the opportunity to steal whatever it was we'd been asked to look for, and what steps we might take to find them. Without my friend I had to ask the questions of myself. I doubted Natty would be of much use, he was so young and had little knowledge of the world beyond mere survival.

Though writing is not one of my better accomplishments, I've enough to make simple notes and I did this using quill and ink sent up by my host. I began by listing what I knew. The names and rough ages of the victims, where they lived, where they died, immediate family, and so on. It would have been useful to include the names of the people who had last seen them, but I didn't have this yet. From the testimony of Annie Reader, it seemed Tom Hurdley had probably been the last to see Beth, though this wasn't certain. All I knew of Daniel's movements was that he'd been at a dance earlier in the evening.

I moved on to possible motives. This didn't take long as I couldn't think of much. Jealousy? This might have applied to Daniel but not to Beth, she had nothing to speak of. The same would be true of robbery, and there was no report that Daniel had been robbed anyway. Revenge? For what? Could they have both hurt the same person in some way? If so, how bad would it need to be for that person to kill the two of them? Passion might be a possibility. Had the pair been lovers and Beth's husband had found out? If so, why would Tom kill Beth as well as Daniel? If a rage had taken hold of Tom Hurdley, what had triggered it? And if it *was* pure anger, from something he'd heard in the town, surely he'd have beaten Daniel, not strangled him. Strangulation with a rope is a much more cold-blooded act. Then, would Tom have gone home, still boiling with anger, choked the life out of Beth, and gone calmly to his bed?

When I'd finished going round in circles, I went round once more and still nothing was clear. I decided to trace who Daniel Powell had been with the night he died. The inn was as good a place as any to start.

George Beard, owner of The Angel, was a giant, broad as a bear I'd seen at Bridgnorth fair. There was no doubt he'd keep order in his drinking house, even though many of his customers would be tough men themselves, coal miners and iron workers. I told him I was trying to find who murdered Daniel Powell.

He frowned and shook his head. 'I don't know anything about that.'

'I'm not suggesting you had anything to do with it, Mr Beard. Daniel was in here the night he was killed. Mr Bagnall has asked if I can find what happened to him after that.'

'Mr Bagnall, you say? Mr Matthias Bagnall?'

'That's the one.'

Beard's demeanour softened, and he waved me over to a corner away from the ears of his customers. The room wasn't large, so this was difficult, and I found myself perched on a box wedged behind three large barrels. For a moment, Beard remained standing, waiting, I assumed, in case any drinks were wanted. When it became clear they weren't, he sat and leaned in toward me. 'Daniel was in here. Nice lad, came in now and again. Don't like his father much, a bit too upright for me. Mr Bagnall though, he's the man you'd want at your side. Tough employer, I hear, but always polite and not one to look down on you, despite having a few shillings to spare. Anything I can do to help him, I'll do. So what was it you wanted to know, miss?'

'Who did Daniel meet when he arrived?'

'No-one that I can remember. No-one in particular anyway. I didn't see him come in, I was below in the cellar, and when I served him, he only ordered one for himself. Did the same another couple of times then took a glass for a woman he'd hooked up with.'

'Would you know her name?'

'Surely. Becky Cole, she's called. Lives down the hill. Her father rows a ferry across the river.'

'And she was a friend of Daniel's?'

'Not that I know of, I never saw them together before.' Beard chuckled. 'But that's what dances is for I expect, bringing lads and lasses closer than they might be otherwise. Not that they stayed close for long.'

'In what way?'

'They seemed to fall out before the night were over. I was too busy to see what they were up to earlier but couldn't help seeing she wasn't happy with him later on. Don't know what he'd said or done. Something she didn't like by the look of it. One time when I went outside, Becky was standing and waving a finger. All red in the face she was. Went on for about five minutes and I was about to go over to knock their heads together when he put his arm round her shoulder and whispered in her ear. The girl smiled then seemed to remember she was angry with him so shrugged him off and walked away. Next thing, Daniel is drinking on his own again and she's dancing with another young lad. Kept looking in

Daniel's direction though, so whatever he'd said must have worked. And he was grinning when he left.'

'She didn't leave with Daniel then?'

'No. She ran after him to the door but don't know if she caught him. Came back inside for a while, then collected her things and left. Home, I suppose.'

I asked the tavern-keeper if I could see the room where the dance took place.

He laughed. 'Room? Not in here. Not a proper dance really. Now and again a couple of the locals bring their instruments in and give a tune outside. That evening, some folk got up and stepped out a jig, then everyone was up for an hour or more. Quite a night it was.' Beard cocked a thumb to a door at the back. 'Out there. Help yourself.'

He returned to his work and left me to mine. There was nothing much to be seen. A patch of soil, perhaps twenty paces each way, a dozen or so seats made from old half barrels, and a rough canopy in one corner. I could imagine the music and laughter ringing off the walls on a warm early Autumn evening, but now there was nothing. The space was as cold and dead as Beth and Daniel.

Becky Cole stood a good three inches taller than me. Her smile, which flickered when I introduced myself, would be sure to set any young man's heart beating fast. I could see why a tall one like Daniel Powell would be attracted to her. They'd have made a handsome couple. Her clothes, serviceable and cheap like my own, hung well on her. She hadn't seemed surprised when I'd turned up at her door.

'I need to ask you some questions, Becky. You know why, don't you?'

'I do, I'd heard in the town that Mr Bagnall'd taken on a thief-taker to find who took poor Daniel's life. Word travels fast round here, even faster when it's a woman doing a man's job.'

For the second time in just a few hours I was facing this stick-in-the-mud stupidity about what a person could do with their life. This time from a girl of similar age and background to me.

'Hardly a man's job, Becky. Don't you think *you'd* be able to do many jobs as easily as a man can? You look fit and strong. I'll bet you help your dad with the ferry from time to time.'

Confusion spread over her face, as if this line of thinking had never occurred to her. It took her a moment to reply.

'I s'pose so. Not sure how I can help you though, I don't know anything about Daniel's killing.'

'Well you were possibly the last one to see him alive. So, first off, tell me how well you knew Daniel? Your sweetheart, was he?'

Becky blushed. 'No, not at all.'

'Really? I heard the two of you were very close at the dance on Saturday.'

'We had a dance that's all. I'd seen him a couple of times crossing the river, and that night we got to talking. I'd gone with some friends to The Angel, and it seemed like good fun to have a dance when the tunes started.'

'It didn't stay fun for long though, did it? I heard you and Daniel had an argument. What was that about?'

The blush deepened. 'We were dancing and getting on fine. Then he suggested more, and I told him to get lost. I'm not that kind of a girl.' Up to this point, Becky had seemed calm and steady in her replies to my questions but with her last words she burst into tears. 'He tried to make up and I was still mad at him so pushed him away. I did like him. A lot. Danced with another lad to make him jealous. I went after Daniel when he left. Just to tell him I'd like to see him there again and he could walk me home.'

'So why didn't he?'

'He'd been drinking after I'd pushed him away, made him nasty. He said he didn't fancy the walk down the hill and back now. Told me I'd missed my chance.'

'I expect that made you angry.'

'It did.'

'Angry enough to follow Daniel home and strangle him?'

'No. I could never do such a thing. I told you, I liked him. I knew it was the ale making him mean. I just collected my outside coat and came home.' The tears which had slowed now came back. 'It's all my fault though.'

'How so?'

'If I'd given in to him, he'd still be alive, wouldn't he?'

'You can't think that way, Becky. Only his murderer would know what would happen next.'

Even if she'd gone with Daniel, there was nothing to say he wouldn't just have been killed afterwards. It was clear Becky had nothing to do with his death, not unless she was a very good liar. Also, though she looked strong, she'd still have trouble overcoming a man, even one like Daniel not used to hard labour. 'What did you do after you left The Angel?'

'As I said, I came home. My dad was still up. Bent my ear for being so late. He'll vouch for what time I got in. Shall I get him?'

'No need. I'll talk to him later if I have to. Did you see anything at the dance? Who did Daniel talk to? Did he argue with anyone?'

'Only spoke to his mates as far as I saw. I'd know most of the ones who were there or at least seen them around the place. We were all in the yard behind the tavern, Jamie James on the fiddle and his brother, Mark, on whistle.'

Becky stopped and clamped a hand to her mouth.

'What is it?'

'Just when we were talking... I remember now. There was a man sitting under the shelter early on, acting a bit strange. No need to be under there, it was a lovely, dry, night. Kept his face covered, just watching the dancing.'

'And you didn't know him?'

I don't think so. As I said, his face was covered. Something familiar about the way he drank and held himself though. Didn't speak to anyone as far as I saw, and he'd gone when I left.'

'Was he tall? Short? What colour hair? Young? Old?'

Becky closed her eyes, as if trying to see the scene again. When she re-opened them, she shook her head. 'Sorry. There's nothing. Just a memory of a man being there, looking out. I didn't really pay him any mind, other than noticing him for a minute.

'You're sure he didn't talk to Daniel?'

'Well if he did, I didn't see him.' She paused for a second. 'God's teeth! Do you think he could have done it?'

Fourteen

I found myself at a bit of a dead-end. Tom Hurdley still hadn't been found, and Annie Reader had told me that Jake Slack, the man who knew him best, was away at market for perhaps a couple of days. Becky Cole's information about the man at the dance was useful but limited. So I had nothing else to go on regarding either murder, Until something new turned up, I thought my time might be best used by talking to more of the theft victims. At least I might make progress on the crimes Mr Bagnall had called me to Broseley for in the first place. I also had a nagging feeling they were somehow connected to at least one of the killings.

If Tom Hurdley *had* killed his wife, could he be the thief and she'd found out? A possibility, though it wouldn't connect him to Daniel Powell's death. He'd face the gibbet, almost certainly, just for stealing from the wealthy and influential. Killing anyone who discovered his thefts would be self-preservation and make no difference to his fate. He could only hang once. Still, I couldn't make any kind of judgement on this until he was captured.

Having called in to New House to get directions, I stood outside a home which had been burgled. Substantial, thatched, and clearly the residence of someone with a deal of money. I couldn't help but be in awe of the beauty of the garden. Though not large, it was filled with every manner of flower and shrub, many in their autumn splendour. A gentleman, by his clothes, rather than a labouring gardener, stood at one end of the house, dead-heading roses.

He had his back to me. I coughed to attract his attention, and he turned. 'Yes? May I help you?'

I pointed to the deep red bloom he had been working on. 'They're very beautiful, sir, the Countess of Clare, isn't it? You keep them well.'

He adjusted his spectacles to peer over the rim. 'You know your roses, miss. Yes, this is one of my favourites. You grow them yourself?'

'I used to, before I moved home.'

His quick appraisal of the quality of my clothes brought a grin which suggested he didn't entirely believe me. Whilst not an out and out lie, it was only true that I had tended the roses of my previous employer. Without the wherewithal for any land or a garden of my own I couldn't hope to grow anything, and he could see this. He politely asked me again what I wanted, and I explained I'd been sent to enquire about his burglary.

A frown replaced his pleasant smile. 'It was a quite horrid experience, Miss ...?'

'Valentine, sir, Meg Valentine.'

'Well, Miss Valentine, as I was saying, very unpleasant. Mrs Exley ... my good wife ... and I had been away at my cousin's in Church Preen for a week. When we returned she was putting away her jewellery and noticed a fine piece was missing. One she had not taken with her. It was a pearl and jade pendant on a gold chain, left to Mrs Exley by her grandmother, and the maids were immediately set on the task of searching for it. It was nowhere to be found. On further inspection, my wife discovered several other trinkets, of lesser value, had also been taken. She was ... is most upset by the affair.'

'Could it have been one of the servants?'

'Not at all. Every one of them has been with the family for a long time and I trust them completely. Two were away with us in any event, and I had given the remainder time off from their duties.'

'And it was only your wife's jewels? Nothing else?'

'A gold watch of mine, and close to two guineas in small coins I had left in a drawer.'

Two guineas left lying around? Half a year's wages when I worked at Cliffe House, and this man could afford to leave it in his bedroom. 'How did the thief get in?'

'We found a window in the pantry had been forced. It could have been any time in the week the house was empty. In some ways I blame myself.'

'How so?'

'I made no secret of our excursion, speaking

freely of it with friends. Not that I would suspect any of them, of course, but they could have spoken of it in front of servants or neighbours. I could, I suppose, have been overheard when I visited local shops. Broseley has some very fine people, and some who are not so fine. Particularly the miners. They might have the shirt from your back if they had the chance.'

It occurred to me that such dishonesty might not only apply to the poorer folk in the town. I didn't share this with Mr Exley.

'Do you think you will be able to find the person who did this, Miss Valentine?'

I said I would try my best, asked if he could send me a full description of the items stolen, then thanked him for his time and left him to his garden.

Ten minutes later saw me at the home of another burglary victim, Mrs Wilkins, a widow. I would have guessed her to be around her fiftieth year, judging by the wrinkles on her face and hands, though her sprightly movement said she might be younger. This lady invited me inside without question when I told her my name, surprisingly trusting for one who'd been robbed. This trusting nature was displayed further by the state of her home. Though tidy and clean, as far as I could tell, her sitting room was cluttered. I could see valuables lying on shelves alongside books, vases, clocks, and all manner of items she must have gathered over the years. Anyone visiting the house would see the lady's fortune on display.

I explained that Matthias Bagnall had asked me

to try to identify the person who'd been stealing from his friends and neighbours.

'Mr Bagnall is such a kind man, Miss Valentine. I know his wife quite well, and a nicer couple you could not hope to meet, None of the airs and graces such wealthy people might be expected to have. I am not surprised he has engaged you. That gentleman was almost the first I told after I found I had been robbed. His brother, too, is a most charming man. And so intelligent and witty. He was very kind and caring when he heard of my misfortune.'

'Could you tell me what happened?'

'Well, my dear, it was all very strange. My departed husband's niece was expecting and, as her parents are no longer with us, I'd said I would go to stay with her in Bridgnorth until her confinement ended. Just to look after the home on her behalf, you understand. Her labour was a long and difficult one, so my maid and I stayed a few days more than I had planned. Two and a half weeks in all.

'When I returned home, I discovered that the kitchen door had been left unlocked. I thought nothing of it at first, then, as days went by, I couldn't find a number of valuable items where I'd left them. Pieces of jewellery, a small travelling clock, a purse, that kind of thing. Initially I blamed my maid for moving the items, though she denied having touched them. Then I thought I may have left them in Bridgnorth. It was only when I received a letter back from the niece, saying they were not in her house, that I began to consider the possibility of a break in.

That's when I spoke to Mr and Mrs Bagnall.'

'Did anyone know you were going away?'

Mrs Wilkins bit her lip before answering. 'I cannot really think of anyone who wouldn't know. I was so excited by the prospect of the birth I talked about it to anyone who would listen. What a stupid woman I am.'

'Not at all, madam, you were not to know that a thief might be listening. It is perfectly natural to let all your friends know that a baby is coming.'

As with the earlier victim I had spoken to, I asked Mrs Wilkins to send a description of her stolen goods to me at New House, and I told her I would do what I could to recover them.

So, we had at least two people who had been away from their homes when the thefts took place. Two people who had told half the town those homes were going to be empty for a good while. Two thefts where only a small number of items were taken, though items of some value which could easily be stuffed into a coat pocket or a small bag. In both cases, the owners had only noticed their losses by accident, there had been so little disturbance in the house.

This wasn't going to be an easy one.

Soon after I left Mrs Wilkins, I bumped into Natty on the street. He looked glum and fell in beside me. 'Mr Bagnall sent me to find you, miss. Said I should say I was sorry for cheeking you and see if you need any help.'

There was little conviction in his voice, and I found it hard to believe he'd changed his opinion of women so soon. 'Are you really sorry, or are you just saying it because Mr Bagnall told you to?'

The boy looked at the ground and shuffled his feet.

'I thought so, Natty.'

I walked away and he chased after me. 'Please, miss, give me another chance. I know I shouldn't have said what I did, I just thought it was funny. If you cast me off, Mr Bagnall will do the same ... he might even take the job off me. Then where will I be? It's not much of a job, picking coal all day, but we need the money. There's nothing else I could do round here.' He must have sensed I was beginning to feel sorry for him. 'Besides, I can help. People tell me things ... and I know everybody in the town.'

I thought for a moment, trying to weigh up if he would be a help or a hindrance, then remembered the way I'd badgered Edwin Hare to let me assist him in his work as a thief-taker. How desperate *I'd* been to break out of the poverty in my life. Despite a gut-feeling the boy would bring trouble, I clapped him on the shoulder.

'Very well, Natty, there is a task you can do for me. But first, you must promise me you'll never again say I'm not up to this job. If I hear one suggestion you have, either to my face or behind my back, you'll be in big trouble. Understand?'

'You can rely on me, miss, I'll not let you down. I

promise. What is it you want me to do?'

'You can go around and ask some questions for me.'

'Happy to, miss. Sounds like it might be a laugh.'

'A "laugh" Natty? It's not a "laugh" as you put it, this is serious. People want the villain behind this caught and it's our ... it's *my* job to catch him. Are you willing to help me properly or are you simply going to mess about?'

The lad looked shocked that I'd picked him up on what he'd said. 'No, no, miss. I can do it. Serious as you want. Just tell me what you need, and I'll be your eyes and ears.' Natty put on what I imagined he thought was a solemn expression. 'You can trust me, miss. What sort of questions do you want me to ask?'

I still had little faith that I *could* trust him. It was only my pity for the lad, and Mr Bagnall's request, led me to give him a chance. 'Questions like has anyone heard of the stolen goods being offered for sale? Has anyone been spending more than they normally would? See if you can you find if there's any connection between Daniel Powell and Beth Hurdley.'

'Will do, miss. Should I ask if there was bad blood between either of them and anyone else?'

'That's a good idea. Now, be discrete about it, and report back to me anything you find. You understand?'

He profusely said that he did and he walked away with a happier face than when he'd arrived. I could still hear his whistling after he turned a corner.

Only time would tell if he could be depended upon to do the job well.

FIFTEEN

Mistress Beddoes was the woman preparing Beth Hurdley's body for burial. Her cottage, up a lane off the main street, was a little bigger than mine. In my head I'd imagined someone doing this work would be an old crone, dressed in dark clothes and wearing a miserable demeanour. Instead, the one who answered my knock would have been only about ten years older than me and beamed a friendly smile.

'Come in, my dear. You're Meg Valentine, aren't you. I heard from Mr Bagnall's men that you'd most likely be coming to call. If you follow me, I'll show you what you've come to see.'

She led me to a room at the back, about four paces square, where Beth's body, covered by a thin blanket, lay on a board. Only her head was exposed. On a dresser against one wall stood a brown bowl and a water jug, a dish of soap, scissors, thread, and a small cushion studded with needles of various sizes. The shelf above held jars marked with names I didn't understand, but guessed it was a foreign tongue, and the contents used in Mistress Beddoes grisly work. Herbs hung in bunches from hooks around the room, giving the air a pleasant smell, not one you would associate with death.

She must have noticed me looking and cocked her head at them. 'Sweet enough now, my dear, but we'd been needing them in a few days if this young woman stayed with me for very long. Now, you just do what you have to, and I'll leave you to it.'

'Where's Daniel Powell's body?'

'Oh, my dear, he's been taken back home. I did my work, cleaned and dressed him ready for his wake, and now he'll be with his family until his remains are put to rest.' She stepped towards the door. 'I'll be in my kitchen if you need anything, just give me a shout.'

'Before you go, did you notice anything unusual when you were cleaning Beth?'

'More unusual than such a fine healthy woman lying dead in my back room do you mean?' With this she laughed, though there was no humour in it. 'Nothing other than that rope burn around her neck. You'd have known about that, my dear?'

'I saw it at her cottage, though wasn't certain what caused it. You believe it to have been a rope?'

'I'd have said so. There's a pattern to it. If it had been a belt or a scarf, say, that wouldn't be there, or at least it would be different. I'll have to cover it somehow when I dress her again. Same as poor Daniel.'

'He had a similar mark?'

'Close enough. Couldn't swear it was exactly the same, my dear, but definitely a rope anyway.'

I let her go and turned my attention to Beth. Though I'd looked on her dead body before, it wasn't something I enjoyed. Who would? I couldn't imagine doing Mistress Beddoes' job and shivered at the thought of it. A colour somewhere between brown and yellow was on Beth's face now, far from the pink cheeks she'd had when we spoke, and it was hard to believe this cold meat had once been a living, breathing, woman. I peeled the blanket away from her right arm. She showed no sign of bruising. Next, I had to lean right over her to check the other arm and despite this unpleasantness I found no bruising there either. She hadn't been held tightly before she was killed. To strangle her in such a way, the murderer must surely have come from behind. If he'd not grabbed her arms, then he must have taken the woman by surprise. A strange way indeed for a husband to kill his wife.

The length of rope I'd found at the Powell house was still in my bag, so I pulled it out and held it alongside the weal on Beth's throat. It looked similar. Sadly, a rope's a rope as far as I'm concerned, other than the thickness, and I could see no difference in that respect. I took the charred remnant which had been in the Hurdley's fireplace from my pocket, checking it first against the undamaged piece, then the wound. Again, I was hard pushed to decide if they were the same. I would need to find someone who knew enough about rope to advise me.

Mistress Beddoes had said she'd found nothing unusual other than the neck wound, so I wasn't hopeful of finding anything either. I ran my fingers deep into Beth's hair, backwards and forwards across her skull. There was no sign of any other wound which might have caused her death. I moved on to look at her fingernails. They were short, as if she bit them, and dirty underneath in the way I recognised from my own. She'd clearly been working in her garden. As far as I could tell, she'd no blood or skin under there, so hadn't had the chance to fight with her attacker.

I called the lady of the house back in. 'I think I'm done here now, Mistress, you may continue with your work.'

'Did you find anything?'

'Nothing more than you mentioned yourself, the marks on her throat.'

'You saw the poor woman was expecting a child?'

A child? Did the husband know about this? If he did, would he really have killed them both? 'That is shocking indeed, Mistress, though I wouldn't have known the signs.'

'She was not far along, Miss Valentine, so not so easy to be sure of unless you know what you are looking for. One more thing, did you look at the girl's eyes?'

I said I hadn't. I obviously had much to learn about examining corpses.

'They're streaked with red, my dear. Just the same as young Daniel's.'

The evening meal in the Bagnall household surprised me. I knew the ironmaster to be a wealthy man, and I'd imagined all such people dined lavishly every night. Many was the time I'd lain on my bench in the stable loft after working all day in my master's garden, dreaming of the food I might eat if I ever became rich. Perhaps those with money are content they can have whatever they want when they want it, so have no desire to gorge themselves constantly. It seems strange to me, as I'm not yet in their fortunate position. The Bagnall's at least, ate simple fare. More than I'd have on my table many a night, simple nonetheless. Bread, ale, cheese. A bowl of potatoes with butter. Beef stew. The one extravagance was a deep fruit pie, layered with apples, plums, and blackcurrants and I didn't refuse a second helping when it was offered.

There were four of us at the table. Me, my hosts, and a gentleman introduced as Mr Lombard, described as Mr Bagnall's brother, though no explanation was given why their names weren't the same. The brothers were as different physically as I'd imagine it possible to be. Mr Lombard looked much younger than Mr Bagnall, and I might have assumed he was a son if I hadn't been told their relationship. He was not so tall as, and decidedly thinner than, his brother, and his skin had a greyish tone. This was much in contrast to the ruddy complexion of Mr Bagnall. His strong spectacles spoke of a man more used to spending his time bent over a desk than in the outdoors. In short, the men were almost like two separate species, a river vole and a harvest mouse, similar enough to see they are related in some way, mismatched in so many others.

Mr Bagnall explained to him why I was staying at New House and explained to me that his brother would only join us for meals occasionally. 'He seems to prefer his own company, in his room, when he's at home at all, which is not often.'

His brother sighed deeply. 'Sadly, it is true, Miss Valentine. I am a solitary soul by nature. I also work long hours and have little energy for polite chatter when I end my day. I hope you will not think me rude for it.'

I assured him I wouldn't think ill of him in any way, and I completely understood how tiring his job must be. Though I doubted his work compared with what I'd had to do in the garden of Cliffe House. Most of the remaining conversation passed me by, being between the two men and concerning the affairs of their business.

Mrs Bagnall flattered her brother-in-law whenever he spoke or made a light-hearted comment, endlessly saying how thoughtful he was, how clever and how amusing. This went on so much that I wondered if there was something going on between them. Nonetheless, Mr Bagnall seemed at ease with it all, and I had to admit the younger brother appeared to be the sharpest and wittiest of the two.

When we'd finished, Mrs Bagnall asked if I'd enjoyed my dinner and I said I had. She nodded and told Eliza to clear the table. 'We will go through to the other room, Miss Valentine, and leave these men to talk the night away on matters of commerce.'

As I rose, Mr Lombard raised a finger. 'It would be pleasant if Miss Valentine could stay a while.' He looked across to his brother. 'We have had enough business for one night, Matthias, it would be good to hear how our young guest has progressed, don't you agree?'

Mrs Bagnall scowled, though her husband smiled and nodded, so I knew I'd be staying. She left us and I ran through what I'd done during the day. I explained I'd discovered little, other than the nature of Beth Hurdley's death, and that Tom Hurdley had gone missing. Both of the gentlemen interrupted with questions from time to time. Mr Lombard was particularly complimentary when I told them of my examination of Beth's neck earlier in the day.

'You appear most fastidious Miss Valentine. 'He turned to his brother. 'Do you not think so, Matthias?'

'Indeed. Most fastidious'

They each offered thoughts on what direction I might take and mused on who might be responsible for the killings. Mr Lombard echoed my own thinking. 'It seems to me, Miss Valentine, that many murders occur when family members fall out. You'll remember the bible story of Cain and Able, and I'm sure the same sad play has been repeated throughout the centuries. The farm labourer's wife, Beth, is found dead after an argument, and her husband disappears. What does this tell us? But how is this linked to poor Daniel?'

'I'm not sure yet, sir,'

'On the other hand, I know that Edward Powell and Daniel disagreed often. Even so, I cannot imagine Edward hurting his son.'

'What did they disagree about?'

'Well, as I'm sure you know, it doesn't take much for a father and son to argue, it seems to be the nature of things. In their case the flames were fed by Edward's religious beliefs, he is a very devout man. Too devout in my humble opinion. He would subscribe to the view that all Papists are evil and should be put to the noose. Daniel, being a gentler soul, did not agree. He often tried to point his father to more charitable interpretations of the Scriptures and this caused friction between them.'

Mr Bagnall raised a palm to staunch his brother's words. 'Now, Samuel, you speak of charity, so try a little yourself. You should not be speaking of our friends in such a way.'

'Would you wish us to give Miss Valentine misdirection, Matthias? What I have said is true, is it not? We cannot allow our friendships, no matter how strong we think they are, to cloud her thinking.' He turned to me. 'My brother is a kind man and always sees the best in people, but Edward and Daniel argued often. Although, as I say, I cannot see that this could boil over to murder.'

It occurred to me that I should perhaps talk to Mr Powell later about their differences of opinion. I moved the subject on. 'Can you think of what connection there might be between the two murders?'

Mr Bagnall interjected. 'Perhaps they are not linked, that's a possibility is it not?'

I admitted it was. Still, inside, I found it worrying and thought it unlikely that two killings might have been committed in the town by different people within twenty-four hours of each other. With its population of poor, rough, miners and iron workers Broseley would be no stranger to violence, but the fact that Mr Bagnall had engaged me to help suggested it rarely resulted in death. I pressed them for any other ideas. 'Would Daniel and Beth have known each other?'

Mr Lombard shrugged. 'I'd think it unlikely, except in passing. We live in a small town but Edward Powell is well paid, and strict. He'd not have his son mixing with a farm girl, I'd wager. The lad spent much of his younger years boarding at school in Bridgnorth so wouldn't have met her playing in the fields. She'd been married a little while, I believe, and I'm certain her husband wouldn't have her in the company of a handsome young man like Daniel. No, they probably never met, and you'll find you have two killers to contend with, Miss Valentine. You mark my words, the woman died by her husband's hands. You should concentrate on who killed Daniel. That's the important mystery.'

We talked round in circles for a while, then the brothers moved on to other topics, of which I knew nothing, and I found myself drifting off. Mr Bagnall must have spotted my half-closed lids. 'You appear to be tired, Miss Valentine, please feel free to leave us old men to our boring business. I will see you tomorrow.'

I was grateful for his consideration and made my way upstairs after I'd wished Mrs Bagnall goodnight. She was cool, though not frosty, and I suspected she was more annoyed with her husband than with me for her exclusion from the table. The lady seemed naturally kind and good-natured and I was sure we'd be on friendly terms again by morning.

In bed, I lay for an hour waiting for sleep to come. My drowsiness had disappeared, and all the possibilities raised by Mr Bagnall and Mr Lombard spun round inside my head.

There *had* to be a connection between the two deaths. For the life of me I couldn't see what it was.

SIXTEEN

Tom woke, aching and cold. It took him a moment to remember he'd slept in a church and, as he surfaced, he fancied he heard a door close. On the pew, by his head, was a lump of fresh bread, some cheese and a flagon of beer.

Whilst Tom ate, he thought of what the minister had said the previous night, and of his own promise to do as had been suggested. To go back to Broseley and give himself up. Not an inviting prospect. He knew he couldn't go on the run. His whole life was in the fields around the town where he'd grown up, where he'd married Beth, and where their child would have been born. Tom had no money to speak of, and only the clothes on his back. He knew his neighbours, they'd be lenient, wouldn't they?

The idea of leaving the sanctuary of the church became even less attractive when Tom opened the door and trod in rainwater which had gathered by the entrance. He cursed, and cursed again, at the torrent pouring down the outside wall onto his bare neck. Even taking the direct route, Tom knew it would be best part of an hour's walk back to the town and the storm would drench him in minutes. He pulled up his collar, ducked his head, and pulled the door behind him, vowing to return and thank the man of the cloth if he ever had the chance.

Tom trudged through the rain, hoping a carter would pass and offer him a ride. There was no-one, not even another walking soul to share the wet day with.

His thoughts strayed to what he'd said to the minister the night before. It was true, Beth was no shrew, and he loved her. What he couldn't understand was the fury which came over him sometimes when he thought of her. He'd had the same feeling of bile about Daniel Powell, and he had no memory of what happened after he left The Angel, other than more drinking. And this rage.

When he reached the Barrow turning, a group of half a dozen men huddled under an oak tree doing their best to keep dry. For a few moments he held back, watching from the cover of an overhanging bush, before grabbing his courage in both hands and approaching them. As he drew closer, he recognised a few, who dropped their heads when they saw him, only lifting their eyes when Tom stopped and spoke.

'I expect you're looking for me.'

The tallest of the party, Ernest Kite, a man not known to Tom, stepped forward and grabbed him by the forearm. 'Too right we are, and it's trouble you're in now, Hurdley.' He turned to his companions.

'Come on, lads, grab him and we'll get him back. Sooner it's done, the sooner he'll swing.'

Most of the group shuffled their feet but stayed rooted. Only two did as Kite demanded, each taking one of Tom's arms and dragging him forward, with Tom struggling to free himself.

One of the men stood in their way and raised a hand. 'Hold steady there, no need to be rough. This here's a neighbour of ours and there's no proof he's done anything wrong, apart from running away. I'd have done the same if I was scared.'

Kite sneered. 'Don't be stupid, man, he killed his wife, and we all know it. You'd best get behind us, or the boss will hear about it.'

'I'm not trying to stop you taking him in, only asking, politely I'd say, to treat him with some respect.' He glared at the taller man. 'And I'll thank you not to threaten me again, Ernest Kite. Not if you know what's good for you.'

He stepped aside and the group parted, letting Tom and his captors lead the way.

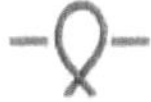

I heard the commotion outside New House from the top of the stairs and started to run down. Eliza gave me such a look from below I stopped halfway and pressed against the wall until she'd opened the door. Seven men stood outside, six of them surrounding another, who I assumed must be Tom Hurdley. There were damp tracks down his cheeks. The clamour died away and Ernest Kite, one of the men

I'd told off at the Powell house, spoke. 'Tell your master we've caught him. Quick, girl. Go on.'

The maid looked at me, then back at Kite, then slammed the door and scuttled off to find Mr Bagnall. I heard his footsteps down the hall a minute later and joined him when he re-opened the door.

'Well done, men, well done.' Mr Bagnall spoke directly to Kite. 'The lad doesn't look like he'll cause any trouble, does he? You bring him in on your own, Ernest, and we'll take him to where Miss Valentine can talk to him.'

He led the way through to the kitchen, then stopped at the doorway of a room on the right. Its white-washed walls, the iron at the fireplace, and wooden shelves stacked with table and bed linen showing its purpose. In the centre was a rough table and two chairs. Mr Bagnall swung an upturned palm in their direction. 'You may use this room, Miss Valentine. It is entirely at your disposal, come and go as you please, and you won't be disturbed. Not unless one of the staff needs fresh linen. Ernest will wait outside to ensure you are safe and you can lock up your charge in the cellar when you've finished. I'll find somewhere more suitable if we need to keep him for long.

'And you, Mr Hurdley, would do well to answer this lady's questions. She is working for me and will get to the bottom of this. If you don't like it, I can just hand you over to the visiting magistrate in Bridgnorth, he'll believe me if I tell him you're guilty and beyond redemption. You'll find yourself on the gibbet within the month.'

Mr Bagnall walked away, leaving me desperately trying to think of questions to ask. I told Hurdley to sit, and I stared at him for a long time before speaking. There was no point beating about the bush. 'So, Tom, why did you kill your wife?'

He looked like I'd slapped him. 'I ... I didn't'

'Everyone thinks you did.'

'Well they're wrong.' His voice trembled. 'I loved Beth, why would I kill her?'

'There's a logic in that, sure enough, but you ran away rather than raising the alarm. Why would you do such a thing unless you *are* guilty of her murder?'

'How could I raise an alarm. I didn't know Beth was dead until Kite and his men told me. I wasn't at home that night and was working early. Helped my friend, Jake, prepare pigs for market then went fishing. After salmon down the river by Apley Hall.'

'Fishing? You don't have a rod with you. Lose it along the way, did you?'

'I don't use no rod, man like me can't afford one. Just a line and hook dangled from the bank. And you're right, lost that. Got a bite from a monster and it tugged the line from my hands.'

I laughed and shook my head. 'That's some tale, Tom. You should take storytelling up for a living.'

'Every word is true.'

'If it's true, explain to me how you walked through your kitchen yesterday morning without noticing Beth's body on the floor? And don't deny you were there, you were seen. She died hours before you'd have been up to help prepare the pigs.' I let this sink in. 'I met her you know. A couple of days ago when I was walking down Lost Lane. We spoke for a few minutes. She seemed very nice.'

He covered his face, and I heard him breathing deeply beneath his hands for a few seconds before he pulled them away. A whisper was all that came out. 'Alright, I admit I lied about not knowing but I didn't kill her.'

'Then why give me the fish story?'

'God help me, I don't know. I knew how it would look. We argued so I went to an alehouse and had more than I should. Came back and we fought again. That witch next door heard us. I drank some more. Lots of gin. I stormed off to Jake's for the night. Went home early in the morning and Beth was there. On the floor. And I couldn't remember anything. My head was so bad with the drink that I couldn't remember how our row had ended. I half-believed I might have done it. So I ran. Stupid, stupid, stupid. Thought about it all day, and in the end knew I wouldn't have hurt her.'

'Why did you argue?'

'Beth told me we were having a baby. Frightened me I suppose. Man does daft things when he's scared.'

'Like killing his wife?'

'No. Like fighting with the woman he loves.'

I'd no actual proof against Tom Hurdley, only the knowledge he'd told at least one lie and that he'd argued with his wife and fled in the morning. Still there were questions. Were there more lies, and did he flee because he killed her or because he thought he might be in danger himself? There was nothing yet to tie him in with Daniel Powell and I really should have let him go, but I couldn't until I'd spoken to Jacob Slack. I explained my decision to Tom then told Kite to lock him up overnight. Mr Bagnall had arranged for a room in the cellar to be prepared and though it would be dark and damp, Tom would be secure. I knew Mr Bagnall would have made it as comfortable as possible.

Seventeen

Next morning, I wanted to explore the possibility of a connection between Tom and Daniel, as well as follow up on what Mr Lombard had said about the stormy relationship between Daniel and his father. It seemed best to tell Mr Bagnall that I intended talking to his mine manager again, so I knocked his drawing room door. He called me in. The curtains were drawn across, and the Bagnalls and Mr Lombard sat in half-darkness, dressed in a most sombre fashion. I explained what I wished to do.

Mr Bagnall sighed deeply. 'That is unfortunate, Miss Valentine. Today will be young Daniel's funeral.'

'I'm sorry, sir, I had no idea.'

'Do not apologise, it is my fault entirely. Confirmation only came late last night, after you'd retired, and with all the fuss this morning I forgot to mention it. I doubt Edward will want to talk to you, but you may attend with us if you wish.'

I tried not to show how annoyed I was by this

situation. Edward Powell had ignored my request not to move his son from where he'd been murdered, and now he'd arranged a burial before I'd had a chance to examine Daniel's corpse. Did he have something to hide? My inclination was to march over to the church and demand the funeral be stopped. The only thing pulling me back was the knowledge I'd be laughed at and ignored. Had I been bigger, stronger … and a man, there'd be a better chance. All I could do now was tag along with the Bagnalls and try to get close enough to Powell to ask him a question or two.

Ten minutes later we'd joined a small crowd of mourners outside St Leonard's, mostly men employed by Mr Bagnall by the look of their work-worn clothes. I recognised some of them from the group who'd brought Tom Hurdley to the house, including Frank Smitheman and Ernest Kite. Natty Preece hopped from one leg to the other beside them, his excitement at escaping the coal-heap for the morning clearly getting the better of him. He waved wildly when he saw me, and I lifted my hand slightly in acknowledgement. Around the fringes of the workers, some of the town's better off residents stood in twos and threes, and most of the men amongst them bowed a head in Mr Bagnall's direction as he led our party to the front. We hadn't to wait long before Daniel's parents arrived, following a horse drawn cart which carried the coffin.

The vicar summoned six of the workmen, who lifted the load and began a sombre walk into church.

Mr and Mrs Powell fell in as the most important mourners, with us a few paces behind. I would have preferred to miss the whole affair, but I needed to stay close to Powell and Mr Bagnall. The latter would give me some credence if I managed to find an opportunity to talk to Daniel's father.

The privilege which money brings is nowhere clearer than in a church. Not only are the wealthy afforded the best seats, where the vicar fawns and frets over them, whilst ordinary folk are expected to treat him as if he's a better. Even the graveyard has the wealth of the richest families on display, whilst the poorest lie in common holes in the worst ground. If I hadn't been with Mr Bagnall this time, I'd have been forced to stand at the back again. Instead, we were alongside the family, right at the front. There were, of course, many tears shed, and the vicar gabbled on and on for an age. To me he sounded insincere, but I didn't know the man, so perhaps I shouldn't have judged.

In the graveyard, when Daniel's remains had finally been laid to rest, I stuck close to Edward Powell, offering my condolences to his wife. I talked with her on the walk back to the house, where refreshments were to be available to the select few. Once again, it would be unusual for a person like me to be invited to join them. It was only the status of being Mr Bagnall's guest which gave me the privilege. I was bemused by how easy it seemed to be to rise through the ranks of society simply by being alongside the right people. I was still the same poverty-stricken woman I'd been when I left Bridgnorth, and my clothes and manners were no better. Yet here I was mixing with the more affluent citizens of Broseley. I took my chance to follow Mr Powell when he went out of the room where the mourners were gathered.

He went up the stairs, so I waited in the hall for his return. The man jumped when he saw me standing there. 'Goodness me, miss, you gave me a shock. Is there something you need?'

'Actually, sir, there is. I'd like to have a word with you about Daniel's death.'

He snorted. 'Haven't I already told you I don't wish to speak to you, and especially here. Now. Have you no delicacy?' He looked me up and down. 'Actually, I know you don't. I've heard that you're really nothing more than a common gardener with ideas above her station. Now, please leave.'

The mine manager moved to push me aside, but I stood firm. 'I will leave, if that's what you wish, Mr Powell, but then I'll need to explain to Mr Bagnall why I can't make progress with the task he's set me. I doubt he'll be pleased. Even though he appears to be a friend to you, he's also your employer and will expect you to work with me.'

For a moment I thought he'd continue on his way, but he paused and rubbed his eyes.

'Forgive me, Miss Valentine, I'm not myself at present. This has been a very trying business and I would have hoped Mr Bagnall might have found someone with a little more experience in these matters. However, I accept he is doing his best and only has the interests of me and my good wife at heart.' He swung a hand towards a door a little further down the hall. 'Please come into my parlour and we can talk.'

Despite Powell's apology, his face was still sour when we sat either side of the fireplace. 'So, tell me what you wish to know.'

'I've just two questions, sir. First, why did you have Daniel's body moved so quickly? I'd sent word to leave him until I could get there, so I could see the exact scene as you found it. There were things it might have told me. By moving him, the men and the cart chewed up the ground, and I couldn't get any impression of how he'd fallen, or the direction his attacker came from. I think it would also have been useful to see the wound on his neck, to identify the nature of the weapon used.'

'I can't see how these would have made any difference. My boy was dead, and I wasn't about to take orders from some slip of a girl.'

'Then I must assume you don't want his killer found.'

Powell banged his fist on the chair arm. 'Nonsense. Of course I do. But it won't bring him back, will it? My grief drove me to do what I thought in the best interests of my son. My logic told me sending out searchers was the most likely way of catching his killer quickly. It's a shame if my actions prevented your little game.'

I'd seen this contradiction in feelings before.

Loss, whether it be of a person or an object seems to do funny things to a person. Often, they want revenge, but they also want to forget about it. To put away their hurt. Edward Powell had taken the biggest loss a parent can, his son had been taken away from him. He had a lot of hurt to put away.

I needed to show him we were both working to the same end. 'I understand this, sir, it's just that your actions might have hindered finding who killed your son. As for this being a game to me, I can assure you it isn't. In the same way Mr Bagnall is trying to help you, so am I. He has engaged me because he has some belief in my abilities. In time, I hope you will feel the same. At the moment, you may not see the relevance of my questions, but I must ask you to humour me.'

Powell didn't seem convinced. 'So what else? You said you had two questions.'

'Tell me about your relationship with Daniel. Was it good?'

'Good. I believe so. At least as with any father and son. We had our disagreements, but not many.'

There was no easy way to ask my next question. 'Was one of them about religion?'

'You say this with a confidence which suggests you know it to be true. What if Daniel's questioning of my faith *did* cause us to fight. It is of no consequence.'

'Except, Mr Powell, as you well know, many men have been killed in recent years over religion.'

Powell stood, his whole body shaking. 'Please

leave my house, miss. I've answered your two questions and now you all but accuse me of killing my son. That son we've just put in the cold ground. How dare you. Get out.'

The walk from Mr Powell's home to New House wasn't far, though it took even less time than usual because I almost ran, with anger boiling out of me. I was angry with Mr Powell for his outburst, I was angry with him for dismissing my worth just because I wasn't a man, but, mostly, I was angry with myself for being so clumsy in my questioning. I should have trodden more carefully. The man was grieving, and I should have respected his grief, shown myself as sympathetic, someone to confide in. Instead I'd charged in like a bull at a gate, and like the gate, Mr Powell stopped any progress. I hoped he wouldn't block me further by telling Mr Bagnall what had occurred.

At New House gate I decided I didn't feel much like going inside. I needed to talk to Tom Hurdley again, but there'd be little point until I'd confirmed or dismissed the story he'd told me, and only Jacob Slack could do this. So I took two deep breaths to calm my annoyance and wandered in the direction of Lost Lane.

The Hurdley's cottage looked different to how it had when I'd spoken to Beth only two days earlier. Empty. It's strange how you can tell when no-one is home, almost as if the life essence of occupants seeps into the walls and makes them somehow warmer. I pulled up my collar and continued past, not envying Tom Hurdley if he turned out to be innocent and had to return to this. A little further on I took the track leading to where Jacob Slack lived, and even as I turned, I could hear his dogs barking. I'm not keen on dogs at the best of times, and these sounded like they were not the friendliest. I kept my eyes peeled in case they were loose in the fields. When I reached his gate, I stayed outside for a few moments. I could still hear them, but they didn't come into view, so I guessed they were tied up somewhere round the back.

A stocky young man with golden curly hair answered my knock, his missing front tooth only emphasising his grin as he looked me up and down. 'Well, miss, what have we here?' The ale on his breath wafted over me.

'Jacob Slack?'

'Aye, if you're the vicar. Jake to everyone else. And who might you be?'

I gave him my name and explained I was working for Matthias Bagnall. This seemed to unlock doors well enough.

'So what can I do for you, Miss Valentine?'

'I'm told you're a friend of Tom Hurdley. Is that right?'

The grin disappeared. 'I am. Why?'

'He says he stayed with you a couple of nights ago.'

'Aye, he did. Said he'd argued more with his wife

after we'd been in the tavern and needed somewhere to sleep.'

'He also says he was working with you on the next morning. Was he?'

Slack's eyes flickered before he answered, and he paused for a second. I guessed the man might not be telling the whole truth.

'If he says he was, then he was. Never a liar, my friend Tom. Why're you doubting him?'

'Why do you think?'

The lad shrugged. 'I dunno.'

'You know his wife was killed?'

He stepped back as if I'd pushed him. 'Beth? No? Can't be.'

'You hadn't heard?'

Slack shook his head. 'Been at market. Went Monday. Got a good price for the pigs over the two days and drank too much. Stayed an extra night in Bridgnorth. Got back early this morning and been sleeping since. Only out of my bed a half hour ago. Who ... who could have done it? Not Tom? Surely not him?'

'That's what I'm trying to find out. Sounds like you think your friend might be capable. Did Tom Hurdley ask you to lie for him?'

'No, he didn't. As I said. Stayed with me until first light, went home then came back and helped me get everything ready before I left. That's the last time I saw him.'

I still wasn't sure if he was telling the truth, but the news of Beth's death had clearly shocked him, and I was unlikely to get anything more out of him at the minute. I told him I might need to talk to him again, then left, reflecting on what an unsuccessful morning it had turned out to be.

Eighteen

The Bagnalls hadn't arrived home when I got back, and Ernest Kite was away at his day's work, so I was a little nervous of seeing Tom Hurdley on my own. Nevertheless, it had to be done. I told Eliza what I planned and said she should fetch help if she heard me shout out. The lamplight flickering on the stairs almost made me lose my footing and I grabbed the rail to steady myself. Then I took a second to steady my breathing. I unlocked the door to the room where Hurdley had been put and pushed it open whilst standing well back. I needn't have worried. The prisoner barely lifted his head to acknowledge my presence. The bread and cheese which had been brought down lay uneaten and the man looked as miserable as a man *can* look.

'You're in luck today, Tom. Your friend tells me you were with him after all.'

He showed no sign that this was good news, only mumbled something which I had to ask him to repeat.

'I said I told you I didn't kill Beth. Don't know why you'd believe Jake and not me.'

'Oh, I didn't say I believed Slack, did I? Only that he confirmed what you told me. I didn't really expect anything else. After all, that's what friends are for, isn't it? But it does mean I have to let you go.'

Hurdley rubbed the stubble on his chin, then stood, but I shook my head. 'Not just yet though. Let's talk some more first.'

'What about?'

'How well did you know Daniel Powell?'

'The man who was killed a couple of days ago? Not at all. Think I've seen him in the tavern once or twice but never spoke to him. Wouldn't mix with the likes of me, would he?'

'What about Beth, did she know him?'

'No.'

'You seem very sure.'

'She's ... she was ... a married woman. Why would she be friends with him?

'Beth didn't need to be a friend, she could just know him from around the town. 'You're certain she didn't?'

'Certain.'

Something about his denial suggested he was either lying, or he didn't want to believe they knew each other. If it was the first, then he might also think there was more than friendship and be hiding a motive for killing them both. If the second, I'd pity the poor man if I discovered something to prove him wrong.

I stood and opened the cellar door. 'In that case you might as well go, but I might need to talk to you again when I've got answers to some more questions.'

Hurdley turned back after he'd climbed the first step. 'I know you still don't believe me, but I didn't kill my wife. I loved her. And now I'm going to find who did. When I do, there'll be no need for judge and jury or need for hanging. You mark my words; he'll get what's coming to him without any of them.'

'Then there *will* be work to be done by the court, only you'll be the one on trial. Is that what you want? Is it what Beth would have wanted, to see you swinging from the gibbet on her account?'

He banged his fist against the wall. 'I dunno, but I can't let her murderer go free, can I?'

'Then help me to catch who did this. Don't take matters into your own hands, it will only end in sorrow. If you're telling the truth, Tom, look for her killer by all means, but if you find them, pass it on to me, or to Mr Bagnall, and we'll see you get justice.'

Without agreeing he'd do as I asked, Hurdley turned and slowly climbed the stairs, leaving me to wonder if this was just a performance. The guilty man playing the innocent. If it was, it was one of the best I'd ever seen.

Tom looked over his shoulder for the tenth time since he'd been released. He could see no-one following. There'd be nothing wrong with him going straight to see his friend, but Tom knew Meg

Valentine would find it suspicious and doubt the line he'd fed her. It surprised him how easily the lie had fallen from his lips. He must be getting used to it. A wash and a shave wouldn't go amiss, but he couldn't face going in to his cottage, with all the memories it held, so hurried past the door, and ducked below the hedge to avoid his neighbour's watchful eyes.

Jake's father's dogs only barked once as Tom approached the house, then must have caught his scent. They were quiet when he arrived at the door. Their behaviour must have told Jake someone familiar was coming, because he opened the door with a grin before Tom knocked.

The grin disappeared when Jake saw who it was. 'You've a damned cheek, Tom Hurdley, coming here.'

'Jake?'

'Don't be acting the innocent with me, man. Why didn't you tell me Beth was dead?'

'Because you'd not have backed me up, would you?'

'Damned right. I wouldn't have lied for you that's for sure. You shouldn't have asked me to do it.'

'What else was I supposed to do, Jake?'

'You should have done what you did in the end. Come back and given yourself up. Even better if you hadn't run away in the first place. Made a clean breast of it and told them you and Beth had argued, and it got out of hand. They'd understand jealousy would make a man mad in the head.'

Tom frowned. 'What makes you say such a thing?'

'You were seen fighting with Daniel Powell last week.'

'Where'd you hear that?'

'Not the sort of thing to stay secret for very long, is it? Mate told me after the market. Said he watched you waiting for him up in the town. Hanging around in the shadows 'til he came out of his house, then went for him, right there in the street.'

'That's not what happened. I was passing and he came out.'

'You saying you didn't have an argument with him?'

Tom looked away. 'No. We did fight. Not fists, just words.'

'What about?'

'He'd been talking to my Beth.'

'That's not a crime, Tom.'

'No, it's not, but I only found out about it when Annie Reader next door told me she'd seen them. Big grin on her face that witch had when she said it, as though *she* knew something was going on. I asked Beth about it, and she didn't deny chatting to Powell, said they'd bumped into each other at the bakery. Seems her dad had worked for his dad ages ago and she and the son had played together a few times Hadn't seen each other for years, she said. Afterwards it was all "Daniel this" and "Daniel that", and I was sick of it. He had a go at me in The Plough, so I had a go back when I met him coming out of his house. Told him he'd be sorry if he didn't keep away from Beth.'

'God's teeth, Tom, you're a fool. You'd been drinking and threatened him?'

'I warned him off, that's all, just the ale talking. Funny enough I almost believed him when he denied doing anything wrong. Still told him to keep away from Beth. What I said was true though, I'd have killed him if I'd caught him chasing round her.'

'Would have, or did?'

Tom stiffened. 'You saying you don't believe me?'

'What I'm saying is I don't know whether to believe you or not. You fight with Daniel Powell and never tell me about it even though we talked about him being dead. Then you ask me to cover for you, lying that you were with me when you weren't. Only when I get back from Bridgnorth do I hear Beth's been murdered and you're accused. How am I supposed to trust you when you weren't straight up with me at the start?'

Tom's knuckles crunched as they bit into Jake's face and within seconds the two were rolling in the mud, first one on top, then the other. Both strong farm workers, who'd wrestled since they were boys, so each knew the other's moves. Jake had always been the stronger, and Tom the quicker, but this time it was for real. Punches came in at all sides, neither taking an advantage for a while, until Tom managed to pin Jake's arms with his knees. With the blood pounding in his head he gripped Jake's throat, squeezing, and squeezing, until his friend's eyes bulged.

At the sight, Tom let go. He stood, gasped, and walked away.

All my time in Broseley seemed to have spent going nowhere. I'd been faced with a series of burglaries and two deaths and could see no link between the crimes. I'd a victim's husband with a possible motive yet the strongest of denials, and a father and son known to fight over religion. I tended to believe both these suspects when they said they were innocent. I didn't like Edward Powell much, but it didn't mean he was a murderer. I was still unsure about Tom Hurdley.

I'd no leads at all in respect of the thefts, other than it looked like they were all committed by the same person. Someone who was selective, stealing only a small number of items. High value, easy to carry, easy to dispose of. They also knew enough of their victims to break into their homes without it being obvious. This gave time to hide or to get rid of the stolen goods before the loss was even discovered.

I knew Peter would help me pull the strands together, and I'd need to talk to him soon if I could make no more progress. In the meantime I'd continue trying to make sense of it on my own.

As I paced the garden, with these thoughts swimming round my head, Eliza came outside, and we chatted for a few minutes about the flowers and the weather. She told me she'd been repairing some cushions and needed thread to finish them but had come out to relieve the stuffiness of her workroom. I said I'd be happy to walk up to the shop and get what she needed. She accepted my offer with profuse thanks.

The late afternoon had become quite humid, as it often does in September, and a haze hung over the fields behind St Leonard's. The loudness of bees dipping into every bloom I passed only made the heaviness deeper. It seemed to me there might be thunder by bedtime.

The half dozen people I saw looked like the very street was dragging at the soles of their shoes. Even the elderly haberdasher served me with no conversation, taking her seat behind the counter as soon as she'd noted the cost of Mr Bagnall's purchase in her ledger. When I stepped out of the shop, I spotted Jake Slack talking to a man across the road, the two leaning against the wall of a tavern. Jake glanced in my direction, and I couldn't help but notice the black and purple bruises on his face. He spoke a few words to his companion then turned and walked quickly away.

I called after him. 'Jake. Wait. I need to talk to you again.'

For a few steps he didn't slow his pace, but then stopped, shrugged, and turned. 'What is it now?'

'You've been in a fight.'

'I can see you'll have no problem solving these murders, miss. You're very sharp.'

'So who were you fighting with?'

'It's no business of yours.'

'Really? I'd say it is. In fact I'd guess it was with Tom Hurdley. Am I right?'

'Wasn't with Tom.'

Some men lie well, others don't. Jake Slack's shuffling feet and averted eyes told me he was one of the ones who didn't. 'Sorry, Jake, I don't believe you.'

Slack swung his arms in front, as if pushing away his friendship. 'Damn. Why should I lie for *him*. We've been together all our lives but now it seems I don't know Tom at all.'

'So what happened?'

Jake folded his arms and pressed his lips tight. I could see he was still wrestling with loyalty to his friend. I spoke to him gently. 'Come on, Jake. Nothing to be served now by keeping quiet about it. Tell me the story.'

His words gushed when the dam broke. 'He came round to my house; day Beth was found. First thing in the morning. Flushed in the face he was and looked like he'd slept in his clothes. Breath stank of vomit and booze. Said he couldn't tell me why, but he had to go away. That I should tell anyone who asked that he'd been sleeping at my place overnight, gone home early and then come back. I told him I wouldn't, but he begged. What else could I do?'

'You could have refused and protected yourself. Instead, you did what he expected and lied for him. I'm not sure who's the worse, him or you. Did Tom tell you about Beth?'

'No he didn't. I only found out she was dead when you told me. D'you think he really did it?'

Always the question they ask. I've little experience of murders, but I've solved enough thefts and robberies to know witnesses and victims assume a thief-taker has some kind of magic power, like a water diviner. Expecting me to be able to sense a guilty man from an innocent one.

'I don't know, Jake. It doesn't really matter what I think. The magistrate won't act until he's clear proof that your friend is guilty, and I don't have any yet. The fact Tom asked you to lie for him doesn't look good though. What about you? Do *you* believe he could have killed Beth and Daniel.'

'Until this morning, I'd have said not. Then we had the fight. We've played at such all our lives, but this was different. Tom was like a madman. Gave me this black eye then took me by the throat. Thought he was going to choke the life out of me. That, on top of what I heard -'

'What did you hear?'

Jake shook his head. 'Nothing. I can't say. I shouldn't have mentioned it.'

I pressed him on this, and he wouldn't budge, he just continued to shake his head at every question. I made it clear I wasn't impressed with him continuing to cover up for Tom. It made no difference.

Now I was faced with a violent side of Tom Hurdley I hadn't seen before. So, he'd lied, more than once, convinced Jake Slack to lie as well, then almost killed his friend in a temper. Despite my doubts of his guilt, the evidence was quickly stacking up against him.

Nineteen

I told Jake Slack to keep away from Tom Hurdley
until I'd spoken with him again, then made my way
once more to Lost Lane, where smoke floated from
the Hurdley's chimney across the surrounding fields.
I knocked and Tom invited me in without question.
The fire, combined with the closeness of the
afternoon, might have made the room unbearable if
it hadn't been for the windows and kitchen door
being open. I asked him why they were.

'The smell. Had to get rid of it.'

An interesting idea given that he spent his days
tending pigs. Though, in my limited experience,
death does cling longer and heavier than other
scents. There was now no trace of where Beth had
lain on the floor, but the picture of her was still in
my head, as it must have been in his. It might have
been the horror of losing his loved one which made
him want to clear the air. Or could it be the guilt
linked with what he'd done?

There seemed little point in dressing up why I'd

called. I stood facing him, making sure I was clear of the spot where she'd died. 'You've not been entirely truthful with me have you, Tom?'

He turned and poked at the fire. 'Why do you say that?'

'Because I've been talking to your friend Jake.'

'He told you I had an argument with Daniel Powell?'

So that's what Jake was holding back. I could see why he would. It would seem like a further betrayal of his friend. He'd been prepared to go some way down that line, but only so far. Loyalty is a strange bond and often defies any kind of logic. 'No, that's not what he said. But did you?'

'What if I did, it means nothing.'

'What it means Tom, is that you lied to me. First you told me you'd been at Jake's and didn't know Beth was dead. Then you gave me some daft story about being fishing. You then said you had gone home from Jake's, which is when you found your wife's body. To top off all these lies, you swore you didn't know Daniel Powell, though you clearly did. Not only did you know him, but I also think you suspected him of chasing after Beth and fought him over it. To make things worse, you ran away. There's more than enough there for me to tell Mr Bagnall to have you dragged off to the magistrate for killing the pair of them, don't you think?'

The clang of the dropped poker made me jump back, ready to defend myself, but Tom simply slumped against the chimney breast, his forehead pressed on the wall. His voice sounded so tired and defeated I could hardly make out the words. 'I didn't do anything. Beth meant the world to me. That's why I had a go at Powell. He was trying to steal her away.' He turned and glared at me, some strength seeming to have returned. 'What kind of man would I be if I hadn't tried to fight to keep her?'

'They were having an affair?'

'No. They weren't. He just wanted to, I reckon. Told me in The Plough I weren't good enough for her. Got the other drinkers laughing at my expense. I knew Beth was a bit sweet on him too, so I had it out with him afterwards.' He hung his head again. 'Only after I'd had a few drinks mind.'

'Fighting to keep your wife is perfectly natural, I suppose. But I'd say killing them both just to keep what you thought of as yours is a step too far.'

'I've told you I didn't. Why won't you believe me? Daniel and me argued a few days ago and that's all. He denied anything was going on between them and I told him to keep away from Beth. Then I came home, leaving him to go on his way. If I'd told you we'd had a fight you'd have made your mind up right then and there that I must be guilty.'

'Well it's not helped by lying about it, has it? So why give me the other pack of lies about being with Jake?'

'Same reason, really. Beth's lying dead in our house and only me there. Obvious I must have done her in, isn't it?'

I sat at the table and gestured for him to do the

same. 'Then convince me you didn't.'

Tom hesitated but pushed himself away from the wall and sat opposite me. 'I don't know if I can. I've told you what happened. Running away was stupid, I know, but my head was spinning. When I first found her, I didn't even know if I'd done it. I remembered arguing. I remembered going out, and coming back and hitting the gin, but nothing else. For a while I thought we must have had another fight, and I strangled her. It was only when I was in that church, I realised I couldn't do such a thing then go off to bed like nothing had happened.'

What Tom said made sense. The trouble was, other than him protesting he wouldn't sleep soundly, it might all apply just as much if he *had* murdered Beth in a jealous, drunken, rage. There was still more against him than for him. The only things I could see in his favour were his threat to find Beth's killer, and the way he seemed defeated by all that had happened.

—♀—

You noticed the sensation when you found the unlocked window at the side. It felt too easy. Breaking in has never been only about the money, though God knows you want it. Part of it is how the blood runs hot in your veins, the dizziness which stays with you all the time you search the house, and for hours afterwards. In the beginning, it had even returned when you relived the memory later, but, as the months and the burglaries went by, the excitement diminished. Your other pleasures had to make up for it. This time there is no thrill, just a job being carried out by an experienced craftsman. The anticipation of a possible kill later sharpens the edge a little, but the excitement of the thieving itself is gone.

You wander the house at your leisure. There are no servants left behind with the owners away. None of the downstairs rooms hold much of interest. Books, lots and lots of books. A harpsichord and a violin in one room. Valuable but far to difficult to carry away. You go upstairs.

Finding Christopher Parfitt's trinkets is simple. People are so trusting, always leaving their most precious objects in obvious places. Sometimes you'd find they'd be conscientiously stored in a locked box, but then the key would be left in a drawer where anyone, servant or thief, could find and use it. This time the valuables weren't even put out of sight, just lying on top of a dark corner cupboard in the bedroom for all to see.

The two lady's gold rings, a ruby necklace, and a fine watch jingle in your pocket as you roam the house. This makes you smile. Not a pleasant sight when you are in this frame of mind. You are tempted to stay until the owner returns, to sate your desire. You even sit in his best armchair, watching the minutes ticking by, and think how it will feel. Your one regret is you had to use your rope to tie Parfitt's dogs in the outbuilding. Then you see the curtain cord, red and gold, which looks strong enough to do the job. You stroke the workmanship, feel its weight. With an end in each hand, you tug. There is almost no stretch. It will do nicely.

The evening light begins to fail, and you pace, knowing your victim will soon be home. You look for a place to conceal yourself. Somewhere you won't be seen or heard but close enough to take Parfitt by surprise. A cupboard in the hall seems ideal, and you practice opening the door quietly, and you count the steps back to the fireplace.

But what if the house owner doesn't return alone? Can you escape without being seen? More than likely they will lock the doors after dark, then you'll be trapped. You consider what you might do in those circumstances. Would killing the whole household while they slept be satisfying? It doesn't take long for you to reach your decision that it wouldn't. Not so much as the others. The struggle of a lone victim adds the jolt which makes it worthwhile. This wouldn't be possible with several and would appear clumsy. What's more, the speed needed would require a knife, much less intimate than your favoured rope.

No, you must go back to your original plan. From your finger you remove a silver ring engraved with symbols of flames. The proceeds of another theft. The attached seal is square with a dragon at its centre and an ornate letter "E" on one side and "P" on the other. You climb the stairs to the bedroom once more, and tuck the ring beneath the bed. Insurance in the game of cat and mouse which is developing between you and Meg Valentine.

Twenty

Soon after breakfast, Mrs Dudley, the Bagnalls' cook, popped her head into the dining room and asked her mistress if I might join her in the kitchen. As I followed, I imagined she wanted to tell me off for diving too deeply into the pound cake and the cocoa, my favourite drink of all time. Such luxuries were never tasted in my home, nor that of my parents, where porridge and toasted bread would be the order of the day. Mrs Dudley wouldn't have dared tell off any of the Bagnalls' usual guests, but she knew I was born as lowly as her, so she'd be happy to bend my ear if she thought fit.

Instead, she simply cocked a thumb towards the back door. 'He wants to talk to you. Please try to keep your urchins outside on the lane where they belong.'

I stayed in the doorway and Natty Preece stood just outside, hands clasped in front, as I suspected she'd told him to do. His hair, face and clothes were grimy with coal dust. I wasn't surprised the cook didn't want him in her kitchen.

I tried to use a tone, for her benefit, suggesting I didn't relish mixing with the likes of this dirty lad. "Morning, Natty. What do you want?'

'Wondered if you needed any help today, miss. Mr Bagnall has said I've to do what I can. Will let me have time off from picking coal to do it. Told me he'd make up my wages, but only if you make use of me.' He cast a glance in Mrs Dudley's direction, fear in his eyes. 'Please, miss, I can't be failing Mr Bagnall.'

Natty sounded so desperate. I could hardly refuse him. 'Meet me in half an hour by that pond along the lane.' I looked him up and down and tutted. 'And have a good wash before you get there.'

I needed to talk to Natty but didn't want to do this in front of Mrs Dudley. Mr Bagnall had said the lad knew everyone in the town, so I hoped he might be able to shed some light on who would be telling the truth. I made my excuses with my hosts, after one more slice of pound cake, and walked up to meet Natty at the agreed time. I'd hardly have recognised the scrubbed boy's face that greeted me if it hadn't been for him wearing the same shabby clothes.

Mrs Bagnall had told me that they called the pool the Delph, and it had been created over recent years from an old mine shaft, with the intention of providing the town with a good supply of water and fish. As far as I could see, this enterprise was a failure, for the pond was murky and didn't look particularly appetising.

Two men and two women, with children

running round beside them, stood talking on the pond side. Natty suggested we moved further along the lane to get out of earshot. When we'd settled against the wall of The Angel, which was still closed, Natty sheepishly popped his question. 'Can I help you today, miss? I'll do anything, anything at all. Just say.'

'What about the things you were to do earlier in the week?'

'I've been asking around. No-one's been offered any jewels or watches, but I'm told they'd probably be sent to fences in Bridgnorth or Shrewsbury to be got rid of. Too easy round here to be recognised.'

'What about someone spending more than they should?'

'Nothing. Makes sense though, don't it?'

'In what way?'

'Man in the mine might make eight shillings in a good week, farm worker and a house servant a lot less. Stands to reason it'd be noticed if they were living above their station, so they'd be careful.'

'That's why I asked about it.'

Natty bit his lip, as if trying to decide his next words. 'Know what I think? It's a rich 'un.'

'What?'

'Rich man would find it easy to hide spending extra money, wouldn't he. Makes sense. Everybody knows he's got a few shillings to spare, so no surprise when he splashes them about. Also, this stolen stuff is worth a lot, I suppose. Poor man would take time off work, might even leg it out of town altogether.

I've not heard of anyone local doing such.'

'Those are good points, Natty. Need to go in the pot.'

The lad looked like he'd won a prize bull, and I was pleased he'd really been thinking about the possibilities. Perhaps he wasn't going to be too bad to have around after all. I moved on to the next question. 'I've found that the murder victims knew each other and Tom had Hurdley heard about it. He denies doing them any harm though. How well did you know Daniel and Beth?'

'Depends on what you mean by "know". Weren't friends or anything, bit old for me. Saw Daniel Powell round the mine sometimes, and met her if she came up to the market. Friendly lady. My mum sold her bits and pieces of embroidery up there.'

'Beth would buy things from her?'

'Nothing pricey, don't imagine she could afford much, but she seemed to like the work and my mum would let her have things a bit cheaper. Said it was nice to see a young woman trying to make her home pretty.'

I'd spotted she liked to do that. Could Tom be thieving to indulge his wife? If he was, she'd hardly threaten to expose him if she found out. 'What about Tom, the husband?'

'Hard worker they say. Never been employed at any of the mines as far as I know, stayed on the land even though so many have left it. Digging coal he'd earn half as much again as being a farm labourer but going underground don't suit everybody.' Natty shivered. 'Not keen on the idea myself if I'm honest with you, miss.'

'Do you think he's trustworthy?'

'Couldn't rightly say. Never heard nothing to say he isn't. You think he's lying to you?'

'Well, he doesn't always tell the truth, I know that much. He told me he'd been with Jake Slack when his wife was killed, and that turned out to be a lie. But I think we'd all do the same if we found ourselves in his circumstances. Could you ask around, see what people think who've had dealings with him?' The grin that appeared when I made this request almost made me begin to like this boy. 'And keep trying to find out what people are saying about Beth Hurdley and Daniel Powell. There's got to be some kind of connection between them other than a passing chat in the street.'

An hour later, Eliza knocked on my bedroom door.

'That Natty Preece is here to see you again, miss. At the back. Mrs Dudley says you've to insist he stops bothering her.'

She turned without waiting for a reply and I watched until she'd taken the first few steps down the stairs, then followed. The sour looks she and the cook gave me as I went through the kitchen said I should know my place. It wouldn't be long before I'd have to put them in theirs.

Natty was up to his habit of hopping from one leg to the other. 'Found out stuff for you, miss.'

I put a finger to my lips until I closed the door. 'Tell me.'

'Everyone seemed to like Tom and Beth Hurdley. Spoke to half a dozen and they all said the same.'

'Well that doesn't take us very far, does it?'

A frown came upon his face as he realised I wasn't excited by his news, but it disappeared as suddenly as it had come, and he tapped the side of his nose twice. 'But there's more, miss. The two was friendly. More than friendly, if you get what I mean. At least that's what I was told by one who would know.'

'Know, how?'

'Said she saw them. On a path down near the river. Holding hands.'

'When was this?'

'Last week I think.'

'And she's sure it was them?'

'Well she knew the woman for sure, related in some way. Said she didn't know the man but everybody in the town's talking about these killings. The description the lady gave sounded a lot like Daniel Powell. Shocked, she said, because they acted just like a courting couple.'

I thanked Natty, saying this was useful. 'Give me the name of the woman you spoke to, so I can talk to her myself. I might get more from her than you have.'

'Oh no, miss. I don't think she'd want me to do that. Very private lady she is.'

'Private she might be, but two poor souls have been murdered. Strangled. You must tell me this woman's name, Natty.'

His agitation, which had calmed whilst we were talking, came back again. 'I can't, miss, not without asking her. Let me go to see her again. Then, if she's happy to talk, I'll take you round.'

'I expect I'll have to be satisfied with that for now. I'd hoped to be able to tell Mr Bagnall how helpful you'd been, but it will have to wait now.'

Natty hung his head for a moment or two, then brightened as another idea clearly came to him. 'There's something else, miss. I'm sure it will be enough to put me in Mr Bagnall's good books.'

'Come on then, let's have it.'

'What would you think if I told you Daniel Powell and Tom Hurdley were fighting only days before Daniel was found dead? Tom said he'd kill Daniel if he didn't leave Beth alone.'

'Where did you hear that?'

'Man in the town had it from a man who heard it at the market in Bridgnorth.'

'So this is just a rumour you're giving me?'

'That's not fair, miss, and you know it. You asked me to find out what I could and I'm doing my best. The man I spoke to had no reason to be making up stories. Told me in good faith. I've no problem giving you *his* name if you want it, he's a different class of person to the lady I mentioned.'

'But even if you do, and he tells me the same tale, it doesn't mean it's true, does it? As it happens, I know Tom and Daniel argued because I got it from Tom Hurdley himself. Unfortunately, your taleteller is at least two places removed from having actually seen the fight. In the same way as the woman who says she saw the couple, she can't be completely certain the one with Daniel was Beth, can she? If you're going to be working with me, Natty, you'll need to be less trusting.'

The leg hopping became much more intense. 'Is that what I'll be doing, miss? Working with you?'

I couldn't help to think back to the same conversation I'd had with Edwin Hare. Me, a grubby assistant gardener, desperate to break out of poverty and drudgery, him, a thief-taker with the respect of the whole town. I'd felt so much joy when he agreed I could help him. It also made me think how dismayed Edwin must have been when he saw this reaction.

Since striking out on my own, I'd welcomed help from Peter, but he was different. Not at all like this scruffy little coal-picker, almost wetting himself from the idea of escaping the lot God had given him. Peter was no better born, and had no ambition, but he was passable looking, had a good nature, more my own age, and I could see him at my side for many a year. There was no doubt in my mind that if I passed on any skills to Natty Preece he'd be taking the bread from my table as soon as he could.

'That's not what I'm saying, Natty. Your employer has taken me on to do a job and has burdened me with you to help me do it. What I'm telling you is you take care. The last thing we want is for an innocent man to hang, and a guilty one go free. Understand?'

'Yes.'

'Good.'

'Now, bearing in mind what I've just said, are you sure your man who heard it from another man, said Tom threatened to *kill* Daniel?'

'Sure as I'm standing here, miss. That's what was said.'

'Then I'll believe it for now. Heaven help you if I find you're making it up just to get in your boss's good books.'

I sent the lad on his way with his head down, and with me feeling I shouldn't have been so hard on him. We were not so far apart in what we wanted out of life, and probably not so far apart in the lengths we'd go to achieve it.

$$-\!\!Q\!\!-$$

Natty had provided me with a new piece of information I couldn't ignore, despite it being second-hand, so I went to Lost Lane again. Tom Hurdley closed the door in my face. I banged on it hard until he re-opened it.

He leant his shoulder against the frame and folded his arms. 'What do you want now?'

'You're not going to invite me in, Tom?'

'No.'

'But we have so much to talk about.'

'Like what?'

'Like why you didn't tell me you *threatened* Daniel Powell.'

'I admitted we had a row.'

'This was more though, wasn't it. You were heard saying you'd kill him if he didn't leave your wife alone.'

He popped out his head and looked towards his neighbour's house, then sighed and swung open the door. 'You'd best come in. Don't want old nosy Annie hearing all my business.'

He didn't ask me to sit down and he glared at me across a table still covered with the remains of at least one meal. 'What is it you think you know now about me and Powell?'

'I've been told he and your wife were seen out walking together.'

'That's not true.' He spat out the words.

'I believe it *is* true, and that you found out about it. This leads me to believe everything else you've told me is lies and you killed the pair of them. If it had been one or the other, I might have accepted the red mist came down and you did it in a moment of madness. But to do away with them both tells me you planned it. So what happened?'

Hurdley dropped down on to a chair by the hearth. 'Nothing. Nothing happened. I had the argument with Powell, like I told you last time, and he went home. But it was only about what he'd said, nothing else. I had a go at Beth because she told me she'd seen him in the town and wouldn't stop talking about him. When I was drinking with Jake, I'd said I thought she was seeing somebody. Just the ale talking though. Jake was right when he said she wouldn't do such a thing. I know she loved me, like I loved her. When I said I'd kill Powell it was words. Just words.'

His denial was made with such strength it made me wonder if what Natty had been given was false after all. I'd warned Natty not to take what was said at face value, and I needed to be sure I didn't either. I decided to change direction. 'Where were you the night Daniel was murdered? The truth mind.'

Tom rubbed his cheeks. 'I was out having a drink. Not for long though, don't make a habit of it.'

'Where did you go?'

'The Angel.'

'Where the dance was?'

'Yes. It got up not long after I arrived. Was sitting in the yard, minding my own business when the music started. I couldn't get the idea out of my head that Daniel Powell was after Beth. Soon after, he was there, dancing.'

Becky Cole hadn't mentioned Tom being there. Was he the mysterious man she talked about? 'Were you hiding your face?'

'God. How do you know that? I only watched him, nothing else. Didn't want him seeing me after our argument'

'But you followed him home to take your revenge?'

'I've already told you. I'm no killer. Saw him dancing with different lasses, just while I finished my drink. Seemed he had no need of Beth with all them chasing him. I drank up and went to another alehouse. I stayed there until just after ten o'clock.

Then came home.'

'And this is the truth this time? No lies?'

'Honestly, it's true.'

'Which alehouse did you go to last?'

'I don't know, could have been any of them. My head was spinning with the drink and the suspicion. Wasn't taking much notice of where my feet took me.'

The man looked so defeated by all that had happened over the past few days, I was tempted again to believe him. I needed to make a decision, and it only took me a couple of minutes. I put my hand on Hurdley's shoulder. 'Are you prepared to swear, by all you take as holy, that you didn't kill your wife and Daniel Powell?'

'I'll swear.'

'And you promise me you won't run away again, Tom?'

'Where would I go? Don't know anywhere other than here.'

'Then I'll not have you taken in just yet. Instead, try to think of anything which would prove to me you're innocent. Also, search everything you know about Beth, and help me figure out who killed her.'

Tom's next action took me by surprise. He dropped down on both knees and clasped his hands in front of his chest. 'I swear I didn't kill no-one. I don't care about Powell but if you're able to find who took my Beth's life, I'll be the first to lift you aloft and shout your praises to the town.'

◊

Twenty-One

Barely quarter of an hour after I returned from Lost Lane, Eliza knocked on my door again. 'Mr Powell wants to see you. He's in the drawing room with the Master.'

There was no hint of respect in her voice, and I knew if this continued, I'd need to have words with her. If I was ever going to climb the ladder, I couldn't let household servants treat me as one of their own. I told her to say I'd be down in a few minutes. A quick check in the mirror confirmed I was as presentable as ever I would be, though it disturbed me that I had no shoes to wear indoors. When I'd arrived Eliza had made it very clear I must leave my boots in the hall and she'd tolerate no mud on the Bagnall's rugs and carpets.

Four deep breaths before I tapped on the drawing room door and turned the knob to open it. Just long enough to gather my thoughts. Edward Powell had told me he didn't want me poking around about his son's killing and he must know I'd ignored his wishes. I was still simmering about what he'd said when we last spoke and wasn't sure I could keep my annoyance in check. All I could hope was that Mr Bagnall would have enough faith in me to ignore Mr Powell if he tried to use his influence against me.

Both men stood as I entered, my host wearing a more welcoming smile than his mine manager, but at least Mr Powell *was* smiling. He was still dressed in black, as was fitting.

Mr Bagnall waved me to a chair. 'Come in, Miss Valentine, and take a seat, we would like a word with you, if you don't mind.'

I could hardly refuse, and he knew this, but politeness is everything to these people. Seated, with my hands neatly placed on my lap, I waited for one of them to begin. Mr Bagnall looked at Mr. Powell, Mr Powell looked at Mr Bagnall, both glanced at my coarse woollen socks. I looked at the fire and thought about the respectable shoes I would buy when Mr Bagnall paid me my due. Eventually, it was the ironmaster who broke the deadlock. 'We hear your investigations are proceeding, Miss Valentine. On both fronts. Is that so?'

'It is, sir. There is very little progress so far, but it is early days. Is there something in particular you wish to know about?'

'Not I, but Edward might.'

For the first time Mr Powell spoke. 'I believe I owe you an apology, Miss Valentine.'

'Sir?'

'Yesterday I was rude, when you were only trying

to help. I beg you to understand I was ... I am ... deeply grieving. I'm not my usual self. Your questions caught me unawares.'

'Perhaps they were a little badly timed, Mr Powell. in my clumsiness I gave little thought to how your son's death must be affecting you. For that, I too must apologise.'

'Then let's speak no more about it. Mr Bagnall and I agree we need help to uncover what happened in this horrible business. My employer appears to have great faith in you so I suppose I must too. Hah - even that sounds grudging and I don't mean to be. Please believe me when I say I would welcome anything you can do to bring to justice the man who killed my son.'

'You're aware there may be some uncomfortable questions I need to ask? You're prepared to answer them?'

'I know I must be treated as much a suspect as anyone else, but as I have nothing to hide I'll tell you anything you need. Please ask away.'

'Can you think of anyone who would have wished Daniel harm?'

'No-one. My son was an honest, hard-working, young man and widely liked I believe. He never caused my wife nor I the least anxiety and seemed to get on well with everyone he came in contact with.'

My next question couldn't be avoided.

'Whilst you say he caused you no anxiety, I understand there were some religious differences between you. Isn't that so?'

'Differences? No. I am perhaps stricter in my faith than Daniel was, and we argued about it from time to time. I did not like him going to the tavern nor the dances, but our disagreements would be no more than usual between any father and son, I imagine. The bible says "Thou shalt not kill" and I hold the commandments dear.'

'I've been told Daniel was having a romantic relationship with Beth Hurdley. That would have been against one of your commandments, wouldn't it?'

Mr Powell spluttered. 'It ... it would. But I didn't know about it. If I had, there would have been a row mighty enough to take off the roof.'

'You'd have been angry?'

'Very much so'

'Angry enough to stop the affair in any way you could?'

The silence which followed this question made the air thick, like an early morning fog, and it hung, unmoving and unbroken until Mr Bagnall intervened.

'Miss Valentine, I beg of you, please be gentler with my friend. He has suffered a great loss, and I believe for him to come here today has taken a great effort. I know Edward to be an honest and upright man. With strong beliefs, yes, but that tells me all the more he couldn't have killed his son.'

I could have done without him interfering, but he was my customer, and I had to take heed of his wishes unless I could dissuade him. 'I'm sorry, Mr

Bagnall, but I did make it clear to Mr Powell that this may not be comfortable. I'd assumed you'd understand why I've to be so abrupt. I've only one suspect at the moment, Tom Hurdley, and I'm finding it hard to see a strong case against him. When I receive information which points to someone else, I'm duty bound to see where it leads even if that person has higher social status than Hurdley. I trust you agree?'

'Well, of course, yes. You must. It's only that Edward has worked for me for nigh on twenty years and I believe I know him well. I am not saying you should attach the blame to Tom Hurdley. From what I know of him he appears a respectable enough person. If you think him to be innocent, and I *know* Edward is, then you must cast your net wider. Do we agree?'

I'd no option but to agree, even though a doubt still lingered in my mind. I continued to ask Mr Powell questions but steered clear of any which might be seen as implying he was involved in his son's death. Instead, I asked about Daniel's friends and his work. Mr Powell said again that he knew nothing of a friendship between Daniel and Beth, nor, in fact with any other women. It was obvious from my talk with Becky Cole, and from the way he'd treated me, that Daniel had a way with the girls and wouldn't often be short of female companionship when he wanted any. Clearly, Mr Powell didn't know everything about his son. He did, however, enthuse about Daniel's commitment to his job.

'A complete master with the figures, he was. Much more so than I. My forte is with the men, his was with his ledgers. He once told me they spoke to him, showing him where to save a penny here or a halfpenny there, and when a particular enterprise might begin to turn a profit.' The father shook his head, and I sensed a tear was not too far away. 'He will be hard to replace. Not only for me and my wife, but for the business as well.'

When Mr Powell finished speaking, Mr Bagnall had nodded vigorously, uttering 'Yes, yes, the lad was so bright.'

So, we had a victim who was well liked by men and attractive to women, trusted by his father and his employer, and had a passion for numbers. Whilst I now had a better picture of Daniel Powell, I still had no idea why he might have been murdered.

My conversation with Mr Powell ended in an agreement that I could now examine his son's room, something he'd denied me on my earlier visit. Though I'd had the urge to dash round to his house straight away, it would have been unseemly, so I waited until after we'd eaten.

His maid was only slightly more respectful than Eliza, but she seemed a pleasant girl and showed me up to Daniel's room once she'd spoken with her master. She stayed by the open door watching me, until I told her she could go. The way she glanced back over her shoulder told me she'd felt obliged to stay and make sure I didn't steal anything.

The room was not overly large, though the ceiling was high and the window wide enough to let the afternoon sun stream across the desk in front of it. Despite this, the room felt chill with its empty grate and turned down sheets. The wardrobe held the outside coat Daniel would have worn the night he died, and a variety of shirts, pants, and waistcoats as would be fitting for a young man of his status. Daniel would have been buried in his best shoes, but there were two other pairs and some riding boots, all of polished leather. Nothing in the room other than these indicated if it belonged to either man or woman.

I turned my attention to the desk, the top of which was as shiny and clear as if it had never been used. Three drawers on the left contained only paper, pencils, and ink. Two on the right were empty, and the third was locked. A search of Daniel's coat pockets for a key proved fruitless, as did my lifting of the mantel clock and my sifting through the other drawers. It might be that the drawer had been locked for some time, and the key mislaid before Daniel had the desk, but I felt sure he wouldn't have kept his curiosity reined in. He'd have had to get into it somehow, so the lock would be broken. Where would I keep a key in a room with so few hiding places? It took me only a moment to think of the shoes, and only another to give them all a shake.

I'd hoped a key would drop out but I was disappointed. There was nothing more than a ball of fluff, which floated down until a draught sent it rolling across the floor. I cursed and went to lift the rug edges. Nothing.

Downstairs, I asked Mr Powell if he had the key.

'Not that I know of. There's a bunch hanging in the kitchen, might be in with those.'

We both went to collect them and trooped back upstairs. Mr Powell paused at his son's door, but after a moment he followed me in. We rejected the keys one by one as being too big or too small. Only two fitted but regardless of how he or I twisted them, we couldn't get the lock to click. After they'd all failed, he told me to wait as he'd had an idea. I imagined he'd thought of where the key might be, but this thought dispelled when he came back with Ernest Kite carrying a hammer and chisel.

The mine manager nodded in the direction of the desk 'There, Ernest, get that drawer open.'

I raised a hand. 'Please don't do any damage on my account, Mr Powell, there might be nothing of interest in there.' It had also occurred to me there may be things in the drawer which Daniel had hidden away from his father's eyes, and nothing would be served by revealing them.

Mr Powell banged the top of the desk. 'Do it, Ernest, my boy has no need for this lump of wood now.'

Kite stepped forward and did as he was told. He inserted the chisel blade into the gap above the drawer and swung his hammer. Two swift bangs, followed by an ear-piercing crack as the wood split, had the drawer open.

I wasn't sure what I'd been expecting to find locked away, perhaps some love letters between Daniel and Beth. Perhaps some correspondence pointing to his killer. At the very least I thought it might be something interesting, preferably useful to me. It wasn't the ledger lying there. On the cover was written the year, 1750, and the word "Accounts". It appeared the young man was just keeping his finances private.

Daniel's father stepped away and left me to flip the book open on the desk top. Inside, page after page was filled with columns of descriptions and figures, titled at the top and totalled at the bottom. Most had ticks alongside, though some had a cross in red ink. Towards the back, a single loose sheet of paper stuck out. The writing on here made even less sense to me than the rest. I showed it to Mr Powell, but he shook his head.

'Means nothing to me, Miss Valentine. Daniel didn't inherit his head for numbers from his father. Mr Bagnall's brother, Mr Lombard, might understand. He has a way with figures I believe. Do you wish to take it with you and ask him?'

'That would be very useful, sir, if you're sure you don't mind.'

'I'll do anything I can which will help catch my son's killer. I'm not sure that ledger will, but if you want to take a look I'll not stand in your way.' He surveyed the room. 'My son lived a quiet life, in the main. He liked a song, and he liked the ale a little too much to my mind, but he was a good boy. Neat and tidy in his habits. Have you found anything else in here which might assist you?'

I told him I hadn't, and I thanked him for allowing me to examine the room. Ernest Kite walked out before me and when I turned at the door to look back, Mr Powell remained standing in the middle, a look on his face of a man who can't work out where his life is going next.

Twenty-Two

When I returned to New House, Eliza told me her master wanted to see me straight away. He jumped up as soon as I went into the drawing room. 'Thank heavens you are back, Miss Valentine, I'm afraid I have some bad news. A message came from Hampton Loade. Your father has had an accident.'

I clapped my hands to my cheeks. 'Is he badly injured, sir? He's not ...'

'No, no, he has hurt his arm, that is all. Worry not, Miss Valentine, he is safe, but he would like to see you. I've arranged for the carriage to take you home. Stay as long as you need. Send word when you are ready and my man will come to collect you.'

Mr Bagnall noticed the ledger under my arm and asked what it was.

'This was in a locked drawer in Daniel Powell's room. Neither his father nor I can make head or tail of it. He suggested Mr Lombard may be able to throw some light.'

'My brother isn't here at the moment. Shall you

leave it with me, and I'll show him when he gets back?'

I didn't want to let the ledger out of my sight until I'd had more opportunity to think about its contents. 'There's no great rush, sir, not if I'm leaving anyway. I'd like to take another look, then I'll talk to Mr Lombard when I return. I should be back later in the afternoon unless my father needs me to stay longer. If you've no objection, I'll ask your carriage driver to wait for me, rather than him having to make the journey twice.'

A little over an hour later, my mother stood open-mouthed when I climbed out in front of their cottage. I could see she wasn't sure whether to curtsy or cuddle until I flung my arms around her. She held me for an age, then, glancing all the time at the carriage, she took my hand and led me inside.

'Look who's here to visit, Richard. Our Meg's come to see you. And in a fine carriage too. My, my, she's going up in the world.'

My father sat in his favourite chair, as always, puffing away on his pipe. His right arm lay across his lap, wrapped in what appeared to be damp muslin. He raised it in greeting and winced. I asked him what he'd done.

'Smashed it under a branch. We was cutting it down and it cracked before I was ready. Must have been more rotten than we thought. Gave me a real clout. Your mam wrapped it in comfrey and this cloth, said it'd help.'

'Is it broken?'

'Might be, but I can't bend my wrist anyway.'

I peeled away the covering and shuddered. From his forearm to his knuckles was a mess of red, black, and purple, and his wrist was half as thick again as his other one. 'You'll not be using that again for a week or two.'

'If I'm lucky.' He glanced at my mother. 'Don't know what we'll do if it don't get better.'

For a while we talked, over beer and bread, about what I'd been doing. My father only nodded as I told the story, and I sensed the pain had his mind elsewhere. My mother interrupted every twist with a question or an exclamation of concern. This went on, her begging for more and more detail, until I got up to leave. She asked if I'd walk down the lane with her first to visit a neighbour.

She didn't speak until we were well away from the cottage. 'He's not saying anything but he's at his wits' end over this. Since he lost his position at Cliffe House your dad's been working all the hours in the day trying to bring in enough to manage. That's what's caused his accident. Trying to be quick and not taking enough care. Until this, we were catching up a bit. The Lord knows what we'll do now.'

My mother is a strong woman, not one for tears and wringing of hands, but this was as close as I'd ever seen her. I put my arm round her shoulder and pulled her to me. 'Don't you be worrying. I'll help. This work I'm doing will pay well, so I'll send some money as soon as I can.'

'You're a good girl, Meg, though it will need to

be soon. The rent's due in a few days. I've enough put by to feed us for a week or two, but after that ...'

These were words I didn't need to hear.

The carriage came to a stop at the old Postern Gate in Bridgnorth and I climbed out, much to the amazement of passers-by who stared and nudged each other. I'd be well known in the town, and none would have expected to see me riding in such style.

The Cartway, where Peter lived, would be far too steep for Mr Bagnall's fine carriage and horse to go down, so I asked the coachman to wait a short while. He was still scowling when Peter and I brought him and his horse a drink and something to eat. When we walked away down the hill the two were munching as merrily as could be. It's amazing how easily a full stomach settles a man's disquiet.

In Peter's kitchen I told him more of my father's injury and brought him up to date with all I'd done in the days since he'd left. As I knew it would be, talking to Peter helped calm the rising panic I was feeling. With no proper ideas about who was behind either the thefts or the murders, I was beginning to fear I'd not finish the job. The murders, strangely, concerned me less than the burglaries. Mr Bagnall had only offered to pay me for the work he'd invited me down for, and I couldn't afford not to be paid. I guessed my parents wouldn't make it through the winter either if I didn't send them something.

In his own quiet way, Peter talked about what

my next steps might be. 'It seems to me, Meg, you can only go on the way you have been. Until you can see a connection between the victims, and between at least one of the killings and the thefts, you'll have to look at them all and see where it takes you. I wish I could join you and help.'

'So do I, Peter. I've a boy supposed to be assisting, though he's not reliable. I'd much rather you by my side than him.'

My friend didn't seem to notice the compliment and continued with his gentle smile as he always did. Often, I wished he'd show some flicker of interest beyond polite conversation. In the year since we met, Peter had never made any amorous advances. I'm aware I'm not the prettiest woman in the town, but I don't believe I'm hideous either. I've certainly had interest from other men, but never the one I'd welcome it from. I started to wonder if it was time for me to make the first move.

Peter broke the spell. 'I've some news of my own, Meg. An uncle of mine told me he'd worked for your Mr Bagnall's father, Gabriel, for a few years. Uncle Charlie come back injured from fighting Frenchies in the Americas and the old man gave him a job. Seems the family was not well off then, this Gabriel having put all his money into inventing something to do with cast iron. They lived in a little cottage down in the Dale when Matthias Bagnall came into the world, not like the place he has now. About five years after, the invention worked and caught on. Family hasn't looked back since.'

There was a look came into Peter's eyes that told me he imagined this might be *his* future, as well as Mr Bagnall's past. This lowly birth of Mr Bagnall explained why his speech and manners were less refined than might be expected. It might also be why he treated his workers well, having come from the same humble beginnings.

I took the ledger from my bag, put it on the table, and flipped it open. 'Well, the next thing we've to do, Peter, is to make some sense of this. It must have been important to Daniel, and he didn't want it left lying around for everyone to see. Nothing else in his room was locked away, only the ledger and the piece of paper inside it.'

Peter ran a finger down the pages, first the ones in the book, then the separate sheet, then back again. 'Did you see the notes on the extra page seem to be linked to the ones in the ledger with a cross next to them?'

I peered at them and shook my head. 'How did you get that?'

'The numbers in each are the same, that's all.' He used a finger on each hand to point to two lines. 'Here, in the ledger, he has ten shillings and fourpence marked, and here, on the other sheet, he has the same number, alongside one of nine shillings and eightpence.'

'So what can that mean?'

He laughed. 'I haven't the faintest idea. I didn't say I understood the numbers, only that I can see a link. You'll have to ask someone a bit cleverer than me if you want an answer to that one.'

We poured over the figures for a while, each spotting where the matches came, but making no progress on why. When I heard St Leonard's bell strike two, I jumped up. 'I must be away, Peter, I've left that poor coachman sitting outside for far too long.'

'Before you go, I need to tell you I had another couple of requests for work after I put out the word.'

'But I can't drop what I'm doing in Broseley, not just yet. You'll have to tell them they must wait.'

'No need for that, they're only simple jobs and I can manage them alone. It's a shame we can't do them together, but I'll send you the proceeds when they're done.'

My gratefulness overwhelmed my caution, and the next minute I'd flung my arms around Peter, leaping away just as quickly when I saw the look of puzzlement and shock on his face. I spluttered a 'thank you, sorry, thank you' and dashed out to the carriage, telling the coachman to take me back to Broseley as quick as he could.

Natty wriggled on the rock, trying to find a spot where he could sit comfortably. He wasn't sure there was one. The ridges and the cold cut right through his britches. Opposite him sat a girl, aged eleven or twelve, watching, with no expression on her face. Everything about Harriet Craven would have made her stand out from the crowd. Though she was never in a crowd. Natty had only ever seen her scurrying through the darkness in the town, scavenging for scraps wherever she might find them. Or here, where she fitted completely.

Her hair, brown as a mouse's, tied in strands knotted with wool, twine and straw, hung long down her shoulders, its fringe framing eyes rimmed with grime. Harriet's stick-thin calves stuck out from a grey woollen dress, which she wore beneath a blackberry coloured shawl.

If Natty hadn't known where the girl lived, he'd never have found her shelter in Greville's Wood. A year before, he'd befriended her, coaxing Harriet with morsels of food he'd managed to sneak from his mother's table or begged from his workmates. She had fascinated him from the first time he'd seen her. It took a month or more before she'd invited him to her home, a hovel made from ripped canvas sails she'd found by the river. She'd told Natty she'd had to level a spot in the hill to put it, only stopping when she'd reached the stony outcrop and could dig no more. Then she'd strung the covering between three birches using whatever she could find abandoned by the boatmen.

Between Natty and Harriet, embers glowed in a circle made of rocks. There was never any shortage of coal to be picked up in Broseley, though the girl would only be able to bring back a small amount in any trip. Natty imagined she would be freezing for long stretches of the winter. Dried fern, herbs, and squirrel skins hung from lines criss-crossing over a bundle of filthy blankets on one side of the shelter. A corner of the bedding twitched, and a large black rat scuttled across the floor to take its leave into the wood.

Natty shivered and he knew if others saw how Harriet lived, they would brand her as a witch, though he also knew she was no such thing. Just a strange little girl with a love of nature and of living outdoors. Today, though, he wanted her to play a part. He pulled open the bag he'd brought and spread the contents on the ground: two blue eggs, speckled with brown spots, which he'd taken from a blackbird's nest earlier in the year; a lady's glove he'd found in the mud; and three ripe golden-brown apples he'd collected from beneath Widow Evans' tree that afternoon.

Harriet's eyes widened. 'For me?'

Natty nodded. 'If you want them. Do you?' She didn't answer but reached for a piece of fruit, sniffed it and was about to take a bite when he held back her wrist. 'If you do, then I want you to do something for me, Harriet. Will you?'

The girl turned her face slowly away from him, paused for a moment, then whispered. 'Yes'

'Good. I have a friend. Well, not really a friend, she's a lot older than me, but I think she likes me. I want to bring her to see you tomorrow. Is that alright?'

Another soft affirmative.

'And I'd like you to tell her what I want her to know.'

Back at New House, Mr Lombard still hadn't returned and Eliza told me he might be away overnight again. This meant I'd get no help with the ledger's mysteries until next evening at the earliest, giving me another day with no money coming in. Despite the promise by Peter to send some in a few days, I needed to be sure I could get a little to my mother as soon as I could. Now I had no alternative than to approach Mr Bagnall. I found him in his garden, taking a pipe in the early evening sunshine.

'Could I have a word with you, sir?'

He patted the bench next to him. 'Of course, please sit beside me, Miss Valentine. It has been a glorious day, has it not?'

I looked around his garden and though not so varied nor as large as the one at Cliffe House, where I'd worked, it was in good order. The colourful flower beds surrounded by low box hedging were particularly pleasant. 'It's a very fine garden, Mr Bagnall, you must have a good man looking after it.'

'I have indeed, though I'm sad to say he is leaving me before too long. He has a sister in the Marches who is unwell and cannot look after herself or her farm. He is moving to live with her. I shall miss him and don't know where I'll find another so good.'

'If you let me know when your man's leaving, sir, I may have someone who can replace him. One who's hard-working and has many years' experience.'

My father might not be willing to move so far away from Hampton Loade and indeed may not soon be fit to work again, but I thought I should put down a marker with a possible employer. It would be a better proposition than the jobbing he was presently reduced to.

'That is most kind, Miss Valentine. I will take you up on the offer when the time comes. Now, what was it you wanted to talk to me about?'

'I'm need of a favour, Mr Bagnall.'

'I thought as much. What is it?'

Though he wore a smile when he said this, it was one which showed a willingness to listen, not necessarily to comply. The ironmaster must have had a good head for business to have kept all his family's wealth, and wouldn't be one easily swayed by a hard luck story. I'd need to present a sound case to convince him to give me what I wanted.

'It's difficult to ask, sir, but I must have an advance on my fee.'

'Must, Miss Valentine? This sounds more like a demand than a request. Our agreement was I would pay your rent for two weeks and provide you with bed and board until your work is done. You were only to be paid your fee when the job is completed. Have you forgotten?'

'I've not forgotten, sir, but things have changed over recent days and there are some bills I need to pay.'

'But that is not my problem, is it? We settled our arrangement, and you seemed more than happy with it at the time. Suppose I pay you something in advance and then you fail in your task, I would be out of pocket and, I assume, you would not be in a position to repay me. No, I'm sorry, Miss Valentine, but I must refuse.'

I didn't want to aggravate a situation where I already felt out of control, but I'd no other way of getting a decent amount of money to aid my father. I folded my arms. 'Then I must put your work to one side for a few days, Mr Bagnall. I've some back in Bridgnorth which I suspect will be cleared up quickly, and which will pay me what I need for the time being. If you still want me to assist, I'll happily come to pick up the threads again.'

Mr Bagnall scowled and shook his head. 'I am not at all happy with this, but you leave me no alternative. If we allow the trail to go cold at this time, you may never pick it up again. Let me know how much you need, and I'll arrange for you to have it.'

I named a figure, enough to keep the wolf from my father's door for a few weeks. My employer's response made me wish I'd asked for more.

'Goodness, Miss Valentine, I thought you would be requesting something substantial. If you had said it was so little, we needn't have had this disagreeable episode.' A polite though sour phrase I thought. 'Come to see me this evening and I will have the money ready for you.' He pulled his watch from his pocket and glanced at it. 'Now, is there anything further?'

I said there wasn't, and thanked him, perhaps more profusely than was seemly, and left to go upstairs to think. Mr Bagnall had made a good point. If I didn't succeed, I wouldn't be paid. I'd also now have to contend with him being displeased.

Time spent in my room after dark, going over what I'd discovered so far, took me no further forward. The figures and notes in Daniel Powell's ledger were still like a foreign language to me. By the end of the hours looking at them, I knew I'd need to do better with my numbers if I was ever to make my fortune. When I lay down to sleep, thoughts of that ledger, the two pieces of rope, the thefts of small items, and the contradictions in Tom Hurdley's testimony, spun round in my head until the early hours.

TWENTY-THREE

Everyone in the household was up by the time I made my way downstairs in the morning, and even Mr Lombard was home. He and the Bagnalls were talking at the table in the dining room. The conversation stopped abruptly when I opened the door, and I'd a strong feeling they'd been talking about me. Mrs Bagnall was pleasant enough with her greeting, but her husband simply sniffed and continued crunching on an apple.

Mr Lombard lay down his knife and raised his mug as if in a toast. 'Miss Valentine. Good morning. My brother tells me you have a little problem for me.'

'I do, sir, if you can spare the time. There's some book-keeping which I'm struggling to understand. I'm told you're good with these things.'

'I wouldn't have thought book-keeping would be something to concern a young woman like you.'

I bit my tongue. 'In the normal run of things, it wouldn't, sir. I just need to understand if it's relevant to what I'm looking into.'

'You think it relates to what happened to poor Daniel?'

'I don't know if it does or it doesn't, only that he'd locked the figures away in a drawer in his bedroom.'

'Then we must look at them after you've eaten.'

The rest of breakfast was a silent affair, Mr Bagnall's annoyance, which I presumed was directed at me, hung over the table like a black cloud. Even the occasional chirruping of the lady of the house was cut short by a glance from her husband. My appetite was dulled by all of this, and I was happy when I could leave. I told Mr Lombard I would meet him in the drawing room as soon as I'd collected the ledger.

Ten minutes later, he and I sat next to each other at a small table beneath the window. The book and Daniel's notes lay before us. Mr Lombard had taken a quill and dipped it in ink, but I begged him not to make any marks on the paper as I was already confused. He laughed and laid it down again, then began to run his finger across the pages as Peter had done.

'You say your friend saw a link between these?'

'Only that some of the figures were the same, but then there was a different one next to it on the single sheet.' I pointed to two of the relevant lines. 'Here, see?'

'Ah yes. Here's another. And another.' He scratched the back of his head. 'Most interesting. Just give me a moment.'

Mr Lombard pulled open the table drawer and took out a sheet of paper. He wrote numbers in two columns. From the way his eyes darted from side to side, the first seemed to be from the ledger, the second from the notes. Once he'd been through several pages, he marked a line at the bottom of each and added up the figures. He did this so rapidly it left me open-mouthed.

'The differences on each entry are small, Miss Valentine, but over the ten days I've examined they arrive at a tidy sum.'

He named a figure close to a month's wages for my father, two months or more of mine as an assistant gardener. I asked if he knew what this might mean.

'Not at the minute. They could all be errors which Daniel had found he'd made and was attempting to correct without anyone noticing.'

'But so many?'

'Daniel was young, and when you're young your mind can wander to things more interesting than dusty old books. I believe he liked the young ladies, and to drink and dance. It would be easy for him to write down a wrong number if his thoughts were on those rather than his work. He'd only notice his mistakes when he couldn't get the balances right at month end.'

'Is that the only explanation?'

'Perhaps not, but it is the simplest. I shudder to think what Daniel's father, and my brother, will say when they find out.'

I asked him, in respect for the dead man, not to say anything until we were sure this was the correct answer.

'I have a duty not to let this lie for too long, Miss Valentine. If you leave the material with me until tomorrow, I can make a more detailed examination and see if there is an alternative solution.'

This was what I'd been afraid of. I'm no expert at the numbers and would be the first to admit I needed help with these. On the other hand, it was the only piece of solid evidence I'd found so far and didn't want to let it out of my hands. 'That's most generous of you, Mr Lombard, but I'd like to be with you when you go through it. If we can't do it now, I'll hang on to the ledger until you're available.'

'That is your prerogative, miss, but I don't have the time today to spend long on it, and I'm very busy this week. Give me a day or two and we can sit together again to look. In the meantime, I'll think about what other possibilities there might be. If I come up with anything before we meet, I will let you know.'

Eliza stopped me on the landing when I was returning the ledger to my room. 'That lad's been round again.' I knew she didn't think much of me, and her tone told me she thought even less of Natty Preece. 'Said you should go and see him. About midday when he gets a break.'

She turned to walk away.

'Did he say where?'

'Huh. Thought you was the one good at figuring things out. Little bootlicker is working, so he'll be down by the master's mine won't he.'

'Tell me something, Eliza - it is Eliza, isn't it?'

'It is. What?'

'You don't like Natty, and you don't seem to like me much either. Why not?'

The maid looked me up and down, scorn written all over her face, but she checked all around to make sure no-one was listening before she spoke. 'I've always been taught to look to my station, not to pretend to be better than I am. I know *you're* no more than a labourer's daughter, yet here you are, a guest in my master's house, making out you belong. And that lad, he's always hanging around the place, trying to suck up to Mr Bagnall with his stories.'

She squared up to me and for a moment I considered slapping her down to size, but this would only end up with us both being sacked if we were heard or seen. Something I could ill afford. If the loss of the ironmaster's fee wasn't enough, I'd also lose his recommendation. I knew it wasn't fair on Eliza either. Instead, I took a deep breath. 'You speak the truth, Eliza, I *am* from poor stock, same as you. But that doesn't mean I shouldn't try to improve myself, does it? I'm not rich, like your master, and doubt I ever will be. The best I can hope for, and work for, is to earn enough so I don't need to worry where the rent is coming from every week. Isn't that all any of us wants? Have I ever treated you with anything less than respect?'

Eliza backed away, her shoulders relaxed. 'I suppose not. I'm sorry, miss. It's just -'

'Stop, Eliza. We'll say no more. Let's put it down to a misunderstanding and start again, shall we?'

'Yes, miss.'

'Good. So what's this about Natty and stories?'

The maid bit her lip, then lowered her voice when she leant in to speak. 'He's well known for making things up, miss. Not sure if it's 'cos he thinks it funny to start rumours running, or 'cos he thinks it makes him look important.' She looked along the landing both ways. 'All I'm saying is you need to watch what that lad tells you.'

I'd never seen the like of the field around the coal pit. Black and barren, except for odd tufts of grass in places where they'd survived the poisoned ground. Carts, horses, and men must have trampled dust here for a hundred years or more, making a wasteland which grated and crunched when I walked on it. Two men with picks stood at the entrance to a tunnel which had been dug into the hillside.

A dozen children gathered small lumps of coal from the ground into baskets, dumping them on a wagon on rails when they were full. Natty was with them. He stood, rubbed his back, and then hobbled over to me. 'God's teeth, I've to get out of this, it's killing me, miss, that's for sure.'

Once again, I understood why Natty was so keen

to work alongside me. His living was hard and would probably never provide more than a crust at the table. At least if he ingratiated himself with the ironmaster he might be offered something easier and a mite more profitable.

'You wanted to talk to me, Natty?'

'There's a girl. She's the "lady" I mentioned. Sees things.'

'What sort of things?'

'All sorts. Future, past ... lost stuff.'

'What's this got to do with me?'

'Harriet, that's her name, Lives in the woods. Been there since her family got too big and there was no room for her at home. Harriet's the one told me she'd seen Daniel Powell and Beth Hurdley together. Now says it's alright to tell you who she is.'

'I already know Daniel and Beth were seen talking in the town.'

'No, not just together near the shop. Harriet said more like her mum and dad were sometimes.' He lowered his eyes. 'Holding hands. Kissing and that.'

'Where did your friend see this?'

'In her head.'

I laughed. 'In her head. Are you joking with me, Natty?'

'I'm not, miss. Ask anyone. She *can* see things. Doesn't have to be there. Found a calf once when it was lost, just by closing her eyes. Another time saw the floods coming down at Jackfield - even before the storm came. Says it's a gift she got from her grandma - burned as a witch *she* was.'

I wasn't sure I believed in witches, any more than I believed in the Devil. Either might exist, chances are they were both invented for the same reason. To keep poor folk on the straight and narrow, either by threats of curses, or by fear of eternal damnation. Natty's insistence made me less sure about this girl though. I'd heard of women with powers before, and she could be one of these.

'Tell me what else she said.'

'I told Harriet I was helping you. She said pictures came to her three times. One was of a man struggling to breathe, then one later, a woman this time. Both had a big, black shadow over them.'

'You said there were three?'

'The third came while she was sleeping. She woke and began wondering what the other two meant. It was then she saw them walking hand in hand. There seemed to be trees and water so Harriet thought they must have been in the woods by the river. They stopped and kissed. She felt it warm on her face, like they were in love.'

'Did she know Daniel and Beth?'

'Only Beth. She and Harriet were cousins of some sort, so Harriet would have met her. She recognised Daniel as the man in her vision when I described him.'

'So it really could have been any man who looked vaguely like him. It could even be Beth's husband, I suppose?' I was unsure why I was even offering an alternative explanation. This was a girl's dream after all.

Natty turned away, bent, and picked up a lump of coal, then slung it as far as he could. When he turned back his face was red as a raspberry. 'If you're not going to believe me, there's not much point in me telling you anything, is there? It's alright for you, you understand what's going on, all I have is bits of instructions. "Find out what you can, Natty" and the like, then when I bring you what I've found, you're not interested.'

'Did I say I wasn't interested?'

'No, but you might as well have. Question after question like you don't believe me.'

'If that's how it sounds, then I'm sorry, Natty, but that's what I do. I ask questions. I've told you before, it's wrong-headed to accept anything you're told at face value. All I want is to be sure we're going down the right path. You've got to admit this story about a girl who dreams things sounds a bit far-fetched.'

'You wouldn't think so if you met her. Come with me and you'll see. I'll need to talk to the mine-head overseer, tell him I've to go on Mr Bagnall's business. Give me ten minutes and I'll take you to Harriet, then you can ask her all the questions you want.'

–ϙ–

You've not been able to get Meg Valentine out of your head since she came to see you. Not so beautiful as Beth, but clever. The way she asked her questions then thought about your answers. Sifting, like a pig grubbing for the sweetest morsels, trying to extract a piece which might be worth consuming. You'd not given her anything, of course, that would be foolish, and despite what others might think, you're not foolish.

The path from the coal pit to Greville's Wood winds its way into shrubbery and small trees, though you've found it easy to follow her and the scruffy mine lad she's with until they reach the steeper slope. Here, you hang back, concerned you might slip in the mud, and your boots dislodge pebbles to give away your presence. You wonder where they're going. Were they more closely matched in age you'd assume it a lovers' tryst, away from prying eyes, but he's little more than a boy. The path goes down, with many a twist and turn, to the river, but there are much more direct routes and you're sure that isn't their destination. So you wait, back against a tree, thinking on this Meg Valentine.

Would she be as satisfying a victim to you as Beth who, for a woman, struggled well against the darkness? Without doubt she'd be better than Daniel Powell, who slumped almost as soon as your rope bit into his soft throat. This other one looks strong, as though she's known heavy work for much of her life. You shake your head, unsure if you want to see her dead at your feet. At least not before she's come to admire you for the man you are.

Twenty-Four

Natty had warned me not to expect too much of the place where Harriet Craven spent her days. I wondered how bad it could be, given the poverty he endured, but he hadn't stretched the truth on this one. Heavy rain had started to fall when we left the mine, and the hill down through Greville's Wood had become slick with mud, causing me to grab each branch I passed to save me from falling. Natty was more sure-footed, so soon had a lead on me. At one point he disappeared from view, and it was only when he stepped out in front of me, I saw the shelter strung from the trees.

'This is it, miss. Harriet's inside.'

The girl sat cross-legged on a mound of blankets, like I imagined a queen would be, waiting to give an audience. Her eyes were closed, and her grubby hands lay flat against her thighs. Natty tapped her shoulder and her lids lifted. She fixed the lad with a stare which appeared to both see into his soul and look right through him.

'Natty?' She shifted her gaze to me. 'Who is this?'

'This is Miss Valentine, Harriet, you remember I said I'd bring her to see you?'

She sat quietly for a moment before she replied. 'Yes. I remember. What does she want to know?'

'Tell her what you told me about Daniel Powell and Beth Hurdley.'

'Who?'

'The man and woman you saw ... in your head ... you told me all about them.'

Harriet shook her head. 'You said it *must* be those people.'

Natty spat on the ground. 'Of course it's them, Just tell Miss Valentine what you saw.'

'They were on a path. By water, it seemed to me. Holding hands.'

I bent and touched the girl's elbow. 'And you knew them?'

'The woman had the look of a cousin of my dad's. Couldn't swear it was her though.' She glanced at Natty. 'He said the man was the one who was killed.'

'Anything else?'

'They stopped, looked all around, then kissed.'

'Then what?'

She blushed. 'Nothing.'

'Nothing?'

'The picture faded away, that's all. Like it always does.'

'So you can't tell me anything else? Just two people who you didn't really know stole a kiss.' I glared at Natty then turned back to his strange friend. 'You have no more?'

'You have anything the folk had touched?'

I started to shake my head, then remembered something and scratted in my bag. I handed her the piece of rope I'd found in Beth's hearth. 'How about this?'

The remnant had barely touched her fingertips when the girl's eyes rolled back in her head and her whole body began to tremble. A voice, though not Harriet's voice, spoke clear as a bell.

'There is pain here. Pain ... anger ... and death. I see paper. And I see -'

She screeched and fell sideways. Natty was on his knees in a flash, lifting Harriet upright and demanding I fetch some water.

I filled a jug from the bucket hanging by the door flap and thrust it at him. He splashed his shirt cuff and offered it to the girl's lips, showing a tenderness I'd not seen in him before. Harriet didn't react for a few seconds, then her tongue flicked out, like an adder's, probing for more liquid. Natty dribbled it into her mouth, all the time begging her to come back.

After what seemed an age, she opened her eyes wide and looked around, seeming even more distant than she had when we'd arrived. 'What happened?'

I took her by the hand. 'You saw something. Maybe someone?'

'I don't remember. I never do. All I know is it hurts,' she pressed a fist to her chest, 'here.'

This poor girl had a gift which seemed to bewilder her as much as it disturbed others. Something over which she had no power, which would come and go, and would use her lips to speak its revelations, but leave no remnant once it departed. I liked her and could see why Natty had worked so hard to become her friend and protector.

Whilst Harriet recovered, I continued to ask her questions. Gently, trying not to upset her, but there was nothing else she could tell me. Should I believe what she'd said, or was it mere performance? She could easily have guessed at the pain once I'd shown her the rope. Equally, the anger. There must always be some kind of raging in the head of a killer. But the paper? What could that be? Was it a reference to the ledger left by Daniel? It might be, but then again it could be banknotes. Many a murder has been carried out for money. And what was the final thing revealed to Harriet? What had made her cry out and faint away?

I left Natty back at the mine, then I wandered through the town towards New House, continuing to ponder on the meaning of what I'd witnessed in Greville's Wood. With my mind elsewhere, I almost bumped into a dark-haired woman coming out of a shop. We both stopped, then moved the same way, quickly shifting back again, still facing each other.

The woman laughed, then spoke with an accent strange to me. 'I hadn't expected to be jigging in the lane when I came out this morning.' She stopped and swung an arm to her right. 'After you.'

I thanked her and began to walk round, but she raised a finger, her smile gone. 'Aren't you the lady thief-taker? The one trying to find out what happened to Beth?'

'Did you know her?'

'My best friend.' Her voice caught as she spoke. 'I can't believe she's been taken from us. I'm Grace Shovelin by the way. Who would have done such a thing?'

'That's a good question, Grace. Have you any idea?'

'Me? How would I know?'

'If you were Beth's friend then you'd know as much about her as anyone, I expect. Had she argued recently? Could someone have been jealous of her? What was her relationship with Daniel Powell?'

The woman looked up and down the street and cocked her head further up the hill. 'You'd best come to my place. My man's out at work and we'll be private there.'

She led me to the edge of the town, where a steep bank ran down to the river, perhaps half a mile away. Patches of greenery had been cleared over time and replaced by crude cottages, all huddled together. They appeared to have been built from whatever scraps of timber and stone could be gathered from the surrounding land.

Grace led me through a maze of paths she called "jitties" between the dwellings until we reached one where the owner had made some attempt at establishing a vegetable garden on the side. 'This is mine. You'll be welcome, but don't expect too much.'

Inside, there appeared to be only two rooms, the one we were in, with a table, three chairs and a corner cupboard. I assumed that the second room, behind a rough plank door was their bedroom.

She must have noticed me staring at the fireplace, much more substantial than suited the rest of the room. 'It's how we got the place.'

'I don't understand.'

'When we arrived here, about five years ago, they wanted miners. We'd left Ireland for my Padraig to work on the navigations, but the job had finished, and he was hunting for something else. Found ourselves in Broseley, him at the mine. Seems the law says if a man can get a hearth up in a day he can hang on to the patch of land and build on it. He grabbed some of the other men from home and they set to. Before the canals, Padraig worked on farms and was no stranger to building miles of stone walls. Had the hearth and chimney up in no time.'

'So then they built the cottage round it?'

'Not "they", Padraig, on his own, apart from where he had that first bit of help. Half a year it took him, digging coal all day and heaving rocks by night. Never been afraid of hard work my man.'

It seemed time to shake Grace from her remembering. 'You were going to tell me about Beth.'

'What? Oh, yes. You've been questioning Tom.'

'I have.'

'Well he didn't do it.'

'You know this to be a fact?'

'As well as I know anything. He was besotted with Beth. He'd never harm her.'

'Not even if she'd taken a lover?'

Grace spluttered. 'Beth? Not on your life. She was as crazy in the head for Tom as he was for her.'

I was beginning to think this conversation was a waste of time. Was this a woman just unwilling to speak ill of the dead? 'Well I've heard she'd been seen walking out with another man.'

'Then whoever said that's a liar.'

'You said Beth was your best friend, but how well did you really know her?'

'She was one of the few who talked to me soon after I came to Broseley, when other local women wouldn't. They accused the Irish of stealing their men's jobs. Truth is they didn't want the jobs. Too hard and no money. Beth took me to one side and told me to pay no mind to them. We'd often walk and talk. That's how I know she'd not play fast and loose with Tom. If she'd been having a hard time, or even thinking about going with someone else, she'd have shared it with me. And she never said a word.'

'Did she know Daniel Powell?'

Grace smirked but couldn't hide the blush. 'We all knew Daniel. Good looking lad he was. He'd flirt with all the girls, but we'd not take him seriously, it was just a bit of fun. Beth was different though. She'd have none of his games and tell him in no uncertain terms to stop. Beth and Daniel were friendly, but in a brother and sister kind of a way. Nothing more.'

Once again it seemed that Natty's story about Beth Hurdley and Daniel Powell didn't hold water. Either the couple had been able to hide their affair from someone who knew them both well, which didn't seem likely, or Natty and his strange friend had it wrong. 'Can I ask you another question, Grace? If you're mistaken, and Beth and Daniel were not quite brother and sister, as you put it, and Tom found out, what would he have done?'

She thought for a minute before she answered. 'He'd not have killed the two of them, that's for sure. Tom's a kind, gentle man. I can't for one moment believe he'd do such a thing. Even if he lost his temper he might go round and punch Daniel. He'd not wait in the shadows and choke the life out of him.'

This was at odds with what Jake experienced. Even Beth had told me Tom could become angry after a drink. If Grace had this wrong about Tom, how much should I trust her faith in him?

On the way back from Grace Shovelin's cottage I saw two men in the doorway of an alehouse, the Red Barn, each with a short-stemmed tobacco pipe gripped between their teeth. They leant together, arms locked around each other's shoulders.

One waved a hand. 'Hey, lady, come join us.' His words were slurred. 'We'll get you a gin and you can sit on my knee.'

I crossed to the other side of the street.

The companion of the first shouted across. 'No need to be like that, miss, we know you'd like a bit of fun as much as us.'

The two collapsed in laughter and I quickened my step. Fearful they might start to pursue me, I kept glancing over my shoulder and almost collided with Natty Preece when he dashed out of a side lane.

'Whoa, Miss Valentine, watch where you're going.'

I stopped in my tracks. 'Are they following?'

'Who?'

'Two men. One tall, one fat.'

He looked round me. 'If you mean them two outside the tavern, then they're not. I can't see no others.'

I slumped my shoulders. 'Thank the Lord for that. I was sure they were coming after me. Just to make sure, will you walk alongside 'til they're out of sight? There's something I need to talk to you about anyway.' He nodded and we walked on. 'Why were you running?'

'No reason.'

'Really? You run about the lanes of Broseley for the fun of it?'

'I do. Always have. Never know when you might need it.'

I wasn't sure I believed him about the running, but it was only one more thing where I thought he might not be telling me the truth, and less important than the rest.

'You said you wanted to talk to me, miss, but can I tell you something first?'

'I suppose so. What is it?'

He pointed back up the street to where my accosters were standing. 'Mr Lyons, the boss of that place, says he has some information for you. Asked if I'd pass on that he wants to see you.'

'Did he say what it is?'

'Not to me he didn't.' He laughed. 'Looks like you'll have to go in there past your two friends. Want me to come with you?'

Much as I wanted to avoid being in the lad's debt, I couldn't see how I'd have the nerve to go in alone. 'It would be good if you could.'

'Before we go, what did you want to talk to me about?'

'I've been speaking with a woman called Grace Shovelin. Do you know her?'

'I do. Nice lady. Irish. That the one?'

'That's her. You say she's nice. Should I believe what she tells me?'

'Definitely.'

'Then if she'd told me something that contradicts your story, I should accept it as the truth?'

Natty stepped away. 'Like what?'

'Like there's not a chance that Beth Hurdley and Daniel Powell were seeing each other.'

'They might have been.'

'No, Natty, they weren't, and the fact you said "might" tells me you were probably making it up in the first place. Were you?'

He hung his head. 'Wasn't lying. Just trying to help you out.'

'Helping me? How were you helping me?'

'You'd already sunk your teeth into Tom Hurdley before I said anything. All I did was give you some more string to tie him up with.'

'But he might be innocent, if we're to believe Grace Shovelin. Can't you see you shouldn't have done that?'

Natty shrugged. 'Huh.'

'That attitude's not good enough, Natty. I'll have to tell Mr Bagnall what you did.'

The lad didn't have my height or build, so I shouldn't have felt threatened when he stepped close and squared up to me, his nose only two inches from my chin, but I did. When a scrawny feral dog growls, you take notice.

'You'll not be telling Mr Bagnall anything, Miss Valentine. Don't you be crossing me, you never know where it will end.'

I moved back a pace. 'And don't you dare try it on with me, Natty Preece. Not if you know what's good for you. I've had little boys like you for breakfast. Get off with you before I lose my temper.'

Natty made as if to move towards me again but then clenched his teeth and shook his head. 'You'll be sorry for this.' He thrust his hands in his pockets and started to walk away. Three steps past me he turned his head. 'All I did was try to help.'

'Well you didn't Natty. You really didn't.'

He turned away again and walked slowly down the street, muttering to himself, and leaving me shaking. I wondered how much trouble I'd just unleashed.

TWENTY-FIVE

Mr Lyons, who ran the Red Barn, pulled back a chair for me. 'Take a seat, miss, and I'll go cuff those two idiots round the ears.'

I'd been so fired up after my confrontation with Natty, I'd marched directly to Mr Lyons' door. When the short, fat, drunk stepped in my way and made a lewd comment, I'd kneed him in the groin. The landlord had barged outside when he heard the commotion, pulled me inside, and asked me what was going on, so I told him. His threat of further violence towards the men seemed pointless. The one rolling on the ground had certainly received the message. I asked Mr Lyons not to bother, and said I'd heard he had some information for me.

'I think I do, miss. I've been away for a couple of days and only heard about you questioning Tom Hurdley when I got back this morning. They said you think he might have killed Daniel Powell.'

'That's a possibility I'm looking at, yes.'

'Well he can't have.'

'Why not?'

'Because he was in here drinking that night. I heard St Leonard's bell strike nine and Tom came in soon after. I locked up then and he stayed on for a while. Not serious drinking, just a mug or two, and chatting. Said he'd been round at The Angel but didn't feel like dancing. Seemed to me he didn't feel like going home either so I let him wait 'til he was ready. He'd only been gone a few minutes before the shout went up about what happened at the Powell's house. Can't see how he'd have gotten from here to there and jumped on young Daniel. Surprised none of Mr Powell's men stopped him on the lane. He'd been in a poor humour when he came in, though he wasn't angry or anything when he left. Not as far as I could tell anyway.'

'You're sure he'd not been gone long when the alarm was raised?'

'Certain. I put the bolt on again after Tom went and I'd only picked up a few jugs before the banging came on the door. I opened it straightway to two lads passing on the news.'

I thanked him for the information and asked him to go through it one more time. His story didn't vary, and there was only one conclusion. It was unlikely Tom Hurdley murdered Daniel, and if the same rope had been used in both murders, then he hadn't killed his wife either.

So who had? Other than Tom Hurdley, I'd found no-one with a motive to kill them. I'd recovered a couple of bits of rope and assumed they were linked to the murders, though they might not be. I'd told Natty not to jump to conclusions and I'd fallen into that trap. My suspicion of Tom, Becky Cole, and even Edward Powell, were all me flailing about looking for the answer. Edwin Hare would tell me to step back, lay out what I know and don't know, and try to see a way through. This would be fine if I had the faintest idea what I was doing.

—Ɋ—

I wouldn't normally go walking after dinner, but the afternoon's events were swimming round in my head. Over our meal, Mr Bagnall and his brother had pressed me on what progress I was making, and I had no ready answers. With Tom Hurdley no longer the likely killer, I'd no idea who to suspect next. The only remaining indication I had were the ravings of a half-demented girl who lived in the woods, and I could hardly present these as evidence to my host.

With a clear show of dissatisfaction, the two gentlemen had taken to their drinks and their business conversation, and Mrs Bagnall settled to her embroidery. For a while I'd sat in the kitchen staring into the hearth, but the fizzing in my brain soon moved me to take some exercise.

There was nothing much to Broseley other than the main street, the houses clustered round the church, and the jitties at the other end. The only other properties I'd seen were farm dwellings, dotted along tracks dividing dozens of small fields.

From New House I wandered down one of these

lanes, between St Leonard's and a fine building I'd been told was Broseley Hall. It led to a tree-lined meadow.

Though the low evening sun had been pleasantly warm on my face when I'd set out, trees soon cast long shadows on one side. I shivered beneath them as it grew dark as my mood. Towards the end of this grove, I fancied I heard a rustle behind me and turned. No-one was in sight. So I continued on my way, hoping to catch some sunlight again soon.

At the darkest point, I was jerked upwards, the unmistakable bite of a rope at my throat. I tried to shout out but all that emerged was a croak. A knee was thrust into my back, and I flailed wildly, trying to escape. The person's bulk and strength gave me no doubt it was a man. My legs gave way, and my attacker stumbled forward. I slammed the top of my head into his chin. For the merest second he loosened his grip, and I reached up to his face. It was covered with a mask or a scarf, I couldn't tell, but whatever it was protected him. I felt soft flesh further down and clawed at his neck with all my might. He yelled and let me go. Before I could vent my anger further, he'd crashed off through the undergrowth. All I saw when I stood and turned was the back of an old brown coat and a three-cornered hat disappearing into the gloom.

I might have given chase, but he had a good lead by the time my breath and my senses returned, and I knew I'd not be strong enough to overpower him. What I'd seen of the man didn't help with recognition. What I'd picked up with my nose was quite another matter. An odour, strong and woody. One I'd smelled before, but I couldn't remember where.

You stare in the mirror, dabbing a tincture on your throat. How the girl got her fingernails in so deep below your collar you cannot fathom. The bleeding has stopped, though you imagine your shirt will be ruined if it can't be washed out. If she sees it, she'll guess where the blood came from, so you'll need to keep it covered.

The response was one you should have expected from this Meg Valentine. From the moment you saw her you knew she was special. The way she handled the search in Edward Powell's garden the night you'd put an end to his son's life. Attractive to you, but not pretty. Handsome in an earthy kind of a way. Often, you'd imagine the women you meet as how they might look dressed in clothes they might wear to impress, as at a dance. You don't see Meg Valentine in this way. You know she comes from poor stock. The long hours spent working outside have the thickened her limbs and textured her skin. Doubtless her morals would be those of a God-fearing country girl as well. Not an easy conquest, but perhaps one worth striving for.

Despite all of this you can't help feeling a desire to win her over, to take her, willingly, to your bed. Deeper than this, just as strong, is more. Your smile broadens, the searing pain temporarily forgotten, as you imagine a different ending to your evening's encounter. One where Meg Valentine lies lifeless beneath those trees, with you standing over her, rope dangling from your sweating hand.

I take another swig from the water jug beside my bed and wince. Mr Bagnall and Mr Lombard have sent two men out to look for my attacker, but we all know it will be no use, he will be long gone. Mrs Bagnall fussed and fussed when I told them what had happened, so much so that I needed to escape to my room to calm my nerves.

Lying still in the darkness helped, and I had begun to piece together what I knew, which wasn't really a lot. First and foremost, I could now be almost certain that Tom Hurdley didn't kill his wife, not if the same person had strangled both Daniel Powell and her. I also knew I couldn't trust Natty's word, he'd twisted the truth on more than one occasion, attempting to tell me what he thought I wanted to hear. Where did that leave me with the revelation by his strange young friend, Harriet? She'd mentioned pain, anger, and death, all of which were obvious and could have been guessed by any fairground charlatan. But she'd also cried out about paper and experienced something so fearful it had broken her trance. Again, I wasn't minded to take her ravings as fact, the paper could mean anything and the vision which appeared to shock the girl could be mere showmanship.

It would be too easy to link this "paper" to the ledger I'd found in Daniel's room, but perhaps there was a connection. Why would he mark it up then hide the ledger it away if it didn't mean anything? Though Mr Lombard had offered to look at the figures again, he couldn't do so for another day or two. Peter had been much more helpful.

As I thought of my friend, I wished he was nearby, working with me on this puzzle. I enjoy his company, and his inner calm rubs off on me. Far better than the chancer of a lad I'd been lumbered with by Mr Bagnall. It had only been a day since I'd seen Peter, but I was already missing him. I shook off the picture of us walking side by side and went back to sifting through what might have a bearing on the killings.

Two pieces of rope, one charred and damaged, the other found hanging in a shrub. I'd no serious doubts they'd been used to strangle the victims, and if I could find where they came from, I'd be well on the way to solving this crime. But rope is everywhere round this part of the country, particularly down by the river where it's used for everything from guiding sails to securing cargo on deck.

Then there were the victims, a young man and woman who knew each other but Grace Shovelin had insisted that was as far as the connection went. Natty and Harriet had given a different view, but I didn't trust it as being true. So, why would a killer target either, or both? They didn't appear to be robberies.

As far as I knew, nothing had been taken from Daniel, and Beth Hurdley was too poor to have anything worth stealing. As well as this, a bash on the head would be more effective in rendering a victim of theft unable to fight back, and, usually, leave them able to recover. Why kill if you don't need to? Strangulation is quite a different matter. It's cruel, painful, and cold-blooded, with only one outcome. Whoever attacked Beth and Daniel wanted them dead.

Both victims had been murdered where their killer could have been easily discovered, Daniel at his father's door, Beth in her own kitchen. Why would someone take such a risk? Daniel could have been taken anywhere between the town and home. Not far, but with plenty of places to keep out of view. To surprise the woman in her cottage would have been difficult. Did she know her killer and let them in, only to be taken unawares when she turned her back?

What of the others? I'd heard nothing to suggest Beth even knew Becky Cole, nor had any contact as an adult with Edward Powell. Daniel's father had disagreed with his son over his style of life, but Powell clearly loved him. These were the only two suspects I was left with and neither very likely. Becky had said she saw a man watching Daniel, but I knew this to be Tom Hurdley. Could there have been a second person watching? I'd need to talk to the landlord of The Angel to ask again if he'd seen anyone.

All the time, I'd been working on the basis the thefts and the killing were connected, and the culprit lived locally. But what if this wasn't true? What if the thief was from somewhere further afield? Close enough to travel in and out of the town, though not known here. And what if another person, the murderer, was just passing through? Stayed for only two nights, then moved on. Miles away by now.

On the other hand I'd been attacked. From behind, with an attempt to strangle me. This must have been the same person who killed Beth and Daniel. A man who thinks I'm getting close. If only it were true. I turned these ideas over and over but couldn't find a way forward. All I *could* do was try to draw together the threads and see what pattern they formed.

Twenty-Six

In the ordinary run of things I'd try to be about my business early but today was different. In my life as a gardener I'd rise with the sun, summer and winter, but in this line of work I have to take account of the hours kept by the people I need to see.

This morning my first task was to talk to George Beard. As keeper of The Angel he'd go to bed late and rise late. Despite my trials of last evening, and the thoughts which had swirled and tumbled into the small hours, I'd slept well when I finally went to the land of Nod. As a result I was in good humour at breakfast and able to calm the fussing of Mrs Bagnall, who remained in a state of shock about the boldness of my attacker.

She sat opposite me at the table, clucking like a fearful hen, and took my hand as soon as I lay down my spoon. 'Stay home today my dear Meg. That horrible creature may still be prowling about.'

I laughed. 'I could stay indoors, Mrs Bagnall, but I doubt he's gone away, and he'll still be around tomorrow. Am I to stay cocooned in your lovely house forever?'

Though I made light of this it didn't mean I wasn't concerned. A man had tried to kill me and that didn't happen every day. I'd need to be more cautious, and I wished, once again, that I'd Peter by my side.

We continued our conversation for a little while until Mr Lombard came in, she begging me to stay and assist with her needlework, and I putting on a brave face and telling her I would be fine.

Mr Lombard took his seat at the table. 'I hope you have recovered from your ordeal, Miss Valentine.'

'I have, sir, thank you. I was just saying the same to Mrs Bagnall.'

'Then what will you do today? You still have the appetite to assist my brother in his search for justice?'

'I do, sir. In fact, if anything, I'm even more determined to find out who killed those people. Some information was passed to me that Mr Beard, of The Angel, may be able to throw some light.'

'George? Well I do hope so. I would expect not much gets past him. Keeps a tidy house and is a good businessman. Would you like me to come with you in case that man is still hanging around?'

Whilst I'd gladly have accepted his offer if I'd been going somewhere out of the way, I thought it unlikely my attacker would try again in the main street of the town. I thanked Mr Lombard for his offer and took the short walk to see George Beard.

He was just unbolting the doors of his establishment when I arrived, and he invited me inside where we could talk more comfortably. 'How can I help you, miss?'

'I've heard a man was watching Daniel Powell not long before he was killed. Did you see anyone?'

Beard folded his arms, his face deep in thought for a minute before he replied. 'Can't say that I did. Saw Daniel with that Becky Cole and a few of his mates, as I told you, but not with anyone else.'

'I don't think he was *with* Daniel. Just a man watching the dancing.'

'What did he look like?'

'I don't know. Becky said she didn't get much of a look at his face, he kept it covered, and she only remembered afterwards that he'd been here. There might even have been two different men keeping an eye on Daniel. Tom Hurdley has told me he was here, trying to see what Daniel was up to.'

'Then I saw neither of them, I'm afraid. It was a busy night, and there were folk in from all around, both inside and out in the yard. I'll have a think and send a message if anything occurs to me.' Beard stood. 'Now, I've an alehouse to run and I won't do it sitting here, will I?'

He accompanied me back to the street but once again the candle of hope had been blown out and the path to solving these murders was in darkness. I stopped at the fish pool and stared into the murk. Like this case, I could see shapes moving beneath the surface but couldn't see any of the detail.

A voice came from behind me. 'Don't drown yourself, Meg, it can't be as bad as that.'

'Peter!' I turned and almost squealed with delight. What are you doing here?'

'One of those jobs I told you of was simple to sort out. Widow Slade thought some money had been stolen but it turned out her son had taken it for safe keeping. He said she was becoming forgetful and always losing things. Even said he'd told her. Anyway, he paid me for my time, so I dropped a little to your dad and jumped a cart to bring over your share. Went to the house and they told me what happened. Are you hurt?'

I lifted my chin and rubbed my throat. 'Bit sore, and hurts to swallow, but no real harm done.' I grabbed his arm. 'It's good to see you, you know.'

'Good to see you too.' His face brightened. 'And I've brought some news.'

'News? What news?'

'I'm to be married.'

I was lost for words when Peter told me of his plans. The best I could manage to squeeze out was "Congratulations. Tell me more". Which he did.

It seems he'd known the girl almost all of his life, the daughter of a neighbour. I remembered he'd mentioned her once or twice, but thought she was just a childhood friend, nothing else. Instead, they'd been walking out for a year or more, long before we'd met. He said he hadn't talked about their growing affection to anyone, as her father wasn't aware, so Peter wanted to keep it quiet until the right time. I didn't know if I should feel annoyed that he'd a secret woman friend or stupid for thinking he had feelings for me. The second one won. All I could do was wish him well.

I *did* wish him well. Peter was the nicest of men and even if he'd chosen another over me, I couldn't argue a prior claim. We'd had a lot of fun and he'd been no end of help over the past months, but he'd never tried it on, never a hand held, nor a kiss stolen. I expect this should have made me see he wasn't interested. After all, I was the one who'd chased him, not the other way round.

As we watched the ducks paddle round and round the pond, Peter told me all about Emily, how she was pretty, funny, and clever. How she could read, and do her numbers, and knew sheep and cattle, and this, and that. If she was half as good as he described her, I could see why he'd be besotted. I let him talk about her, and about their plans together, for a full ten minutes, nodding and smiling until I could stand it no more.

'Can you help me, Peter?' He looked surprised that I didn't want to talk about Emily all afternoon, and I felt sorry straight away but pressed on. 'I'm really stuck, and I need your eyes to see a way forward.'

'You know I'll do all I'm able, but if you can't figure it out, then I'm not sure I'll be up to it.'

I told him not to put himself down, and that he often saw what I'd missed. Like the patterns of the figures in the ledger I'd showed him. This seemed to pull him back in.

'What do you need, Meg?'

We found a wall to sit on, and I went through everything I'd sifted the previous night in my bed. Peter said very little, other than to be sure he had particular facts correct in his head. Often, I'd find just talking with Peter would help me become clearer, but this time it didn't help, it only confirmed my confusion.

When I'd finished, Peter shook his head. 'It's certainly an odd one. It seems to me the stranger at the dance is worth chasing. Do you have any idea who he is?'

'None at all. It could just be Tom Hurdley, he's already admitted he was there. Perhaps I'm clutching at straws.'

'Is it worth talking to any of the others who were there?'

'Can't see how it would be, if his face was hidden, as Becky Cole said, then he'd have done it on purpose and not let anyone see him.'

'What about this witch? She saw something.'

I snorted. 'Peter Turnstone, are you suggesting I take seriously a little girl who lives in the woods with rats and spiders as her friends?'

'I don't see why not. Lots of things in the world we don't understand, Meg. My ma says her granny could see into the future. Knew stuff, she did.

Reckoned she always had.'

'Nothing more than superstition and silliness.'

Though my words were dismissive, I felt far from sure. Harriet had been very convincing, and if there's good and evil in the world, why couldn't there be other forces as well, ones that guide us in ways we can't explain? And ones that are only revealed to a select few? I decided I'd put what she'd said with to my "doubtful but possible" ideas, ready to grab again if needed. 'Can you think of anything else?'

'Do you think there's any connection between the burglaries and the murders? Seems funny a little place like this should have so much badness going on if there's not.'

'That's another thing I don't know and can't fathom, Peter. I've not been able to spend much time digging into the thefts, all this with Daniel and Beth blew up before I got very far. I haven't worked out any links yet, but that means nothing.'

'Then you'll need to get on to it, won't you? Think what was stolen at each of the houses and who might have wanted it. Could this Daniel and Beth have found out who the thief was and threatened to expose them?'

'It's definitely a possibility.' I clapped Peter on the shoulder. 'There, I said you'd find something which hadn't occurred to me. It might not take us very far but at least it's something to consider.'

But if they both found out, how? And why would they only threaten to expose the person rather than just do it. I couldn't see either of them wanting to extort money. Perhaps they knew the person behind the thefts and wanted to push them to mend their ways. If so, who did both the victims know well enough to want to them give a second chance?

Twenty-Seven

Peter and I walked back past the church to where he'd set off back for Bridgnorth. He'd offered to stay, but I told him I needed no protector. Nonetheless, his concern touched me, and I thanked him for it. Perhaps I was a little too enthusiastic when I flung my arms round him, given his recent betrothal. I quickly recovered myself and wished him a safe journey home. The next minute, a waggon came round the bend, and the carter shouted for Peter to climb on board. I looked back in less than twenty paces, but my friend was already on his way, deep in conversation. Probably about his Emily.

Peter's question about who Daniel and Beth knew in common was certainly an interesting one. Mr Lombard had told me Daniel spent his later childhood at school in Bridgnorth, but Broseley is only a small place so he and Beth must have mixed with many of the same people. The question was, who might both victims be close to, so close they'd try to protect them, rather than turning them over to the magistrate? Even more mystifying, how could they be so close without realising this person could be a killer? In this whole affair I seemed to be going round in circles, like I was trapped in a maze with no way out.

Back at New House, Eliza passed me a note. 'Left by Mr Parfitt's servant. Said to give it you as soon as you came in.'

I took it to my room, away from her prying eyes.

My dear Miss Valentine

My name is Mr Christopher Parfitt, and Mr Bagnall has said I should contact you with a matter which is concerning me. Three days ago my wife and I were away visiting a friend over the border in Wales. We had left early in the previous morning, stayed overnight, and travelled home after midday, arriving not long before dark. As we hadn't needed them, we had allowed our maid and manservant the chance to visit their families and had made sure the house was secure before we left.

When my wife was unpacking on our return, she noticed two or three items of jewellery were missing. Items which she had felt too valuable to take on our journey and knew she had left at home. She searched thoroughly and has since checked that our maid did not move the rings and necklace, but they seem to have quite disappeared. It would also appear that a fine watch left to me by my late father has also been taken. What is strange is that there were other items of some value in our room, but they do not seem to have been touched.

I have used the word "strange" and this applies to two other things.

The first came about last night. The missing items were still niggling at me in the evening before I retired and I decided to search our bedroom to see if my wife had inadvertently moved them and then forgotten. There was no sign of anything in the wardrobes or our chests, but under the bed I found a signet ring, which I know not to be mine nor Mrs Parfitt's.

I only thought of the second strangeness later. Before Elias, our manservant, left, he had put away our dogs in the barn, as would be our habit, leaving them food and water enough to last. The door is on a simple latch and there has never been any problem with them escaping. However, when I went to let them out, the handle had been tied to the frame and well knotted. I imagined that Elias had found the latch to be faulty and had added some extra safety to make sure the dogs didn't escape. I thought no more of it until today. This morning I asked Elias, and he said he hadn't fastened the barn door in this way.

Putting together the missing jewels, the mystery of this ring, and the tying in of the dogs, it occurred to me that we must have been burgled. As soon as I guessed this, I called round to speak to Mr Bagnall for advice. He told me there have been a number of similar thefts, and I should pass on to you what has happened in my home.

If you would like to call upon me this afternoon, I can show you the ring and answer any questions you may have. Perhaps what I can tell you may get you closer to the person behind them.

> *Yours, most sincerely,*
> *Christopher Parfitt*

I didn't know the address he gave, so went downstairs to consult Mrs Dudley.

'Oh, Mr Parfitt is a good friend of the master, he is. Comes here often. You'll find him on the left down Rough Lane. Farmhouse. Been in his family for generations.' She nodded at the note still in my hand. 'Written to you, has he?'

She paused, arms folded across her not inconsiderable bosom, clearly waiting for me to say why I wanted to see him. I didn't oblige and she returned to kneading dough, casting me a look as if she wished her knuckles were pummelling my skull rather than the evening's bread.

I found Mr Parfitt's house easily enough from Mrs Dudley's directions. It was a rambling place which looked like it had been added to over the years. Surrounded by a garden much in need of love and attention, its most striking feature, and possibly the most recent addition, was a huge window set high in the wall. The sun glinted off something inside, but I couldn't make out what it was.

Mr Parfitt's maid led me through to a room at the back of the house, knocked, and then showed me in when she'd spoken to her master. An elderly gentleman wearing an ill-fitting wig and mismatched clothes welcomed me inside. He asked me to sit, though he had to lift a pile of books from a chair in order for me to do so. I had never seen so many books or papers in my entire life, nor so much disarray. Mr Parfitt must have guessed this.

'I'm sorry, Miss Valentine. This room is in such a mess. It has been my life's work, you see.'

I asked him what it was he studied, and he waved a hand around the unusual drawings around the walls. 'This, can you not see? The stars, the planets.' He drew aside a curtain covering the tall window I'd noticed from the outside, to reveal a large instrument of brass and glass.

'Goodness, sir, what is that?'

'With this I can see all of God's wonderful universe. It is called a telescope.' He tapped the part nearest to him. 'One looks through this eyepiece and anything the telescope is pointed towards appears much, much, bigger. Would you like to see?'

'I would, sir, if you can spare the time.'

He made some adjustments to the height and direction and gestured for me to put my eye to the end. What I saw made me jump back and gasp. Leaves on the trees across his garden, with as much detail as if I held them in my hand. I viewed again and spied a sparrow, large as a peacock, every brown and grey feather beautiful in the sunlight.

Mr Parfitt swung the machine round to point across the fields. 'Take a look here, Miss Valentine.'

When I'd looked at the scene through his

window all I'd seen were two tiny dots in the distance. Now they were clearly cottages, their chimneys sharp against the sky.

'And you can see up to the heavens with this, Mr Parfitt?'

A grin split his face from ear to ear, like a child with a ripe berry.

'Indeed I can. Our moon, if only you could see. And planets. Tiny Mercury, close to the sun, Saturn with its amazing rings. Stars, so far, far, away ... but you didn't come here to indulge my little research, did you? We must now talk of more unpleasant things, mustn't we?'

Despite the man's obvious desire to share his excitement, I knew it was necessary for us to move on. 'That would be helpful, sir. Perhaps I could come back another time, when it is dark and all these things might be visible, and you can show me what you mean.'

'It would be my pleasure. You will eat with Mrs Parfitt and myself, then we can look at the wonders of the heavens together.'

'I look forward to it. Now, you said in your letter that you noticed your wife's jewellery missing when you returned from a night away with friends. Is that right?'

'Yes. At first, I thought we had simply put them away for safekeeping from their usual place on the corner cupboard.' A smile not quite a smile came to his face. 'It is one of the trials of old age that we forget some things. Most inconvenient. You know,

Miss Valentine, I can remember an entire astronomical text, but some days cannot remember where I left my favourite cravat. With this in mind we searched all the places we may have hidden our valuables but to no avail. They had quite disappeared.'

'But you found some things of interest later? The ring and the rope?'

'Shall I fetch them?' Without waiting for a reply he went to a drawer and returned with the items he'd discovered. At first examination the rope looked the same type as the other pieces I'd recovered, though couldn't be sure until I had them together. The one obvious difference was that this piece had been dipped in something like tar to stop it from fraying. It also had a grey cotton label stitched into it, bearing the legend *GB17*.

'Do you have any idea what this label means, sir?'

'Not a clue, my dear. I had never seen that cord before in my life.'

The ring was most unusual. Silver, with a carved square centrepiece, about the size of my thumbnail, where a gem might have been on a lady's ring. The carving was of a dragon with an oddly formed letter *P* on the left side and a number 3 on the right.

'Would you know of anyone owning such a seal, Mr Parfitt?

'I haven't the faintest idea. Do you see that everything is the opposite to how it should be?'

'How do you mean?'

'My telescope uses a similar principle. In order for that dragon and the initials to look right when pressed into the seal, everything needs to be as you'd see it in a reflection. The two characters you see are therefore the wearer's initials, *EP*.

'I take it the *P* isn't you or your wife, Mr Parfitt?'

'Not at all. My first thought was it may belong to a family member, but none who might be in our bedroom would have a Christian name beginning with *E*.'

'And you found it under your bed?'

'Only about the length of my fingers in. Almost as if it had been tucked there.'

'Or perhaps it came off and the wearer didn't notice it was missing. Did you check if anything else had been pushed in?'

'My wife and I lifted the bed as best we could and found nothing else. Most odd don't you think?'

'Odd is right, though it may have nothing to do with your burglary, the ring could have been there for some time.'

'I thought of that, but our maid said she and our manservant moved the bed for cleaning only two or three days before we went away and the ring was not there then.'

I asked if he'd mind me taking the things away with me.

'Of course not, Miss Valentine, anything which will help us get back our jewellery. If you think of anything else you need to ask, please do call round. Also, don't forget to come to dinner. I will ask my dear wife to find a suitable day, and our maid will bring you a message.'

Mr Parfitt waved me from his door, and I wandered back to the New House, a little wiser than when I'd left.

Back in my room there was very little doubt about it. The three pieces of rope lay side by side on the table and they were clearly from the same coil. All were the thickness of my middle finger. Two the same length, more or less. These, and the burnt remnant I'd taken from Beth Hurdley's grate, looked to be the same pattern, though I'm no expert. Thicker than the string we'd use around the garden but thinner than what my father would use to tie down haystacks at home. It seemed to me to be the sort of rope used on boats and carts to hold the cargo in place.

What I now had was a vital piece of information. Two of the lengths of rope had been used to strangle Beth and Daniel. The other was discovered where one of the burglaries had been committed. The killings and the thefts of crimes *were* connected.

I examined the ring again. Within the crevices, flecks of red stood out against the metal. Sealing wax. The initials, if they didn't belong to a member of Mr Parfitt's immediate family, suggested only one other person. Daniel's father.

Edward Powell seemed paler than when I'd seen him only two days before, and a sadness was on his eyes. I believe grief comes in waves, and with Mr Powell's son taken from him so suddenly in such a violent way, the poor man must have felt bewildered. He greeted me at the mine workings with neither friendliness nor the animosity he'd shown to me when first we met. Simply resignation, another tribulation to be endured.

I took the signet ring from my pocket and showed it to him. 'Do you recognise this, Mr Powell?'

'Where did you get this?'

'I might ask where you left it.'

'Leave it? I didn't leave it anywhere, I lost it.'

'Then where might you have lost it?'

He laughed sourly. 'Surely that's the point of losing something, if you knew where it was then it wouldn't be lost, would it? Are you going to tell me where you got it from or not?'

'It was found under the bed in the burgled house of a Mr Parfitt.'

Mr Powell frowned. 'Mr Christopher Parfitt?'

'You know him?'

'Of course. A fine old gentleman, though a little absent-minded, and a friend of Mr Bagnall. He has been burgled?'

'He has, and your ring, I assume we're agreeing it *is* yours, was under his bed. So how could it have got there?'

'How would I know? I use it once, perhaps twice, a week to seal letters intended for important customers. We have a plainer one in the mine office for the day-to-day correspondence. The last time I remember using this one was a little over a week ago, for a personal letter to an old friend sadly ill in Dorset. I wrote to him before retiring for the night. A day or so later I noticed I wasn't wearing it and assumed I'd simply forgotten to put it on in the morning. When I returned home and found it wasn't by my bed, I imagined I'd dropped it somewhere or it had been stolen when my house was broken into. You do remember that don't you? I am a victim here, not someone to be accused of I don't know what.'

'No-one is accusing you of anything, Mr Powell. I'm simply attempting to get to the bottom of what happened to your son. This ring was found where it shouldn't have been and I'm trying to find out why. Are you sure you can't think of any reason it might have been in Mr Parfitt's house?'

He held out his hands, palms upwards, in front of him and shook his head slowly. 'Look at me, Miss Valentine, I'm a hard-working and God-fearing man. From what you have said, I can only guess that you've made a connection between these thefts and my son's murder. How you can believe I'd have done such a thing is beyond me. I was sitting in my home with my wife at the very moment Daniel was taken from us. She will vouch for that.'

'I'm sure she will, Mr Powell, though it wouldn't be the first time a wife has lied to protect her husband. The story you've given matches the one you told me the night your son was killed, but we have a mystery. As you've worked out, the terrible killings of your son and Beth Hurdley are linked to the thefts which have taken place. Your ring has been discovered at the scene of one of the crimes, and you can't explain it.'

'No, you're right, I can't explain it, because it makes no sense. Earlier I said I'd thought I might have dropped it, but I couldn't have done so in Mr Parfitt's bedroom as I've never been there. I've never even visited his house. The only other possibility is that it was stolen from my home with the other items and was left at Mr Parfitt's to lay the blame at my door.'

'Who would wish to harm you in such a way?'

'There would be plenty, I suppose. I've hired and dismissed enough men over the years to have made enemies along the road. Doubtless there are also suppliers and journeymen who might think I've driven too hard a bargain for their goods and services and might wish me harm. I've no reason to believe any of them would want to kill my son, though. And none come to mind who would be in the burglary game.'

I know it isn't a good idea to judge what people may, or may not, do just because we know them, but it seemed likely that most thieves would be less discerning in their choice of what they stole. The one active in Broseley took only a few choice items from each home, valuables which would be easy to carry, easy to store and easy to dispose of without arousing much suspicion. Also, each of the victims had been away from home for a short time, as had their house-servants, when the burglaries took place. This suggested the thief knew their travel plans. How likely would it be for miners, journeymen, and tradesmen to be so well acquainted with the movements of the richer folk in the town? Mr Powell was also correct that if he'd upset a man by driving down the price of a job, it would hardly result in the aggrieved murdering two people in cold blood. Even if Daniel *had* been taken as revenge, why would Beth be killed as well?

'There's something in what you say, Mr Powell, and, for now, I'm prepared to accept your explanation. Though be sure I'll come back if I need to. Now, before I go, I need to ask you to do something for me.'

'Anything, if it helps catch my son's murderer.'

'I'm not sure it will, but it may. We never know where these things may lead us. I have a feeling Daniel must have been killed by someone he knew. If you give me a list of all his friends and acquaintances it may provide the sunlight which this seed needs.

Twenty-Eight

Natty's grandfather was used to the lad calling to see him at all hours of the day or night. They lived only a short distance apart and Natty had hidden with him many times in his young life, when his father's short fuse was made even shorter by drink. Or he found another reason to vent his anger on one of his children.

Often, they'd sat by this same fire, the old man toasting lumps of bread over the glowing coals. The two would share it in silence, with a thin spread of butter, until Natty was ready to reveal his father's latest cruelty. When the grandfather had been a younger man, less rigid in his joints and bones, he'd tried to defend the boy. Now he knew he'd not be fit for such a task and wasn't prepared to have his son's fury rain down on himself.

This time, though, Natty had come to talk of something else. 'Can I ask you a question, Grandad?'

The old man laughed, a deep, husky, croak, like the bull frogs on the Delph pool at sunset. He leant forward in his chair and prodded the fire. 'Can I stop you?'

'I've met this woman -'

'Bit young for that, aren't you, son?'

Natty frowned, then tutted. 'Not like that, Granddad. She's much older than me. Nearly as old as my ma. She's a thief-taker and I want to be like her.'

'A thief-taker? Chases ne'er-do-wells for money?'

'Exactly that. Meg, that's her name, though she tells me I've to call her "Miss Valentine". But plain Meg will do when I'm with you. She goes round following a trail, puts it all together, then finds out who's done the crime and collects the money.'

'So what's she doing here in Broseley?'

'Mr Bagnall called her over to look into some burglaries, but now there's been these two murders and I'm helping her with them.'

The grandfather raised an eyebrow. 'Helping her solve murders? This ain't another of your stories is it Natty, because if it is, you can go home now, I'm fed up with them.'

Natty's eyes crinkled, but he remembered he was not a small child, and beyond tears. 'I'm not telling you stories, Granddad. I don't understand much of what she's doing - yet - but she *has* asked me to help a couple of times.'

'So what's the problem?'

Natty didn't reply. His grandfather stood and placed an arm round the boy's shoulder. Come on, lad, what is it?'

'I've told her some fibs.'

'Big ones?'

'I don't know.' This time the tears came running, leaving pink tracks on his coal dusted cheeks. 'I only wanted her to think good of me. Told her what I thought she wanted to hear. Trouble is, she found out it wasn't true, and we had a big row. She won't believe anything I say in future.'

'Then there's a lesson to be learned in it, isn't there. Don't tell lies to them that trust you. You'll just have to do better when you get another chance.'

'But if Meg doesn't ask me for help, Mr Bagnall will see me in a bad light, and I'll end up down that blasted - sorry Granddad - down that mine for the rest of my days.'

'And that's a bad thing, is it? It was good enough for me, and it's still good enough for your dad. Worse ways to put food on the table.'

Natty stood and clenched his fists, fierceness in his eyes. 'I don't want that for me. Scratching in the dirt from morning to night and starving at the end of every week 'til pay day comes. I've had enough of that already.'

'Then you'll have to learn right from wrong, Natty. You can't go through this life saying whatever you think will get you what you want. You mentioned Mr Bagnall. Now there's a good example. Honest, truthful, and reliable. Does the right thing even when it's against his best interest, and that serves him well in his business. Can I tell you something about him?'

'What?'

'When were both a lot younger, children really, I came upon him being bullied by some of the miners' lads. Throwing stones and calling names they were. I'm only a year older than him but I was bigger and stronger then, so I stepped in and stood his corner, chasing the others away. He's never forgotten it. Always made it a bit easier for me and your dad. Made sure we had jobs when they were short, and dropped a bit extra our way if he thought we needed it.'

Natty sat again, his head full of questions but his voice calmer. 'So what are you saying, Granddad, That I should bribe people to like me?'

Another croaking laugh. 'Not at all, lad. I'm just trying to say if you do the decent thing by others, they'll do the same for you. I helped Matthias Bagnall when he needed it, and he's helped me when I've needed it. Now, it seems to me, if you want that woman's respect, you're going to have to earn it.'

'So what do I do?'

'You start by telling her the truth.'

The evening had become fine and sunny, though the nip in the air was increasing with each passing week. In Lost Lane, the chestnut leaves had started to droop and shrivel, always an early sign that winter will soon be on its way. In my pocket I had a list of Daniel's friends and acquaintances put together by his father in the afternoon. My plan was to ask Tom to go through it with me, so we could see who Beth had also known.

I stood for a moment across from Tom's cottage, looking up into the branches of an especially fine tree, which spread fully twenty-five paces on all sides. Just beyond, there was a gap in the hedgerow. Whether caused by the shade from the tree, or by starvation from its roots, I couldn't tell, but as I looked through and across the fields, I could see a house on the hill in the distance. The sun glinted off its most distinguishing feature, a high, wide, window, and I knew it to be the home of Mr Parfitt, the man with the thing he'd called a telescope. It seemed that the dwellings I'd viewed through it were the ones belonging to Tom and his neighbour, Annie Reader.

When Tom opened his door, I could smell the drink on him. He was unwashed and leaned forward, as if trying to focus his bloodshot eyes on me.

' You again? What is it this time?'

' Can I come in?'

'May as well, no point doing this out here.'

It was clear that keeping his home tidy wasn't top of Tom's list of things to do. A beer jug and a brown pot tankard sat on the table, alongside three unclean bowls and a spoon. Clods of earth and something unpleasant were scattered around the floor. Even above his beery breath, Tom stank of pig.

'What's going on here, Tom?' He looked confused. 'This mess. Guilty conscience, is it?'

He stepped forward, leaning in towards my face. 'I've told you before. Nothing to be guilty about. How would you be if you lost the one you loved? Eh?' He stepped away, then slumped on a chair with his head in his hands. 'She's gone... my Beth's gone. With our baby. Why would I bother keeping this damned place clean? No-one here but me to care about it now.'

He was right. I'd guess Beth would have looked after her house, as part of the duty she would have thought she owed to her husband. While she was alive, he'd never have given a thought to the fact it was clean and tidy when he came back from the fields. Now she was gone, guilt, grief or plain idleness meant he wouldn't see the point in sweeping mud from the floor when it would only be back again tomorrow.

'We have to find out who did this, Tom. Will you help?' He slowly nodded. 'Good. Then let's get this room cleaned up and you can answer some questions while we do it.'

I set him to washing his pots, while I swept the floor. I wasn't sure how drunk he was but, judging by how slowly and deliberately he answered, I guessed he must be well on the way. When I asked him to tell me about Beth's friends, it took time to get anything out of him.

As I might have expected, Beth knew a lot of people. She'd been born and grown up in Broseley, right in the middle of the town. Much of her family still lived there and had done for generations. Tom knew of only a few close friends, Grace Shovelin being one, and three other women of a similar age.

He became agitated when I asked about men friends.

'Why'd she have any of them? She'd be a decent respectable girl my Beth.'

'I'm not saying she wasn't, but she *must* have known some men in the town.'

'That all ended when we married.'

This I knew not to be the case. We'd already clashed about how well she knew Daniel Powell, and Grace had confirmed he and Beth had been friendly. I let it go and trod another path.

'What about Jake?'

'He's my friend, not hers. What're you saying?'

'Nothing, Tom, nothing. Don't be so touchy. I have to ask these questions if I'm to solve the puzzle. You know that don't you?'

A drop of the head. 'Yes.'

'Then you're sure there's no-one else? Someone who could be so angry with Beth as to wish her harm?' Someone jealous?'

'Why would anyone be angry with her. She was so nice. Everyone she knew liked her. And jealous? Look around you. We have nothing. A tumbledown old cottage and barely enough to live on. Beth had no enemies, why would she?'

My only thought was that she must have. One who hated her enough to slip a rope around her throat and squeeze until every breath had gone. I shrugged and took from my pocket the list that Edward Powell had made and laid it on the table.

Tom sniggered. 'No good to me, miss, I don't have no letters.'

'They're names, Tom. People Daniel Powell knew. I'll read them out and you tell me if you recognise any as ones Beth knew as well.'

Edward Powell had marked the ones his son met at school in Bridgnorth, and I wasn't surprised that Tom denied any knowledge of those. Of the rest, he indicated the ones Beth knew, though the only close friends were those he'd mentioned earlier. I put a cross next to those known to them both. I noticed Mr Powell's list didn't include Becky Cole. Did this mean Daniel's father didn't know about her, or that he didn't want *me* to know about her? 'Did Beth ever mention Becky Cole?'

'Don't remember her talking about her.'

'But you know her?'

'Know her dad. Takes the ferry over the river and back. Seen her there with him. Can't see how Beth would have known her though unless she bumped into her in town sometime.'

We went through the names again, with me checking and double-checking each one, but there were no differences to when we'd been through them the first time. I was left only with Grace Shovelin and the three others as friends of Beth, and nothing to suggest any of them would want to kill her or Daniel. On the other hand, I had nothing to suggest *anyone* would want to do them harm.

Twenty-Nine

Sunday can be restful, or a time of entertainments at some times of the year. Other than church, which I'd felt obliged to attend alongside the Bagnalls, this one dragged beyond measure. We didn't eat until after the service, which was hours after I'd risen, then the day was spent sitting either attempting conversation, or avoiding conversation when Mr Bagnall felt the inclination to snooze in his chair. I was glad to take to my bed when the light faded.

On Monday, a knock on the bedroom door woke me. It was Eliza. 'That Natty Preece is outside asking for you. What should I say to him, miss?'

'Tell him I'll be down shortly. You might offer him a bit of bread and cheese while he's waiting.'

'We can't be giving food to the likes of him ... miss, whatever would the master say?'

'If you're so concerned about that, Eliza, you'd better go and ask him. Tell him I've a visitor and I've asked you to show him some hospitality, but you've refused. Let's see what Mr Bagnall thinks of that. I have to say I've no great wish to see Natty, but he's poor, just like you'd be if not for Mr Bagnall's generosity, and he'll be thankful for a little extra to eat.'

The look on Eliza's face was worth the chance I'd taken in challenging her again. She reddened, she spluttered, and she turned on her heels away down the stairs. I'd hoped our earlier talk had cleared the air between us, now I wasn't so sure.

Soon afterwards I strode into the kitchen. Natty sat at the table tucking in to the food which had been put before him. He was eyeing Eliza and the cook, clearly wondering what he'd done to deserve such treatment, and they were eyeing me, probably concerned at what this mad woman would do next.

I said nothing, just sat opposite him and waited until he'd finished. When he had, I nodded towards the outside door. 'Come on, young man, let's take a stroll round the garden, it's fine enough.'

Once outside I put on the sternest look I could manage, though it was difficult to be annoyed in the clear sunshine with a boy who grinned from having a full belly. 'Why've you come to see me, Natty?'

He shuffled his feet. 'I've something to tell you, miss.'

'It had better not be another of your stories.'

'No, no, miss, it's not. I promise.'

'Go on'

His confession gushed out, like water in a new land drain when the last spit is dug. 'I've told you fibs, miss, I admit it. About that Daniel and Beth.

About Harriet. I only did it to impress you, so you'd put in a good word with Mr Bagnall. I'm sorry, I really am. I shouldn't have done it. Shouldn't have said the things I said the last time either. They were spiteful and I'm not like that. Please don't tell the boss on me -'

I put up my hand. 'Whoa, slow down a minute. First of all, what's this about Harriet?'

'I told you she sees things.'

'Not sure I believed it anyway but are you saying it isn't true?'

'No, she does. Or at least I think she does.'

'What then?'

Well when we went to see Harriet, I'd asked her to *pretend* she'd seen a man and woman together. It didn't take much to prod you towards thinking it was the two who were killed.'

'So Harriet was just play-acting?'

'Some of it. I didn't tell her to do that last part, all the shaking and going into a trance. I think that bit might have been real. Scared me anyway. Harriet's nice, she wouldn't have put it on just to convince you.'

'But why do all this, Natty? What were you hoping to get by lying?'

The lad stared at the ground and twisted his fingers together. 'I don't know, miss. Not really. It's something I do to make myself look better than I am.' He paused for a moment, then looked me in the eye. 'It's not easy, this life of mine, you know. I work and I work at the coal, at bits and pieces wherever I can get them, and every penny goes to my mam without a word of thanks. Sometimes my dad gets it first for the drink, and even then, he thumps me all the time when I've done nothing wrong. All I *do* know is I've got to get out of it.'

'What do you imagine I can do about that?'

'I just want to be like you, Meg ... Miss Valentine.'

'Like me?'

'Free. Doing interesting things. Making more money than I'd ever do underground.'

I laughed. 'You have a funny idea about what I do, Natty. Most of the time I'm counting the pennies to find a way of paying my rent and feed myself. Some weeks it's one or the other. I can't say it's boring though. Not when I can get the jobs anyway.'

'But you are your own boss. Nobody telling you what to do is there?'

I couldn't exactly argue with that. Something I didn't think about often, but I was grateful for it. My dad had been in charge at Cliffe House, with me and the other assistant gardeners under him. He gave the orders, and we had to follow them, or else. Though I'd never known anything different, I can't say I enjoyed every minute of every day controlled by someone else, even if it was my dad.

I was still annoyed with Natty, but I understood why he'd want to break free of the chains of poverty if he could. 'If you promise, and I mean *really* promise, to always tell me the truth in future I'll let you help me. Perhaps you'll learn a trick or two and, when you're older, it'll help you get some work. Just make sure you don't pinch any of mine.'

Natty worked all day in a grindingly hard job, and he had to fend for himself a lot of the time, but this didn't mean he wasn't still a child, with a young boy's hopes and fears. He jumped up and threw his arms round my waist. 'Thank you, miss. Thank you. You'll not be sorry.'

I could feel him shaking against me and couldn't believe the lad might be weeping. Nevertheless I left him for a while before prising his arms away. 'Now this is your last chance, Natty. Don't let me down.'

'I understand, miss. Can I tell you something else?'

I ran a hand through my hair. 'What now?'

'Mr Powell called me in after Mr Bagnall told me to work with you. He said I had to tell him everything you found out.'

I took a minute to take in what Natty had said. It raised more questions about Powell. Was he lying to me stone-faced? Was his wife covering up for him? If so, why? The signet ring was a strong piece of evidence he'd been in Mr Parfitt's home, yet his story of it going missing was plausible. Could he have killed his son, on their own doorstep, calmly returned inside to join Mrs Powell, then made a pretence of hearing a noise at the door?

And why, with the planning this took, would he carelessly fling the rope into the bushes? Perhaps he hadn't bargained on anyone properly searching for clues to his son's murder. 'So, what did you tell Mr

Powell?'

'Not everything.'

'Natty!'

'What else was I supposed to do? If I'd told him nothing, he'd know I was keeping stuff back and I'd be in trouble. So I dropped him the odd word, things I didn't think important, said you never told me much. Didn't tell him you'd found that rope at his house.'

'You saw that?'

'Course I did. I also saw you tuck it in your pocket when you thought I wasn't looking. Like you didn't want anyone to know you'd got it.'

At least it showed the lad was observant. 'Did Mr Powell say why he wanted you to watch me?'

'Huh. He's not going to explain himself to the likes of me, is he? He gives his orders and expects them to be obeyed. No need to tell me why he wants something done.'

The thoughts about Edward Powell continued going round in my head. At first, he'd resisted my attempts to look into his son's death, and now I'd found he'd made Natty spy on me. What was he hiding?

I was finding it hard to imagine he'd strangle his son, even though he and Daniel argued often. If he had, why would he raise the alarm and have his men look for the killer? It could be a decoy, but it surely would have been easier to kill Daniel somewhere away from his own doorstep and hide the body. Powell could then simply pretend the young man had gone away to work or stormed out after one of their arguments. And with Daniel dead, what would be the point in killing Beth Hurdley? Even if Mr Powell suspected them of committing adultery, a crime against his strong Christian beliefs, it would be ended when Daniel breathed his last breath.

These thoughts tumbled round my head for a good few minutes until a cough from Natty brought me back. His next question floored me.

'Is your Peter coming back soon?'

I didn't reply, just rubbed my forehead with the palm of my hand.

'What's wrong, miss?'

'I don't think Peter will be coming back.'

'Why not?'

'Because he's not "my Peter" and he's to be married.'

'But I thought you -'

'Don't you dare, Natty Preece. This is nothing to do with you. Peter's a friend, that's all. We hardly know each other, if truth were known. He's just someone I met last year and who's worked with me a few times.'

'So you're not sweet on him? Only I could have sworn you liked him. A lot.'

I glared, then turned my head away. 'I'm not sweet on him, as you put it, and even if I was, it's none of your business. Now, come on, I've things to do. You wait here while I go back upstairs. I'll be down again shortly.'

As I moved to stand, Natty placed a hand on my

forearm. 'Please don't be mad at me again, miss. I didn't mean to cause upset. Anyway, if that Peter's gone for someone else over you, it's only his loss I'd say.'

Despite myself, this brought a smile, though I gently lifted away his hand. Sometimes the most unlikely people can surprise you.

'Perhaps you're right, Natty. Perhaps you're right.'

Having left Natty in the garden, I went inside to finish getting ready for the day as I'd dressed quickly after Eliza woke me. I couldn't help smiling when she and Mrs Dudley glowered at me on my way back through the kitchen. Upstairs, I slipped on an extra layer and gathered the notes I'd made along the way. I also cut off a piece from the end of the rope I'd found near where Daniel had been murdered.

I joined Natty outside again. 'Come on, let's walk. You can help me think.'

He led me from New House to a path between St Leonard's and a large home he said was the vicarage. The way ran only a short distance from where I'd been attacked two nights earlier, and I have to admit to keeping one eye over my shoulder until we reached the open fields.

Even without looking at my notes, I knew the key to this mystery lay in working out the links between Beth, Daniel, and the burglaries. I said this to Natty.

'Why do you think they're connected, Miss Valentine?'

'The same rope was used in both killings and in the theft from Mr Parfitt's house. I'd wager my boots on it. I showed him the piece I'd brought with me. 'This is it. And, by the way, if you *are* going to behave, and tell the truth as you promised, you might as well call me "Meg".' I'd known for some time the "Miss Valentine" nonsense wasn't for me.

'Then ... Meg ...' This was accompanied by an even bigger grin than when he'd gobbled his breakfast. 'We'll need to find out where the rope came from, don't you think?'

'Will you be able to do that?'

'Well if it's from round here, I probably can. Not too many places would use something like it. Carters perhaps? The mine? Think I've seen that thickness down there but wouldn't bet on it. Then there's the river. All the boatmen use rope. Do you want me to see what I can find out?'

I told him it would be a great help. I read him the number from the tag. 'You'll remember this, Natty?' I made him repeat it back to me several times until I was sure he'd got it, then gave him the piece of rope.

He tucked it into a pocket. 'I'll go down to the wharves first, see what I can see.'

This might take him some time, there were a large number of boats and boatmen on the river below Broseley. I'd heard one time that there were even more than in Bridgnorth due to the mines and iron works.

I told Natty to do the job thoroughly, then asked if he could think of any friends Beth and Daniel might have in common. 'You're around the town all the time, have you ever seen the same person with either of them?'

Natty went quiet for a minute. 'Not that I can remember. I'd see her with Grace Shovelin, and him with different lads. Course they'd *know* other folk, both came from Broseley, but no-one close as far as I know.'

I read him the names given by Tom Hurdley and Edward Powell, and he said he recognised most, even some of Daniel's school friends, which made me doubt he was being truthful. When I challenged him, he gave me a snippet about them, their family or their habits which was convincing enough to confirm he did know them, or that his lying skills exceeded my expectations. I gave him the benefit of the doubt but made ready to pounce on any slip he might make. It seemed that Mr Bagnall's assertion that Natty knew everyone, and everything going on in the town, was accurate. Once again there seemed to be nothing connecting those who were close to the two murder victims, other than what I'd already heard from Tom and Powell.

I decided to change direction and look at Beth in greater detail. I was beginning to think I could rely on Natty to know of any secrets she might have had. 'How long had Beth and Tom had been married?'

'A bit over a year I'd say, but they were courting

for a year or more before. Tom lived with his dad in that cottage down Lost Lane, and they tied the knot only a couple of months before the old man died.'

'Did she walk out with anyone before Tom?'

'Not that I ever heard of. All the men seem to think she was pretty though, so there may have been one or two.'

'What about Daniel?'

'How do you mean?'

'We knew she and Daniel were friendly, so any word on them being together before she met Tom?'

'No.'

'And Jake Slack?'

He thought for a moment. 'I didn't hear of them walking out, but there was a whisper at work he'd made a bit of a fool of himself with Beth not so long ago. Shall I try to find out some more?'

'If you can.'

'I'll talk to the men at work again, see what else they know.'

Natty waited, saying nothing, without going off to do as he'd said, so I asked if he had something on his mind.

'It's just I had a thought. What if there wasn't anything between them but Beth had witnessed him being strangled, and the killer had found out about it. He'd then go after her as well, wouldn't he?'

'That's a possibility, I suppose. But why wouldn't she have told anyone? Tom hasn't mentioned it, nor Grace Shovelin, the two people she was closest to.'

'It could be though, couldn't it.'

This poor boy was so desperate to please it made me smile. 'Yes, Natty, it could. Ask around about that as well, while you're at it, and we'll see if anything comes up.'

I couldn't think of any more lines to follow, and I'd moved no closer to figuring out who'd committed these crimes, so we walked on in silence for a while before turning back. When we reached the gates of New House, I sent Natty off to do what we'd agreed.

The only niggling doubt now was Jake Slack. Tom had insisted there was nothing between Slack and Beth, but Natty's workmates had thrown a different slant on them. Was this a loving husband being blinkered, or was he ignorant of the truth? Or was it just idle gossip?

Thirty

Natty called to see me after lunch. He said he'd found the source of the story about Beth and Daniel.

'It came from a man name of Moses Slater. He works at one of the other mines and his brother works at ours, that's how it was floating about. Seems this Moses was laying coney traps out in the woods and overheard a couple. He recognised Jake Slack's voice and when he peeked from the trees, he saw Jake was talking to Beth. They were enjoying each other's company by the looks of them, until Jake took hold of Beth's hand. She stopped smiling and pushed him away. Jake said he was in love with her and said they should run away to be together. Moses told me he saw Beth look shocked then burst out laughing, telling Jake not to be so silly.

Then Jake was angry, shouting at Beth and telling her she'd be sorry. Beth began crying and he stormed away.'

'You trust what this Moses Slater says?'

'No reason not to. Don't know him that well but

his brother is well-regarded.'

'Did he say when he heard them?'

'Most particular about that he was. Said it was a week last Sunday. Only day he gets off.'

Sunday. The day Beth was killed.

I banged on Jake Slack's door more ferociously than I intended, but I don't like to be lied to. There were no pleasantries when he answered.

'You threatened Beth Hurdley.'

'What?'

'Last Sunday. You were heard, so don't deny it.'

'I never threatened her. I wouldn't.'

'You're saying you didn't warn her she'd be sorry for refusing to leave her husband? She laughed at you, didn't she?'

'Well ... she did, and I did say that, but it wasn't a threat. I'd been drinking. It was just words.'

'But you were seeing each other?'

'No. At least not like that. I saw Beth most days, like I had for years. Tom works with me and I'm his friend. Even if I wasn't calling on them, I'd be passing their place all the time, so couldn't help but seen Beth about the place. We'd always share a nod or a word.'

'So why would Tom say you were his friend, but not close to her?'

'He said that? Don't know why he would.' Jake swung open the door and waved me inside. 'You'd better come in and I'll tell you what I know.'

His father's cottage was bigger and tidier than Tom Hurdley's. Jake asked me to sit at his table and took a place opposite me. 'Can I get you a drink?'

I refused and asked him to tell me about his friendship with Beth.

'I've known her since we were small. My mum and hers were close, both regular at church on Sundays. We'd be taken along and sat next to each other. I thought she was wonderful. Always laughing and kind, I expect she thought we were like brother and sister.'

'But you wanted more?'

'I suppose so. As we grew up, she'd have different lads chasing after her. So pretty she was. None of them stood a chance except for one called Dalt Adams. Lives on his dad's farm out towards Much Wenlock. Beth saw him a few times when she was about nineteen but soon stopped. Violent man. Heard he was very unhappy when she packed him in and took up with Tom. Tom said he went round to the cottage one night, drunk as you like, and started raving at him. Dalt Adams is the one you should be talking to, not me.'

'Strange you should only just mention him. And that you didn't say earlier you were sweet on Beth Hurdley. Not pointing the finger at this Adams just to take my eye off you, are you?'

'No. Been racking my brain ever since you came to see me before, and the bother with Adams only just came back to me. I didn't say anything about Beth because I knew you'd take it the wrong way. It made me mad for a day that she wasn't interested in me that way, but deep down I'd known all along how she'd feel. When she found Tom there wasn't anyone else for either of them. That's why I trusted him. He'd never have harmed Beth.'

'I'm fairly sure he didn't, but when we spoke a few days ago you said you were having doubts. What's changed?'

'Nothing changed. I thought about it, that's all. Even though Tom fought with me it was only because he wasn't right in the head, having lost Beth. As I say, they might have a tussle now and again, like any man and wife, but Tom adored her and wouldn't hurt her, of that I'm certain.

I asked Jake to tell me properly where Dalt Adams lived and trudged off to talk to him, sure it was another dead end. Why would a spurned lover wait three or four years to take his revenge?

As I'd suspected, Dalt Adams had nothing to do with either of the deaths. He'd been away, driving cattle to market in Shrewsbury, on the days Daniel and Beth were killed. It was just as well, because he made no secret of a simmering anger against the woman who'd turned him down, and against the man who had won her affections.

He left me in no doubt he was a nasty piece of work, and I'm convinced he'd have tried to beat me if I'd been a man when my questions touched a nerve. But in this instance, I had to accept he was innocent, so once again I was in the position of having no suspects.

My feet dragged even more on the way back from Adams' home than they had on the lane out to it. If I had no suspect, then I had no solution and without a solution I wouldn't be paid. The money which Peter had brought might see me through another week, two at most, then I'd be taking my dad's charity or sleeping in the hedgerows. On top of this, without a commendation from Mr Bagnall there'd be no more work for *me* as a thief-taker. Gardening would be the best I could hope for, and I so wanted to escape that life.

Mrs Dudley must have seen some of this on my face when I pushed open the kitchen door. 'You look terrible, Miss Valentine, are you sickening for something?' Though there was concern in her voice I could still hear she thought I was one to be wary of. 'Take a chair and I'll fetch you something to revive you.'

I did as she asked and sipped at the warm brown liquid she put before me.

'Tis tea, miss. The master lets us use the second brewing when the family have had the best of it.'

Not so bitter as the coffee I'd drunk once with Edwin Hare, nor so delicious as the cocoa given to me by Mrs Bagnall, I found it did indeed make me feel better. Cook poured herself one and sat opposite me, slurping it down in a most gross fashion. She stretched her pudgy arms above her head and yawned. 'Been a long day already, miss. Are you any closer to finishing your work?'

'It doesn't seem so, Mrs Dudley. I can find no-one who wished harm to either Beth Hurdley or Daniel Powell and I'm running out of ideas where to look. That's why I was in such poor humour when I came in.'

'I didn't know the woman, though I'm told she was well regarded around the town. Young Mr Powell was here often and always polite to me. It saddens me to think the poor man visited only the day before his life was taken from him.'

'He came to New House?'

'Why yes. I thought you knew. He came in the mid-morning. Mr Bagnall and his wife were out visiting a neighbour. They only returned a short while before you and your friend arrived.' Mrs Dudley leant back in her chair and covered her mouth with her hand for a second. 'Perhaps I shouldn't be telling you. Maybe Mr Bagnall didn't want you to know.'

'I think it's more likely he just didn't think it important enough to mention, don't you?'

I'd worked around a big house for long enough to know that gossip is the meat and drink of the servants, brightening their menial lives with tittle-tattle about their masters and visitors. The cook didn't need much encouragement to loosen her tongue.

'Eliza, who's too nosy for her own good, said she answered the knocker to young Mr Powell, and he seemed agitated. He asked to speak to Mr Lombard, so she put him in the drawing room whilst she fetched the master's brother. A little while later she passed down the hall and heard them arguing. I'd wager a year's pay she stuck her ear to the door, but she claimed she didn't. Eliza said she'd needed to sweep the rug near the front door ... not that she was listening, of course ... and young Mr Powell seemed in a much better mood when he came out to leave. I expect it was something and nothing.'

Thirty-One

In my time at New House I'd found that most evenings Mr Lombard would either be away or would eat his evening meal in his room while he worked, so I was thankful when he joined us for dinner. It gave me the opportunity to raise Daniel's visit without needing to search him out.

The conversation at the table was much as it was most nights. The weather, events at the foundry and the mine, visits Mrs Bagnall had made that day, and so on, until Mr Lombard asked how my investigations were going. I told him they were moving along slowly, not wishing to alert my host to the fact that I was completely stuck in the mire. 'There are a number of possible suspects, Mr Lombard, though I'm having trouble pinning down any firm evidence to their guilt. All is circumstance.'

'How so?'

'Well, as a simple example, Tom Hurdley ran away after supposedly finding his wife's body. Is this the act of a killer or of a man who's shocked and scared? He's lied to me more than once and I know he can be violent, but on the other hand I'm told he was completely besotted by his wife and would never harm her. The more I do this work, the more I come to know that people are complicated, and the most obvious answer isn't necessarily the right one. Take you for instance.'

'Me? This seems like fine amusement.'

'I'm told that Daniel came to see you on the morning before he was sadly taken.'

'He did, but that would not be so unusual.'

'I'm also told you argued.'

'Who said this? If it was one of the servants, I'll have them thrown out.'

'It doesn't matter how I heard of it, only that it happened. Are you saying you didn't have a disagreement with Daniel?'

'Yes, there was no argument really. He was a little concerned about a small matter at the mine, that's all. We disagreed about how it should be handled and, as with many young men, he became slightly heated when he couldn't get his own way. Voices were raised but it was nothing of any consequence.'

'There you have it, Mr Lombard, this is my point entirely. What looks suspicious on the surface can be easily explained away by looking at it from a different direction.'

Mr Bagnall laughed loudly. 'She has you there, Samuel. I think you'd better confess, and we'll have the magistrate over first thing in the morning. How about me, Miss Valentine? Have you unearthed anything that would link me with this awful affair?'

'Hmm. Not so far, sir. All and sundry say your character is without blemish.'

I'm not prone to giving praise to gain favour, unlike many I could think of, including Natty Preece, but in this case it was true. Mr Bagnall *was* highly respected by his neighbours, and I'd found nothing to suggest he would commit such terrible crimes. Indeed, it was only his concerns which had led to even the thefts being investigated. I turned to Mr Lombard again. 'Could I ask about another matter, sir?'

'Please do, Miss Valentine, before my brother proceeds with his threat to have me arrested.'

'I brought you a ledger to look at a couple of days ago. Have you had any further thoughts on what the notes in it might mean?'

'I'm afraid not.'

'And Daniel didn't mention them when he came to see you? I hear he was quite distressed.'

'No he didn't. As I said, he came to discuss an issue at the mine, something very practical where he had an idea. Our disagreement became a little more heated than it warranted because, I think, the young man was upset after rowing with his father. We didn't discuss the ledger at all.'

'Do you know what the row between them was about?'

'I told you before, I believe, that Edward Powell and his son often disagreed about religion. Daniel was young, with more modern views, his father is traditional, takes his scriptures seriously, and thought his son should do the same. I'd imagine it was just part of this same story. Nothing much was said, but I could see Daniel was upset. So much so that I almost conceded to his wishes about the mine, despite my own feelings. If he hadn't dug his heels in over the detail I may well have done so. I am really sad to have fought with the lad on the last day I saw him alive.'

This put a damper on the conversation at table, destroying the light-hearted silliness which had existed only a few minutes before. We all finished our meal in silence, and I left for my room, with an apology for taking the conversation down such a sad lane.

I couldn't rest after we'd eaten, and knew I'd not sleep if I didn't talk to Edward Powell about what I'd just heard. Thankfully, I could go to his home along the road in plain sight, without exposing myself to the possibility of attack as I had a couple of nights earlier.

The sun hadn't set, though the evening had become cloudy and dull, so I stayed well away from the dangers I imagined lurking in the darkness beneath trees and bushes. Two waggons hauling coal trundled past as I walked, and I felt safer when the carters called out a greeting.

Edward Powell met me at his door and invited

me in more warmly than he had before, though I could still hear his grief when he spoke. 'Please join me, Miss Valentine, and tell me of your progress in finding my son's murderer.'

He led me inside and we sat by his fire, where he waited for my reply.

'I'm afraid there's still not much progress, sir. The enquiries I've made have as yet led nowhere. I've compared the list of names you gave with those provided by others, and it's taken me no further forward. You know already that Tom Hurdley, the suspect we had under lock and key, has now been shown to be blameless.'

'It cannot be easy. Whoever took the lives of my son and the young woman must be as devious as they are evil.'

I didn't relish what was to come, but I had no choice but to confront him. 'This may be true, Mr Powell, so I hope you'll excuse the directness of the questions I've to ask.'

'I have already said I will do anything in my power to assist you in finding Daniel's killer, so please ask your questions.'

'The first is about an action you took when I visited your home the night Daniel died. You asked young Natty Preece to spy on me and to report back to you. Why?'

For a moment I saw the animosity begin to rise in Mr Powell again, but he relaxed back into his chair. 'I believe you must try to understand this from my side, Miss Valentine. Barely an hour before you arrived, I had found my only son dead at my door. I was beside myself yet had to show some mettle in order to support my wife, and to command the respect of the men and women who had come to help. Some of this bluster spilled over in your direction and, let us face it, I had no idea who you were, what skills you might have, and, just as importantly, what damage you might wreak with your digging. Any degree of incompetence may have resulted in Daniel's murderer escaping unpunished.

'Consequently, I asked Natty to watch you. So I could step in if it seemed necessary. I had the same reason for keeping you away from Daniel's room and his ... his body. I'm pleased to say I was mistaken.'

I thanked him for his candid explanation, though I was still displeased with his actions. He nodded and asked what my second question was.

'There's no easy way to say this, Mr Powell. I've been told that you had an argument with Daniel on the morning of the day he died. I understand it was of such a nature as to leave him quite upset.'

Mr Powell pressed his thumb and forefinger onto his eyelids, and I could see he was shaking. 'This is the biggest regret of my life, Miss Valentine, to have crossed words with my son in almost our last conversation. It is something I will never forgive myself for. I doubt the Lord, even in all his goodness, will forgive me either.'

'Why did you argue?'

'Only the same things we always fought about. He told me he was going to the dance in the evening and was hoping to meet a young woman he was sweet on. I knew he would be in an alehouse with all sorts of temptations, and I told him he'd be better served staying home and reading his Scriptures. Daniel laughed, as he always did, and told me the Lord would want him to be out enjoying himself, not stuck in his room reading old stories. I'm afraid I saw red and warned him not to blaspheme in my house. The shouting between us became far beyond what it should be, and it was only the intervention of my dear wife brought me to my senses. Daniel stormed off upstairs, leaving me to simmer. I went to the mine to take my mind off our argument.'

'Was this the last time you saw him?'

'Not quite. He was eating when I came home later but only stayed a few moments before wiping his lips and making to leave. I'd calmed down by then and I spoke his name, hoping to make amends, but he glared at me and left. I heard him slam the front door a short time afterwards. I... I didn't see him again until I found him outside.

The man's shoulders shook as he spoke these final words, then he stood and walked across to a bureau, where a small leather-bound book sat. Mr Powell lifted it and showed me the first page. The title read *The Book of Common Prayer*. 'This is what I try to live my life by. Will you pray with me for the soul of my son?'

I could hardly refuse, even though the act meant very little to me. In Greville's Wood, Natty had asked me to believe in witches and magic, and now here was a man asking me to accept his beliefs of how our lives are in the hands of a greater force. Still, it would be insulting, and perhaps unwise, to deny him, so I knelt at his side, bowed my head, and copied his words as best I could.

THIRTY-TWO

When Eliza came through to breakfast with an "it's that boy again" I made my red-faced apologies to Mr and Mrs Bagnall and went through to find him at the kitchen table, munching on a lump of fresh bread. Mrs Dudley smiled at me with the slightest shake of her head. She'd obviously accepted what I'd done the previous day as a kindness she should copy, and I guessed she'd been hungry enough in her younger life. I asked what he wanted but had to wait for an answer until he'd finished chewing.

'Went round and talked to the boatmen yesterday afternoon.'

'And?'

'None of them use rope the same as the ones you found. Some were as thick, but the weave pattern or the number were different. I didn't talk to all the boatmen, but enough.'

'If you found nothing, why was it so important to interrupt my morning meal?'

'Hold your horses, Meg, I'm getting to it. I asked

a couple of them where they got their rope, and they gave me some names. After I'd been down the river, I cadged a ride into Bridgnorth to talk to the men in the yards where the boats get their supplies.' If Natty had beamed any more, I'd have sworn his face would split in two. 'There were four who sold rope. Three of them only had the sort the boats use.'

'But one had ours?'

'He did. Coils and coils of it. With numbered labels just the same as you showed me. I went and found the yardman. He didn't want to talk to me at first, knew I wasn't buying, but I told him I'd been sent down by my master to check what he'd got because we had a big job coming up and would need plenty of rope like his.'

The lad was quick on his feet; there was no doubt about that.

'Greedy people can be fooled so easily don't you think, Meg? Anyway, he opened up quick enough and said he could get as much rope as we wanted, as long as he had time to buy it in.'

'But we don't want to buy any rope.'

'No, I know we don't, but it's what he said next that's important. That label *GB17* is ordered in for just one customer.'

I knew who it would be before he replied. 'Mr Bagnall's mine?'

Natty's chin fell. 'How did you guess?'

'Because you told me you'd seen it there. If it's a special order and the boats don't use it, who else could it be? I'd guess those letters are Mr Bagnall's father's initials. You've done well, Natty.'

He puffed up like a pigeon and bowed. 'You're very welcome, my lady.'

We both laughed at his playacting, though his humour disappeared when I told him I didn't need him for the rest of the morning. I didn't want him under my feet and, besides, Mr Bagnall was paying him to help me, not follow me round like a pet dog. I wasn't sure how much assistance he'd be in the next part of the job.

You wait outside the door, listening. Only when you're sure there is no-one close by, you creep inside. Six steps down the hall and you are at the bottom of the stairs. You listen again. Somewhere at the back of the house you hear a woman singing tunelessly. A rough, untrained voice, croaking out the words. She is not going to bother you. She won't even know you are there.

It takes only seconds to reach the landing, and you count the doors to the room which the thief-taker is using. She is not there. You know because from your hiding place across the road you saw her leave. One more glance to the floor below before you push into her room. You do not think you are in danger of discovery but as a precaution you pull the curtains together, leaving just enough of a gap so you can see what you are doing. The ticking of a clock calms you as you scan the room for what you seek.

What you want is there, in plain view. You lift it

then hear someone whistling on the landing and you step back. In a flash you draw the curtains to where they were and move to the door. You grab the handle and fling it open, a smile on your lips. The boy standing there is known to you, but unexpected. 'Natty? My, you gave me a shock.'

He looks you up and down and you can see him wondering why you are there, though he does not speak and you see him shaking. You throw him an excuse. 'I'm looking for Miss Valentine, have you seen her? Mrs Dudley thought she may be in her room and said I should come up. I knocked but had no reply so nipped inside in case she had not heard me.'

You know the likes of him would not dare argue with you, and you are safe.

It is a surprise when he finds his tongue. 'She isn't in here then? I ... I wanted her and Miss Eliza thought Meg ... Miss Valentine ... had gone out, but, same as you, said I should just see if she was still in her room.'

There is little chance he is telling the truth; the maid wouldn't let this boy wander the house alone. It is of no matter. 'Well I'm afraid she's not.' You turn, place what you'd taken back in its place, then step past him, cursing inside that he has thwarted your plan.

In another situation you might have ended his young life, just for the pleasure of it, but not here. The thrill, indoors, with people in the house and likely to come upon you at any time, would be immense. So would the risk. Instead, you bid a farewell to the boy, saying you'll tell Meg Valentine he is trying to find her. You tread nonchalantly down the stairs and leave the house by the door through which you'd entered.

Close to the entrance to the mine stood a long, narrow, shed built from Broseley brick, with the word "Stores" painted in rough white letters on the side. Inside were stacks of pickaxes, shovels, spikes, and many tools I didn't recognise. Alongside these were barrows, buckets, and iron helmets, and, at the far end, what I had come to see.

The ropes stored there were of varying thicknesses and lengths, some used, judging by the black dust on them, but most were new. The piles of thicker ones were closer to the wall and the thinner, like the pieces I'd recovered, by the aisle. As I reached down to lift a coil which looked most similar a voiced boomed out from the doorway. 'Hey, you, what are you doing?'

The storeman, for that's who I guessed it was, stood a full six and a half feet tall and a lot more than half that around the waist. He was an even more impressive a specimen than his employer. His fearsome appearance was made more so by a bald head as big as a bull's and one eyelid stitched closed, the skin flared red around it. He lurched towards me, but I jumped away before he could grab me by the scruff of the neck and fling me outside. 'I'm working for Mr Bagnall.'

This stopped him in his tracks. 'Mr Bagnall? Prove it.'

I couldn't help but grin. How on earth could I prove such a thing. Even if Mr Bagnall had given me a letter of introduction, I'd doubt this man had the wit to read it. He'd manage well enough with the tags on the stores but probably not much more.

'That would be difficult, sir, but if you like I could go and fetch our employer to tell you himself. I'm sure he'd be glad to leave his office to oblige.'

The giant's jaw dropped, and I could see him weighing up the consequences of such a request. After a moment it was clear he thought it wasn't worth losing his livelihood over it. 'Huh. I expect I'll have to believe you. So what do you want?'

I showed him the fragment of rope bearing the label. 'You have some of this?'

He pointed where I'd been looking. 'Some. Mr Lombard is ordering more all the time.'

'Mr Lombard? I thought Mr Powell manages the mine.'

'He does, but he tells Mr Lombard what's needed and because he pays the bills, he places the orders. Why are you interested?'

'Because I think there's a story behind it. You're sure it's the same as that stuff?'

He took my piece and peered closely. He even sniffed it. 'Got to be. Same number, same pattern. Only made for us.'

'What's it used for?'

'They tie the covers over the coal waggons with it. Keeps the dust from flying everywhere.'

Having seen the state of the ground in this part of the town, it clearly didn't do a very good job. 'So most of the carters at the mine would have some?'

'Not just them. Anybody can get it really, either new or old. A lot of the men would find it useful for odd jobs and that lot would have no conscience about lifting a coil or two.'

The church bell struck ten in the distance, and the storeman raised himself up to his towering height. He folded his thick arms across his chest. 'Now, is there anything else? I've work to be getting on with.'

⚱

I'd hoped finding the source of the rope would be the final clue which would lead me to the foul person who'd taken the lives of Daniel Powell and Beth Hurdley. Like everything else, it had led nowhere, half the town might own bits of the same rope.

In the afternoon I walked down to Mr Parfitt's house and was lucky enough to find him home. 'I'm sorry to bother you again, sir, but could you show me the telescope again?'

He appeared more than happy to do so and took me through to the room where he kept it.

Once there I pointed through his window to the buildings in the distance. 'The day before yesterday I went to Tom Hurdley's cottage. Over there across the fields. You know the one?'

'I do indeed, Miss Valentine. I often use those buildings when I am adjusting the instrument. I do it most days, in fact. They are about the farthest things I can focus on without actually looking at the night-time heavens.'

'Can I ask if you've noticed anything peculiar over there in the last week or so?'

'Usually all I see is smoke curling from the chimneys. Occasionally I will see one or other of the occupants going in or out. I don't know them, and cannot recognise them from this far away, but I am aware an older lady lives in one and a couple in the other. No children as far as I have seen.' He stopped in his tracks. 'My Goodness, isn't that where the young woman was found dead?'

'It is. *Have* you seen anything strange?'

Mr Parfitt scratched his chin. 'One night I'd been cleaning my lenses. In my previous observations I'd found some interesting stars out by Saturn. During the day I'd checked my records because I did not remember seeing them before and I confirmed this. When night fell, it occurred to me that what I'd seen might simply be specks of dust on my telescope. So I took it apart. Once I'd re-assembled everything, I trained the telescope across the fields to adjust the focus. A storm was unfolding but there were breaks in the clouds, which was why I thought I could make my observations. The light from the moon was enough to see the cottage clearly.

'Whilst I was looking at the one on the left, a man opened the door and went inside. It took me some time to make my adjustments, switching between the heavens and the cottage. On my last check I saw another man go to the same door. He was let in by the young woman, then he came out soon afterwards and crossed back into the bushes from where he'd appeared. A few minutes later, I caught a glimpse of him again, striding along the lane toward the town. I thought nothing of it other than it being late at night for the couple to have a visitor.'

'Can you describe him?'

'I'm afraid not. It was dark and though my telescope will pick up good detail on the planets, they are brightly lit. The lane across the fields was not, other than that glimmer of moonlight. Is it important do you think?'

'Important to Tom Hurdley I'd say. Once and for all this shows he *was* telling the truth. Someone else was in his cottage, and murdered Beth that night.'

Thirty-Three

I wandered over the fields to tell Tom Hurdley what Mr Parfitt had seen, then I tramped back to New House. My feet felt like clay as I prepared to explain to Mr Bagnall I'd need to give up on the investigations because they were leading me nowhere. I'd racked my brains for inspiration from the lessons Edwin Hare had taught me, but nothing had come. The only consolation was that there must be cases such as this, where the thief, killer, or other villain, leaves no trail to be followed, either by luck or by cunning.

It was small consolation though. If I couldn't capture this man soon, it might mean ruin for me, and starvation for my parents. Only days earlier, things were tight, but I'd still felt I had prospects. With Mr Bagnall's recommendation, this could only improve. Without it, where would I be? A failure. Not worth engaging. And poor again.

This final thought hit me as I reached the turnpike and, instead of turning right for the final couple of hundred steps to New House, my legs took me left, on the road back to Bridgnorth and home. I trudged for a quarter of an hour or so, until the weight on my soul forced me to sit by the wayside, staring across the open fields. There was no sound other than birdsong. Even the wind was still. On the bank opposite, a thrush tugged at a worm relentlessly until the morsel came free and was gulped down. The picture came to me of Peter once watching a similar scene with wonder on his face, lost in the mysteries of the world. The memory of my friend reminded me of his encouragement and his belief that I could solve any case if I set my mind to it. I could hear him telling me I should speak to Mr Bagnall, tell him where I'd reached, and then give it one more go. I stood and turned back towards Broseley.

⚲

Despite my renewed resolve, I was glad when I found the ironmaster was out on business, so my embarrassment was spared at least for a little while. Mrs Bagnall invited me to join her in the drawing room, and did so to take my mind off the difficult task ahead.

Knowing I'd previously been an under-gardener, she asked my advice about some plants she was struggling with, and I did my best to assist her. All the time we talked, my eyes were drawn to a pendant she wore on a gold chain.

'That's a most pretty jewel, Mrs Bagnall.'

'Thank you, my dear. I do love it. I do not know what I have done to deserve such a generous brother-in-law.'

'Mr Lombard gave it to you?'

'Why yes, only last week.'

A quarter of an hour later I was on the doorstep of Mr Exley, the second of the burglary victims I'd met. When I explained why I'd come, he went inside and fetched his wife. I lay on my palm the pearl and jadestone pendant that a surprised Mrs Bagnall had allowed me to borrow. 'Do you recognise this, Mrs Exley? It seems like the one you had stolen.'

The woman squealed and clamped both hands to her cheeks. 'It is the very one, I would know it anywhere.'

She reached to grab the jewel, but I closed my fingers over it. 'I'm sorry, madam, but I must hold on to this for a little while longer. You'll have it back soon enough.'

I collected Natty from the mine when returning to New House. He'd been a part of finding the solution to this mystery, so deserved to be in at the end of it. I'd had second thoughts when I saw him, he was filthy from picking coal, though so grateful to see me I couldn't resist. I decided I'd ask Mrs Dudley to let him use the scullery to clean himself before taking him further into the house. I was sure she'd have some bits of clothes he could change into.

As we walked, he told me he'd sneaked up to my room earlier looking for me, and when he explained who he'd met there, it confirmed what I'd already worked out.

Back at New House, Eliza told me that Mr Bagnall still hadn't returned. When I asked if Mr Lombard was home, she said she didn't know, and I should check his room. In the normal course of things I'd have suggested it might be her job to go and find him, but this time I let it go by without comment.

I knocked on Mr Lombard's door and received no answer. As I pondered what to do next, the faint whiff of a smell I recognised caught me. I went into the room, and the odour was stronger. When I swung open a wardrobe door, there was no mistaking it was the scent I'd smelt on my attacker. There was also no mistaking the bloodstain on the collar of an old brown coat hanging alongside a three-cornered hat.

I pulled open each of the drawers in the bottom of the robe and found nothing of interest, only more clothes than I'd owned in a lifetime. On one side were three smaller drawers and when I drew out the first, I saw it was not so deep as it should be, so I removed the rest. Behind, there was a small door. Inside, I found a box, stuffed with all manner of small jewellery, gold watches and trinkets. From what I could see, several matched those reported to have been stolen.

In the drawing room, Mr Bagnall perched on an armchair opposite me, and Natty stood behind mine. On the table between us lay several items.

'What are these, Miss Valentine?'

'They'll help me explain how I know who stole from your neighbours and who killed Daniel Powell and Beth Hurdley. One of them perhaps tells us why Daniel was killed but we'll have to wait to talk to the killer to understand why he took the life of that young woman.'

'So you know who committed these terrible crimes?'

I took a deep breath. 'I do, Mr Bagnall, though I suspect you're not going to like the conclusion. Nevertheless, I know in my heart you'll do the right thing.'

'This sounds like it might be someone I know, which is distressing. However, the truth cannot be denied, so you had better give me your reasoning and we will bring this sorry episode to an end.'

The first item I lifted was a grey pot containing brown seed husks. I passed it to Mr Bagnall and asked him to sniff it. He screwed up his nose and turned his face away. 'It is camphor, Miss Valentine. We have it with our clothes to prevent insects from destroying them. Common enough.'

'In your world that may be so, sir, but not in mine. It's clearly a precious commodity, so much so that it isn't used in the guest bedroom where I sleep.

The odour is strong and can't be mistaken for anything else. I hadn't noticed it on you or your wife, neither have I smelt it on Mr Lombard around the house.'

'But you *have* smelt it elsewhere?'

'Certainly, though I didn't recognise what it was at the time. It was on the clothes of the man who attacked me behind St Leonard's. Only when I found those seeds did I make the connection.'

'And where did you find them?'

'I'll come to that shortly, Mr Bagnall. First let me take you to the next step.' I pointed to the lengths of rope. 'These connect the crimes together. I found the plain one hanging from a bush outside the Powell's house. As far as I can tell, the pattern matches the marks on the throats of both Daniel and Beth.'

The shock on Mr Bagnall's face was obvious. 'Why did you not show me this before?'

'Because when I came upon it, and you'll have to forgive me for this, I had no notion who I might trust and who I might not.' I cocked a thumb over my shoulder. 'I even tried to hide it from Natty here, though he proved too sharp for that.'

Natty grinned from ear to ear.

'What about the other pieces?'

'All three are the same thickness and pattern. The burnt fragment came from Beth's fireplace. Too damaged to be of much use, but enough to link the murders to the same killer. The third length was found at the home of your friend, that very fine gentleman, Mr Parfitt. It had been used to tie in his dogs. This showed me the murders and the burglaries were committed by the same person. You see the label fixed to it?'

He nodded.

'That label, Mr Bagnall, led me to the only place it's supplied to.'

'Where?'

'Your mine, sir.' I let it sink in. If I had thought he appeared surprised before, it was nothing to the expression now on him. 'True, it is regularly stolen by your workmen, but it is only ordered by one person.'

Surely you're not saying Edward Powell is behind this?'

'I don't believe I said that sir. Let me continue.' I flipped open the ledger. 'I don't have enough learning to understand these figures. Peter couldn't understand them much either, but he *was* able to point out that Daniel had been making notes. See there, all the way down the page. Small differences but adding up to a lot of money. Your brother came to the same conclusion. The significance eluded me until this morning when the clinching clue came to light.'

I took the final piece from my pocket and dangled it in front of him.

'My wife's necklace?'

'Only for the last few days, Mr Bagnall. Before then it belonged to Mr Robert Exley.'

'But ... but ... my brother gave it her.'

'That, I'm afraid is where the trail takes us.'

I turned to Natty. 'Please tell Mr Bagnall what

you told me earlier.'

The lad grinned from ear to ear. He was so excited the words just spilled out of him. 'I was at the mine this morning, sir. One of the men was talking about the night Mr Powell's son was killed. He had an accident next day and been off work since. Said he'd been in The Angel that night and saw Mr Lombard there. Thought it odd. Mr Lombard walked past him without saying hello. Usually very friendly to the miners, he said, but went by as though something on his mind.'

Mr Bagnall smiled kindly at Natty. 'It's good you have brought this information for Miss Valentine, but it may mean nothing. My brother occasionally like to go into a tavern and he's a busy man. He *would* have a lot on his mind.'

'Yes, sir, that's what the man thought. But there's something else.'

'What?'

'Mr Lombard was in Meg's room earlier.'

'And why were *you* in her room?'

'I wasn't in her room, sir. I was on the landing. Slipped past the cook to tell Meg what I'd heard and to see if she'd let me help some more. I didn't want to be out picking the coal. Mr Lombard came out of her door. I told him Miss Eliza had sent me up,' Natty pointed at the ledger, 'had that under his arm. Put it back when he saw me.'

Mr Bagnall spoke directly to Natty. 'You're sure about this, my boy? It was my brother you saw?'

Natty nodded so hard I thought his head might

fall off.

I asked Mr Bagnall the question which had nagged at me for a couple of weeks. 'Forgive me, but you've referred to Mr Lombard as your brother each time we've spoken of him, yet he doesn't carry your name.'

'Because he is a stepbrother, our parents are different. When I was about fourteen years, my mother became sick. Though coming from humble beginnings, my father had risen and become successful in his business endeavours by this time. He took on a nurse to look after my mother's needs. This woman, much younger than either of my parents, had lost her husband to smallpox, alongside most of her children. The only one remaining, and still barely able to walk, was Samuel.

'My mother passed away a few months afterwards and though his heart was broken, it seemed to my father that the most practical arrangement to attend to my care was to marry Samuel's mother. They became closer as the years passed and before my father died he made me promise to continue to look after Samuel.'

'What you've told me perhaps explains why he doesn't have your high morals, sir. It's my belief that alongside his other crimes he's been stealing money from your business, and that Daniel discovered this when he looked through the mine accounts. Mr Lombard told me he couldn't see what Daniel's notes meant, but this was just a smokescreen. With his skills he would surely have understood them as clearly as Daniel had. Daniel came to New House the morning before he was killed and I think he confronted Mr Lombard, probably telling him he'd a period of time to put things right. Instead, your stepbrother waited for Daniel to return home, then strangled the life out of him.'

I'm also sure he burgled the houses of your friends. By his association with them through you he'd know of their wealth, something of the layout of their homes, and what arrangement they'd have with their servants when they are away.'

Mr Bagnall rubbed his forehead, his eyes closed. 'This is all very convincing Miss Valentine but there must be some other explanation. Samuel is at the mine today. I'll send for him, and he can put us right, I'm sure of it.'

'I think he *should* be sent for, Mr Bagnall. And you might ask that storeman to join us as well.'

THIRTY-FOUR

In the half hour it took to bring Lombard back to New House, Mr Bagnall peppered me with questions, checking my reasoning from every direction. Each time I replied, he would nod, pause, then ask another.

Eventually a calm came over him, and I could see he'd finally accepted my version of events. 'This is indeed a sad state of affairs, Miss Valentine. I shudder to think what my father, or Samuel's mother, would make of it if they were still with us. Though it pains me to do so, I will send for a friend, Mr Woodall, who is good with figures, and he can take a further look at the ledger you found. I can only pray he discovers you are mistaken.'

When Mr Bagnall's friend joined us, he was put to work on the ledger in another room. Soon afterwards, Eliza came through to say Lombard had arrived home and was waiting in Mr Bagnall's office as he'd asked. My host indicated Natty and I should follow him, then, erect and commanding, he strode through to where his stepbrother stood looking out of the bay window into the garden. On the way, Lombard had nodded for the storeman, Rodrick, to stand guard outside the door.

When Lombard turned, his eyes were full of fury. 'What is the meaning of this, Matthias? It is unforgiveable to have me pulled me away from the mine in the middle of the day without a word of explanation.'

'I'll thank you to soften your tone with me, Samuel. I'm the master in this house and do not forget it.'

'Forget it? How could I forget it? I'm completely beholden to you for everything. My home, my job, even all the meals I eat are at your pleasure, not my own.'

This was the first time I'd heard a cross word between them, but the flush on Mr Bagnall's face showed it wasn't the first time they'd had this argument.

'Please let us not go through this again, Samuel. It is none of my fault that my father favoured me in his will. As I've said many times, it was because I was his son, and you weren't. You were left an allowance of your own and, as you've just said, you have employment for as long as you want it, you have a roof over your head, and you are fed well.'

Lombard banged a fist on the side-table. 'And it's never been enough. You have land, the mine and the ironworks, this house, a comfortable income, and a loving wife. I have nothing in comparison.'

Mr Bagnall walked round his desk and sat. His voice was all calmness when he spoke. 'Is that what all of this is about, Samuel? Jealousy and greed?'

'All of what? I say again, I was at my business ... your business actually ... and told I must return here straight away. I've not yet had any explanation of why.'

'You are not a stupid man, Samuel, and I am sure you now realise the time of reckoning has arrived, but I will let Miss Valentine reveal what she has discovered.' He waved towards an armchair. 'Please feel free to make yourself comfortable'

So, I stood there and took him through every twist and turn. At first, he blustered and protested, only quietening when Mr Bagnall told him to, before rising up again at my next point. He ceased his open aggressiveness when I talked of his attack on me, though the hatred was still on him. By the time it came to my discovery of the stolen pendant, Lombard's head was down and he seemed to be resigned that the game was up.

When I'd finished, Mr Bagnall spoke gently to his stepbrother. 'Why, Samuel, why?'

'In the beginning because I needed the money. The wages you provide did not go far for a man of my tastes. I'd built up some debts, and suppliers were demanding to be paid. Two small thefts sorted those out, but by then I had begun to enjoy the risk of being caught, so it became a habit of sorts. You and Mrs Bagnall are acquainted with all the more affluent folk in the town, and you talk freely at dinner of their comings and goings, so finding suitable houses to rob could not have been easier.'

'But you stole from me too. You must have known I'd have gladly given you what you needed if you'd asked.'

'There you have it wrong, Matthias. I would not steal from you. Who says that I did?'

Mr Bagnall told him to wait a moment for his reply and sent Natty to fetch Mr Woodall. We waited in silence until he came through and Mr Bagnall spoke to him. 'Have you found anything, sir?'

Mr Woodall sighed and spoke directly to Mr Bagnall. 'It is quite clear, Matthias. What young Daniel found were clever little inconsistencies in the figures. Each week, most of them are correct. However, some are not. There is a difference between the invoice or bill amount and the sum entered in the ledger, there is then a balancing figure applied and an adjustment to the cash recorded as placed in the bank. The nature of the book-keeping system enables such practice to lie hidden to the casual eye. Daniel is to be commended to have spotted it. His notes made it considerably easier for me to see what was going on.

'I've heard complaints from men down the river for some time that the quantities of the coal they've received have been different to what they've been charged on the waybill. I imagine Daniel heard the same from your customers and decided to do a little investigating.'

The ironmaster stepped towards his stepbrother,

shaking, and I thought for a moment he was going to hit him. Instead, he clenched and unclenched his fists before speaking. 'So all of this, the thefts, the embezzlement, the murders even, have all been because of your jealousy of me?'

Lombard threw back his head and laughed harshly. 'There's no point in denying it now, is there? Even taking money from you was only a part of this adventure. At first, I wanted to see how long it would take before you noticed your profits were down. If you had, I would have lied and explained I'd been testing the accounting system against fraud. I planned, once my affairs were straightened, to return what I had taken, but soon it went beyond recovery. I dipped into the cash I'd put by, and then there was no going back.'

'And Daniel Powell discovered what you'd been doing?'

'If only he hadn't, I did like the lad. The sums I was taking each month weren't large, but he was sharp enough to spot them when he took over the book-keeping whilst I was away for a time.'

I interjected. 'So you killed him for threatening to expose your thieving?'

Lombard didn't reply. His eyes darted around the room, and he leapt, like the cornered animal he resembled, for the door. He hadn't a chance of escape when the tree-like arms of Rodrick encircled him.

With Lombard trapped, I asked Mr Bagnall to remove the cravat from around his stepbrother's neck. There was the final damning evidence of his wrongdoing. Four deep scratches on his throat where my nails had ripped away his flesh.

Thirty-Five

As you lie on this gaol cell ledge, you feel again the pleasure of dispatching your last victim. You see yourself in the shrubbery opposite the Hurdley's meagre cottage, a cloak around your shoulders and a hood hiding all but your eyes. You knew you would not be seen as you watched, but took the precautions anyway, savouring the secrecy. Minutes passed and there was no movement. You did not realise you were holding your breath until the woman you knew as Beth appeared, silhouetted in the lamplight against the kitchen window. It took but a moment to cross the lane and tap the door. The lightest of taps. The heaviest of import.

The woman looked quizzical when she opened up, then turned away into her kitchen when you explained you urgently needed to speak with Tom. She'd said he was sleeping but you'd insisted. Moments later, you'd imagined her eyes widening when she felt the tightness around her throat. Your knee went into the small of her back and her arms flailed, fingers outstretched, like a life-size dancing doll. The cord almost slipped in the sweat pouring from your palms. You hung on. It was all too delicious to allow her to escape through such a small mistake.

The dance stopped as quickly as it began, and her head slumped. Then her legs buckled. You strained to stop her dropping and lowered her gently to the floor. Lying there, you felt the woman looked like she was sleeping. So peaceful.

This had been much more satisfying to you than the previous night's episode with Daniel Powell, which you felt was rushed and messy. Despite this, his death gave you more pleasure than you would have anticipated and woke something inside again that you thought you'd lost. It excited you, yes, but it was done out of necessity, to keep him quiet. Disposing of the rope in such a haphazard way had started your undoing, though you thought nothing of it at the time. Taking this Beth's life seemed to you to be better planned, something for yourself. You were not to know that the fire wouldn't do its work on the ligature you threw to its heart, forging a second nail for your coffin.

With Beth gone, you took two steps back and looked down on her. You paused, just for a moment to take in the scene, then moved forward once more and began to arrange her pose. She would soon stiffen, though for now she was still supple enough to turn on her side. Next, you stretched out her legs, with the slightest of bends at her knees, before placing both hands, palms together, under her head. The pretence of sleeping was complete and you're sure anyone coming in would be convinced.

A creak upstairs shook you from your game and quickened the blood already rushing through your veins. You looked to the front door for escape, lifting the latch for a second before turning back, realising it was only the husband shifting on his bed. A cloak hung behind the door. It would have taken no time to cover Beth, but this struck you as absurd. She'd take no warmth from it, so you let it stay where it hung. One more look around the room, then you left. Quietly, and not far. Waiting. Hoping to see the husband's reaction. But he did not appear and for a moment you considered going back into the cottage for one more look. There was no point. Young Beth was cold, and her pleasing days were done.

You recall the tune you whistled, *Good Morning, Pretty Maid,* as you strode home in the cool night air.

The approach to Shrewsbury gaol made me pleased I was only visiting. Large gates opened from a filthy lane, so different from other parts of the town where the grand houses of merchants looked over every form of commerce, the River Severn, and the Shropshire countryside.

If I'd thought the outside depressing, the inside was ten times worse. The gaoler, black-haired and swarthy, led me, with nothing more than a grunt, down a dozen stone steps to a passage where the stench of human waste was unbearable. A grating in the ceiling which I assume had been put there to remove the smells, had been covered over by a slab of some sort.

My guide banged on the fourth door we came to. 'Thissun's yours.'

The chain hanging from his belt rattled and clicked while he found the key he wanted. I drew a deep breath, almost gagging on the stink, and stepped inside. A minute later, and without another word, the gaoler was gone, with me and Samuel Lombard securely locked in. The cell was bigger than I'd imagined it would be, and fitted with sleeping spaces for four felons. In a corner was a pail and though covered by a lid, it was obvious this was one of the sources of the offensive odours. There were no windows, nor decoration of any kind, but a bible, parchment, a quill, and an ink bottle lay on a rough table in the centre of the depressing space. These, at least, might provide some distraction for men who'd be held here.

Lombard stared at me from his seat on a board below a lamp. I remained standing, with my back against the wall. I said the first words that came into my head 'So, Lombard, how do you like your new home?'

He grunted. 'Is that the best you can come up with, Miss Valentine? I would have expected better of you.'

All the way from Bridgnorth, I'd rehearsed the questions I needed to ask but they had flown away as soon as I walked through the prison gates. It was only the disparaging leer on Lombard's face when he replied which brought them back to me. 'When your trial was reported in the broadsheets, I received messages from bereaved families around the county and beyond saying a loved one had been killed in the same way you dispatched Beth Hurdley and Daniel Powell. Might you have taken their lives too?'

The leer deepened. 'It's possible. You will need to give me dates and places.'

The matter-of-fact way Lombard freely admitted this sent a chill to my very core. I pressed my shoulders even more firmly against the wall, and kept one eye on the door, even though I knew the gaoler wouldn't reach me in time if I needed him. 'So, how many did you kill before I tracked you down?'

'More than I can remember. The first was such a long, long time ago.' Lombard shifted his gaze to the flagstone floor and clicked a tooth with his fingernail several times. 'Just a boy, like me. We'd fought over a frog we'd captured if I recall correctly. I pushed him and he cracked his skull on a rock. It made me laugh how quickly the life seeped from him. I can feel that exhilaration again now, as we speak.'

The questions I'd planned hadn't prepared me for this. 'The judge has said you'll hang for all the lives you've cut short.'

'No, he didn't, did he? He only knew of Daniel and Beth. The families of the others will never find the justice they seek.'

'The day after you've swung on the gallows, I'll

have letters sent to every one of those poor people who contacted me, and they'll know you have gone. That, I think, will be enough. But tell me two things that bother me.'

'What?'

'Why try to have the blame fall on Edward Powell? Hadn't he gone through enough by you taking his son's life?'

Lombard laughed. 'Enough? You know nothing, Meg Valentine. My stepbrother, damn him, thinks the world of that man. It should have been me in charge of the mine. I should even have owned it. But no, Matthias cheated me out of my inheritance then gave the mine over to his friend. Once Daniel was gone I saw a way of getting Powell out of the way as well. A fitting kind of justice, don't you think?'

'How twisted you are, Lombard. There's nothing just about putting an innocent man in danger of hanging.'

'Innocence depends on how you see it. Powell took what should rightly belong to me. In my view, he stole it. He's the guilty one. But you said you had two questions?'

'This is the one which really mystifies me. I know why you took Daniel's life, to hide your wrongdoing, but why Beth?'

Lombard continued to stare at the ground but gave me no reply. After a few moments of silence, I summoned the gaoler and was soon relieved to be out in the sanity of Shrewsbury streets.

As I wandered on my way to my night's lodgings,

I pondered on Beth's death, as I had since we'd challenged Lombard at New House. For a time, I'd thought, as Natty had suggested, that she might have witnessed Daniel being strangled. Then wondered if she'd spurned Lombard's advances and he'd killed her in a fit of rage. Now I knew that neither were true.

Beth Hurdley was just the last act of pleasure for this force of real evil. There was no reason for her death.

Thirty-Six

The weeks after I exposed Samuel Lombard brought many changes. For me and for those around me.

Mr Bagnall's neighbours gave generous donations, even those who didn't get their jewellery back, satisfied they'd discovered what became of their stolen goods. One of the kindliest offerings, if not the largest sum of money, came from Mr Parfitt. True to his word, he invited me to dine with him and his wife one evening and later he showed me the delights of the stars and the planets through his telescope. It was a most wondrous night.

These contributions, along with the sum Mr Bagnall paid me meant I didn't need to worry about the rent for a good while to come. The successful arrest of a murderer and thief was the talk of Broseley, Bridgnorth, and beyond, aided in no small way by a letter penned by Mr Bagnall to the local newspaper. As a result, I faced a daily visit from one person or another wanting to engage my thief-taking services. Some were intriguing, some boring, but they all paid well enough for my time, and I could sense my fortunes, not to mention my skills, improving every day.

Peter benefited from this upturn in my fortunes, which enabled me to use him more and pay him regularly. As a result, he was able to announce a date when he and his Emily would marry.

Even my parent's lives changed. With my father's arm fully mended, he became the Bagnall's gardener, settled in a nice cottage in Broseley, with a vegetable plot at the back and a flower garden at the front.

The last time I saw Natty Preece was the day they hanged Lombard. Mr Bagnall had sent a message, asking me to attend the hanging with him, and he arrived at my door that day in his carriage at a time we'd agreed. Sitting beside him, as neat and tidy as ever I had seen him, was Natty. I'd already sent the lad what I thought was a decent amount for the assistance he'd given me, certainly more than he might have expected from his job in the mine.

When we arrived by the gibbet. Mr Bagnall asked to be excused for a few minutes, and I suspected he wanted to compose himself for the ordeal to come. Natty thanked me for the payment.

'You deserve it. I'd never have painted the complete picture without your help.'

'Does this mean you'll take me on?'

'If I'm needed in Broseley again. There's a good chance of it, so then I certainly will. I can't use you permanently, not yet. Perhaps when you're older and when I know my own future is secure, we can work together more often. In the meantime, will you go back to the mine?'

His face turned sour. 'Not if I can help it. I gave half the money you paid me to my mum, didn't tell her about the rest. That'll keep me going long enough to find something else. Mr Bagnall had me in to New House and told me how he was in my debt for what I'd done for him, I expect I have you to thank for that. Said something about "must run in the family" then laughed. He dropped me a good few shillings anyway. Never seen so much at one time. Mr Bagnall offered to have me trained up to become his bookkeeper, but I don't think that would suit me at all. I put what he gave me with the wages and I'm thinking of heading to Birmingham if you can't employ me. It's a growing town. Plenty of work there and fortunes to be made they say. I might take Harriet with me. She'd find it strange, but she deserves to be looked after.'

I'd wished him well just as Mr Bagnall returned. By this time, the crowd had grown, and I could taste the excitement in the air. There were three hangings, one after the other, Samuel Lombard being the last, and I thought I saw his stepbrother shed a tear when the trap dropped. Lombard had never said why he'd murdered Beth Hurdley, though to his eternal credit he'd admitted to every one of the killings before he was sent to his Maker.

The more I thought about it the more I knew he'd come to enjoy the act of strangulation; in the same way he couldn't stop himself from stealing once he'd developed the taste for it. All the more fitting then, that it was the rope which took his life too.

When Mr Bagnall dropped me on the lane outside my cottage, and I'd said my final goodbyes to him and Natty, I walked to my door, the delightful sound of coins jingling in my purse.

A WORD FROM THE AUTHOR

If you've reached the point of reading this note, I'm assuming you've read the rest of the novel. I thank you for this.

There's a famous British TV comedy sketch in which a very bad pianist claims he has all the right notes, but not necessarily in the right order. So, it seems to me, it is with writing a novel. We write one word, followed by another, then another, and another. Eventually, we arrive at 80,000 or so. Individually, we're probably pleased with our choice of words - they're more or less the right ones. Then we have to put them in the right order. This is where the redrafting starts.

Not all authors are the same, but in my case, I spend a good chunk of time redrafting and there are always two big questions. Does the story work? Have I told it as clearly as I can? If it doesn't, or I haven't, then my apologies - and I'd like to hear your comments on these. I'd also, of course, like to hear your comments if you've enjoyed it. Contact me at charlie@charliegarratt.com

Having mentioned redrafting, this isn't the same as proof reading. In my experience there will always be typing errors and punctuation issues left, no matter how many times the manuscript has been read, and how many people have read it. If you find any (and I'm sure you will), I apologise again and hope they've not put you off.

Lost Lane is the second in the Meg Valentine series, the first was *The Thief-Taker's Apprentice.* I'm also author of a series of crime novels featuring Inspector James Given, set in England and France in the late 1930s and early 1940s. I've also written a family saga, *A Handkerchief for Maria*, a novel with stories drawn from research into my family.

I now live near Ironbridge, Shropshire, the cradle of the Industrial Revolution. The *Meg Valentine Mysteries* series draws its inspiration from this area.

I hope you enjoyed reading *Lost Lane*, Follow my writing through the links below.

charliegarratt.com
charliegarratt.substack.com

HISTORICAL NOTES

Lost Lane is set in late 1751. King George II was on the throne and England was a very different place to now.

There was no municipal police service, and victims of crime, particularly theft, had to seek redress through private services, such as thief-takers like Meg Valentine.

At the time, there was still widespread belief in witchcraft, despite the passing of the Witchcraft Act in 1735. In April 1751 a woman, Ruth Osborne, was drowned at Tring in Hertfordshire as a suspected witch, though the Act was used to prosecute and hang her killer. Harriet Craven, a character in the novel, is the type of person who would typically have fallen foul of this belief.

This story has Broseley, Shropshire, as it's setting. A real place with a real history - though not necessarily the history depicted within these pages. Some aspects are true. The 'Ironmasters', the experimenters and entrepreneurs who developed techniques from which the Industrial Revolution grew, lived in Broseley. The coal which fuelled their furnaces was mined there. The makeshift cottages around the lanes known locally as 'The Jitties' existed, and some survive today. St Leonard's Church, attended at times by Meg Valentine and the

Bagnall family was a real church, later replaced by the current one, All Saints, in 1845.

There is a reference in *Lost Lane* to coal waggons on rails. This predates steam railways by several decades, but systems using wooden rails were in existence for a long time before this. Evidence exists from as early as the beginning of the 17th century of a railway, using horses and manpower, carrying coal from Broseley down to the River Severn.

Whilst the technology and some of the locations are real, *Lost Lane* is a novel. Much of the setting is imagined. Houses and cottages are sometimes based on actual buildings in Broseley, though most aren't.

To find out more about the heritage of the town, check out the website of the Broseley Local History Society (www.broseley.org.uk).

One further interesting fact about this period was the change in calendar from the Julian to the Gregorian. This changeover involved a series of steps, one of which was the change in the date of starting the new year. So, December 31, 1750 was followed by January 1, 1750 (December was the 10th month and January the 11th month on the old calendar). Then, March 24, 1750 was followed by March 25, 1751, because March 25 was the first day of the "Old Style" year). The year then changed again after December 31st. *Lost Lane* begins in September 1751, in the midst of this transition. However, such matters probably wouldn't have bothered Meg Valentine. But in the following year, 1752, eleven days were taken out of the calendar, and this would have been a topic of conversation and may have had an impact on wages. Watch out for this in the next in the series.

If you enjoyed *Lost Lane*, please give it a review on Amazon or Goodreads – this helps spread the word.

To hear about new releases from Charlie Garratt, please sign up at charliegarratt.com